CW00428190

Wee Davy

Andrew Doig

Copyright © 2012 Andrew Doig

All rights reserved.

ISBN-10: 1478137290
ISBN-13: 978-1478137290

This book is for Debbie
and dedicated to the memory of Russell Deans.

This is the story of a black-hearted wretch. A nasty, dirty, selfish narcissist. A user. A bastard abuser with a foul mouth and a twisted, lecherous, unquenchable lust. This is the story of the incubus, the night prowler, the leach. This is the story of Davy and it's the story of me.

PART 1: TULLY

CHAPTER 1

The first time I met Davy was in Tully. I was standing at the washblock sink, scrubbing at the sap stains in my jeans, when I heard a noise from inside one of the washing machines – a sound like a pair of trainers in the wash. The banging stopped. I turned over the jeans, found a new stain. Electric insect noise buzzed through the empty frames of the doorway and window. Clouded, starless night sat over the campsite. A mosquito spun and landed on my arm. I slapped at it and missed, drawing a red mark on the sun-tender skin. My mind wandered back to the day in the fields, the sound of the machete cutting a stalk above my head, angry shouts, endless rows of trees, green and heavy with bunches to hump.

Then the banging returned. Bang-bang-bang. Knock-knock-knock.

I dropped the jeans, moved closer to the machine and peered through its door. It splashed and sloshed with a tumbling layer of froth. I watched for shoes, but instead, a hand came forward and, while turning and twisting with the wash, it rapped against the glass. Knock-knock-knock.

I reeled away, appalled.

Then I lunged for the latch of the door. The machine had sealed itself. I sat on the floor and grasped the handle with both hands, pressed my feet against the base of the washer and pulled with all the strength I could muster. The seal gave with a suck and a jerk, and as I fell backwards, the contents spilled out onto the floor: silted water, suds, sodden clothes and a tiny, naked, withered old man.

He spluttered, coughed and tried to lift himself onto his hands and knees, failed and wheezed back into a slump.

I stalled, sinews locked. I had no instinct to tell me how to cope.

The wee man's wheezing came out in syllables, 'Fu.. huh.. fu… huh bas… bas… turt.' Then he spewed a stream of foamy water and collapsed. His chest heaved, but his limbs gave up twitching. His overlarge hands and feet reflexively stretched then curled. Hair clung to his scalp in clumps and straggles of a white beard splayed across his cheeks and neck. Grey flaccid skin sagged on his emaciated frame. He was not much more than two foot tall.

I was panting too, from the exertion and shock. A puddle spread around me. From a basket, I grabbed a towel and used it to bundle him up, not daring to touch his flesh. I kept his head uppermost, outside the folds; his face was tense, pinched around the eyes and clenched at the mouth. I clung tightly hoping that the towel would rub him dry and abandoned my washing.

Clouded, starless night sat over the campsite. No-one else stirred and I passed unnoticed along the aisle between tents towards the row of fixed cabins. Cane toads croaked and bellowed in a nearby field. As I marched, the man's wheezing subsided and when I looked down on his face I saw it relax.

My shoulders and back were tense, aching. I had to manage the bundle in one hand against my chest while I dug in the pocket of my shorts for the key then shunted the sliding door across. My stride across the room caught a chair and knocked a pile of folded clothes to the floor. I levered my arms through the overlap opening in the mosquito net and placed the towel, and man, on top of the sleeping bag spread out on my bed. For a while I held the net apart with open arms, looking down at the unmoving lump, then stepped back letting the net fall closed again.

I scooped the clothes up and left them on the table so that I could sit facing the bed. A fan mounted in the far corner panned around the room, billowing the net inwards then letting it sigh back. I watched the bed breathe and tried to follow it with my own breath, to slow down, hoping that my pulse would stop racing and the pounding would subside enough to let me think.

And then the shadow of the shape behind the net began to move. It jostled at first, rocked and pushed upwards. The apparition of a head rose. The silhouette of the man shucked off the towel. It padded around on the soft-sprung mattress in bouncing steps, then the shape bulged out the side of the net and slipped down to the floor. A hand appeared. A long nose poked under and sniffed.

The wee man burst through, flung himself upright, his arms thrown above his head and shouted,

'Crivvens and help ma Boab! Whit a blaw that wis!'

I was dumbfounded.

'Man, but it's braw tae be up an aboot.'

He stretched high, then bent over and touched his toes, straightened up and spread his arms wide. All the time he hopped with a nervous energy, agitating himself across the floor like a toddler on jelly beans. In his turns, he kept banging against things: shunting the table, clunking against cupboards, springing them open and peering inside. But this was no child. He had lost the grey sag the water had given him and looked full-flushed and sanguine. His face was covered in a white puff of beard except for sharp eyes and pointed nose. The wisps of his hair were long around a shining bald patch. His limbs were long, but his body squat, thin except for a bulging pot-belly. The sight of him jittering around the hut also gave me the unsettling sight of his tackle. It was obscenely large, flapping around between his legs and slapping across his skinny hips.

Tins tumbled out of the open cupboard where I had neatly stacked them; the sleeping bag was dragged across the floor; the bin tipped over and rattled as he banged into it. He tumbled over it, scattering cans. 'Oof, aw ya bas... Sorry boot that. I'll jist...' He flipped the bin up with a long finger, too hard, and it tipped again, rolling away from him. And then, he stopped to stare at me.

The wee man said, 'An how you keepin, laddie? Ye well?'

Strongly and distinctly Scottish.

He pinned his fists to his hips, gave me a wink and set off on an inelegant jig, grinning broadly. His heel caught my backpack toppling him backwards against the table and bringing over the plastic cup that held my pens.

I jolted forward. 'Mind yourself.' But couldn't bring myself to touch his flesh. I picked up the pens. 'Are you OK?'

He sprang back to his feet, dusted off and looked around, startled. 'Och, wid ye look at the state o this place?' His long fingers swept over the ruin of my room. 'I'm mighty sorry. I seem tae huv got a bit carried away.' He picked up a pen and handed it to me.

I took it from him, solid and assuredly held.

'I'll tell ye whit,' he said, 'Afore we go ony further, let's gie the place the wance ower.' He picked up an empty coke can, tossed it in the air, and deftly righted the bin before it clonked in. 'Aye, and there's nae better way tae tidy up than wi a chirpy wee song. Noo, how wid Mary Poppins huv it?'

He began to dance in jerky shuffles and leaps. His song started, 'Da da dee da da dee da.' He bent to pick up a sock, sniffed it and flung it in the air.

'Aw, a spoon fu o sugar makes the medicine gae doon,

'The medicine gae doo-oon,

'Medicine gae doon.'

He danced and spun round the room, bounced off the walls and hopped over objects. He picked up the odd bit of rubbish and threw it to a corner. Objects moved, flew, redistributed around the room without any sign of tidiness developing.

In a few circuits, he had transformed the lyrics into,

'A hof poon a butter makes the medicine gae doon,

'In a simply slimy way.'

A naked, two-foot septuagenarian doing Julie Andrews with the words all messed up.

'Stop. Stooop. Hey... mister. Hey old... please stop. You just... you can't... can't you just stop, please?'

He caught himself in mid-air, snatched a breath and landed with his hands clasped in front of him, looking up at me. 'I jist thought I'd try tae ingratiate maself, y'knaw?'

'Who are you?'

'Aw, I'm Davy.'

'But what are you?'

'I'm jist yer wee big bollixed pal.'

I was taken aback. But it was true. I just wished that he would put them away.

'Hey, mister... eh... Davy, please, let me get you something to put on.'

The first clean thing I could find was an old work t-shirt streaked with stains. As he pulled it over his head, he muttered something, but the words got lost behind the cotton.

I asked, 'I'm sorry, you said something there.'

'Eh? Aye lad, I said it's the comfort o family and kindness o strangers that means the maist tae a needy man.'

The t-shirt touched the floor, the sleeves cuffed around his hands.

Davy looked down at himself. 'Aw, that's braw.'

'Davy, I don't know what to say. It's just I... Davy, what happened to you? I mean, how did it happen? Or why? Are you alright?'

'I'm fair pechin if truth be told.' He rubbed his hand along his throat.

'Aw, man, I'm sorry. I should have asked. After what you've been through. Would you like a drink or something?' I went to the little fridge. 'I've only got a bit of orange juice, or there's some milk, or some water as well, but that's not chilled. And I could fix you something to eat if...'

A hand thrust in under mine, startling me.

'I'll help masel tae wan o these, if ye dinnae mind.' The hand came out again holding a can of beer.

'Eh... ah... yeah, sure.' I heard the pop before I turned to see Davy chugging back a big swig. He let out a gurgley burp and said, 'Awwww jings. That's the business. Will ye no huv wan yersel?'

I opened mine as Davy finished his. He crunched the can and flipped it into the bin.

There were two more cans of beer in the fridge, and he was eying them.

'Go ahead.'

He was at the fridge in a few quick steps, bare feet slapping on the linoleum. With the second can, he took a slower, smaller sip and I noticed that though he wasn't much taller than the fridge, the beer can sat in his hand much as it did in mine; his fingers reached most way round it.

'Mighty me, better than soapy bubbles, that's fir certain.' He lifted the short green can towards me in a toast, one bushy eyebrow raised, the corner of his mouth curled up below it.

I raised mine. With a couple of sips, my tension slipped a little and the mad whirl in my head began to settle.

'So, young laddie, whit dae I call you?'

'I'm William. I... I guess...' He held out his hand. I hesitated, then took the handshake. 'It's nice to meet you.'

His palm was wet and cold from the can, but the skin was rough. He didn't let go. 'You guess? Whit d'ye mean, ye guess?'

'Well, I'm sorry. It's just... really, you're not...'

'Whit? Not normal? Wid ye go up tae an auld boy in a wheel chair and tell him he's no normal? Some poor wee chap wi nae legs and nae arms, You're no normal, pal. That's very nice that is.'

'No. No, I wasn't gonna say that. It's just... you're... not... from... round here, are you?'

'Aye, right ye were. I am but. Queensland through n through. Gawd streuth, mate. Don't cahm the raw prawn wi me, cobber, and aw that. Nah, but, fair play tae ye wee man, I dinna suppose I'm whit ye were expectin on a Monday night at the laundry. Probably doon there hopin tae meet the lassies.'

'Well... maybe, but, the thing is... What happened in the laundry? How did you end up inside that machine?'

'Och, there's no much tae tell, just a wee accident. Didnae knaw the lassie fae Adam. Jist a wee mix up, accident like I say.'

'What lassie? Did someone put you in there on purpose?'

'Naw. No. Nane ae that. It was only, someone like me, there's folk oot there take exception tae us, cause we're a bit special. It's prejudice like, y'knaw.'

'But, it's just... I'm sorry but you've gotta see that it's a bit difficult. I mean... what is someone like you?'

'Well...' Davy walked over to the chair and still holding his can, levered himself onto it in one deft movement. '...I can tell ye a story, but ye may find it a bitty hard tae believe.'

'Try me. Please, because I don't...'

He held up a hand to stop me, took a deep breath and began, 'Lang ago, in a land far away, there lived a poor auld peasant farmer and his wife who longed tae hae a son.' The note of his voice dropped, more soothing. 'Wan day they struck a deal wi some nasty wee goblin who promised he wid bring them a son if he could sleep in their hoose jist the wan night. Durin that night, a helluva storm blew up that rattlt and shook their hoose. It soonded like aw the hoonds ae hell battrin oan thur walls. But come the mornin, the storm had passed, the goblin wis gone and low n behold, there was a wee bonnie bairn asleep in a basket next tae the hearth. The thing was that this wis nae ordinary boy. He was very, very wee indeed.'

'What, and that was you?'

'Aye, and that'll be right! Ye think I was born in a fairy tale! Naw, away wi ye. I'll tell ye though, ye ever heard o a leprechaun?'

'Aye.'

'Or a brownie?'

'What, like a girl guide?'

'Naw, ya gowk, a brownie. It's a wee Scottish leprechaun pixie thingy, y'knaw? Breaks intae yer hoose at night and daes aw the dishes n that.'

'Are you trying to tell me you're some sort of pixie or something?'

'Well, I'll tell ye, but I kin only whisper it tae ye, so come here.'

I bent over and Davy cupped his hands around my ear.

'YER ARSE!'

My head shook and ears rang.

Davy rocked with laughter until he tumbled off the chair. After giggling on the floor for a while, he climbed back up and sat with his legs apart, his hands propped on his knees, shoulders pushed back. 'I'm nane ae they things. I telt ye, I'm jist yer wee pal.'

I shook my head to stop the ringing as Davy sat there, looking certain and resolute. I tried to smile an acceptance. 'Well... that's... good to know. I guess.'

'It is lad. A pal is aboot the best thing ye could ask fir in life, except, mibbe, a lassie tae call yer ain.

'Now laddie, you have done me a service, and I am indebted tae ye. Saving the life of one soul such as me is no small thing and it gies us a bond that will no easily break. I owe ye, and will repay ye.'

*   *   *   *

CHAPTER 2

I'd been thinking about mum. Mum and home. Perhaps because I was towards the end of my year. It was so dull, so contrived, to be craving the hearth I had so badly wanted away from. But I knew comfort there, a bit of boring, quiet, unremarkable respite.

'Oi, Soft! Stop fackin scratchin yar arse and get the fack over ere. These bastards won't hump themselves.'

I slipped and stumbled across the rows. The treads in my boots were clogged with mud and offered no grip. I came down onto a knee and a hand deep in mud, shuddering at the thought of the excrement mixed in there.

Roy stood at my next tree, pushing on it so the bunch hung down.

'What the fack ya doin here if ya can't keep up, Soft Jock?'

I got under the bunch and readied myself, hands at my shoulder for the weight. Roy thwacked his machete into the tree, toppling it over. My right knee buckled to the ground. A second blow just above my head came as Roy cut the bunch away. Sap splattered and the tree dropped behind me, but I couldn't heave to my feet.

Roy rumbled, 'Jeez, I end up doin all the fackin work with you pricks,' and he lifted the bunch allowing me to straighten then begin my stagger toward the trailer. 'That's only a little un as well.'

I'm pretty scrawny; my legs are spindly. I tripped and panted along the furrow, my back screaming. Sweat poured from my forehead, caught in my eyelashes and stung my eyes. Mentally, I tried to conjure the living room in Glasgow: the electric fire, mum, a blanket over her knee, the telly on; I'd be bundled up on the couch, deep in a book; the sky's black outside; rain rattles the window; the wind sucks and blows the pane against its frame; the standing lamp warms the room's browns and burgundies. The smells are all tea and fruit loaf.

I tried to keep my eye on the trailer, measuring the distance, but the sun glared behind it, the sky achingly blue, the green of the trees fluorescing.

Footwear always got wrecked in the fields; your trainers, your new pair of Blundstone boots, your best hiking gear bloated and split at the seams from day after day of saturation. Some fellas just went barefoot, letting the mud squish up like soft clay between their toes. But they were putting up with the risk of pig-itch. Wild pigs roamed the fields at night and their droppings mixed in with the mud unseen. The air was always heady with damp earth, ripening fruit and excrement.

Old Graham was sat in the tractor as I tried to lever my bunch onto the trailer. 'Speed it up son.'

One of the English guys strode up, flipped his bunch on and bounded off, shirtless, bronzed. I walked back slowly, feeling the sun on the damp back of my t-shirt.

Any backpackers or Aussie drifters were generally made humpers while the locals gave themselves the job of cutter. They stood by the trees calling out, steadily getting nastier as the day wore on.

'Come on ya slow bastard, I'm stood here waiting.'

'Oi Soft, pick yar fackin feet up.'

'Fack's sake yar a slow cunt.'

Normally, we didn't see anyone else in the field, but a ute with a stringing team parked up next to ours that morning. The stringers were women who tied the laden trees together to stop them toppling, and they were just a few rows away, all in shorts and vest tops. Our gang kept glancing over to see their shoulders tense and legs tighten as they reached to wrap a string around some high palms.

Roy had been on my case right through the morning, but as I trudged toward him, I heard him booming on another favourite subject. 'I'm tellin yar, Beersy, that Emma, she's a roit dirty little cow.'

'You aint never been near er, mate.'

'Fackin roit I have. Last Froiday noight, her and her mate were in Top, fackin pissed as. I took her back ta moin and saw er off proper.'

An English voice shouted, 'Leave it out, Roy.'

'What, ya think she's yar fackin girlfriend? Fack off. They want a bit of Aussie cock. That's why they're here.'

'Can't be Emma, she's sucking on me every night.'

A lot of the English guys felt the need to keep up with the leering and lechery. I craved again to be back in my own country, back among my own people, the ones I chose, ones that talk like me, think like me. I played with the thought that maybe I should bring my ticket forward, speed my exit from this working 'holiday'.

But I wanted to see it out, my big adventure: off with my mates to Australia, finding the world, finding myself – that's how it goes, isn't it? Even my mum was proud. My passage. My severance.

I was fairly certain the English one, Rob or Paul or Nick or... I don't think he had got anywhere with Emma. Not for want of trying; I'd heard him talking, seen him running. I hated him for not standing up to Roy properly over her.

The worst if it, chances were that Roy had been where the English guy couldn't. Roy was that type, all bare chest and tattoos, work-hardened and rough, crass and nasty. It seemed that was the allure, the dark bit that girls, maybe it was just the girls on holiday, wanted to touch. Whatever; Roy went after it, and he got it.

Beersy hollered back, 'Tell yar what mate, wouldn't mind a piece of that myself. Pwoar, take a look at that.'

Roy was sitting on a felled tree, rolling a cigarette, glancing towards their bare legs and uncovered shoulders.

'You can have er, mate. Dirty slag. Not enough foight in er. Tell yar what I'm havin, that Swedish bit.'

Beata.

'What that one there?'

No. That was just, too wrong.

'That's er,' Roy husked, 'She's a fuckin piece, int she?'

'Too noice fa you, mate.'

That was the truth. Beata was the difference. He couldn't have her.

I had thought all Swedish women were big, blonde and fresh pale. Beata was auburn, dark tan, with the face of a pixie: everything gently pointed, large eyes that dominated and a mischievous curl to her lips. She was small and light, but not delicate; there was a firm line to her jaw that marked a definite profile, hinted determination, strength of will.

Roy licked the edge of his roll up. 'You watch me at smoko.'

Beersy's eyes widened. 'Yeah, yeah. You do that Roy.'

Roy bellowed, 'Oi, Graham! Aint it time far lunch yet?'

Everyone in the gang stopped for the response. 'Yeah, alroit, go on fellas.'

The smoko truck was a big old wagon with a gas burner and a couple of benches. I got back there quick as I could, stuck my hand in the slatted side and grabbed my packed lunch. The women had taken the cue to down their strings. I was determined to distract Beata, get in the way, avoid them coming into contact.

But she didn't know who I was.

Beata was with some friends, laughing, relaxed together. I'd never spoken to her before. My stomach lurched up under my ribcage, too tight.

Could I tell her that I had seen her first arrive three weeks before, approaching the morning trucks, looking for work? Or that I had once watched her coming down an outside staircase of the hostel, moving idly, caught in thought, and that she had seemed to me so serene?

Then Beata turned away from her friends and said, 'Hey, I like you're t-shirt.'

Blood rushed to my ears.

She came closer.

I said, 'Aw... Thanks. I....' I stared at my t-shirt. Not her. 'Actually, I ...'

She reached her hand out towards me, not quite touching my chest. 'Is that... No, I'm not sure, what album is that with?'

'Actually, I... ah... I bought this when I went to see them in Glasgow.'

'You have seen the Cure? Wow, that's cool. I don't know if they ever come to Sweden. They was good?'

'Yeah, really. It was like... just a couple of years ago.'

I found we were lowering down to sit next to each other on a hummock of grass. She started to unwrap a sandwich, glancing at me as I spoke.

I nearly choked. 'Aw... it was... It was an amazin gig... You should really try and see them if you can.'

She smiled.

All of the bold adventure, taking chances, gaining experience, making new friends for life, all those reasons to travel, right there. Better times.

Beata said, 'So, you're from Glasgow? That's Scotland, yes?'

I cracked a smile too; the homeland hadn't been far from mind. 'You're right. Have you ever...'

Something cold, hard and moving dropped around my neck.

A snake.

I screamed and leapt to my feet. My lunch fell to the floor as I wriggled and twisted and ... I couldn't help it, I squealed.

The snake was thin, brown, maybe three feet long and it wasn't happy. Its tail whipped, slapping against my chest, and its head curved up towards my face, mouth spreading wide. I bent over and flicked it off my neck, practically crying by now.

Roy stood behind us, howling with laughter, doubling over, putting his hand on Beata's shoulder to steady himself. Behind and around him were a group of the pickers, some of the girls among them.

'What... What the...?'

Roy barked, 'Ah, fackin noice one. See the look on yar stupid spotty face?'

It was hilarious, for everyone.

'How... Why...' I finally managed, 'But, but, but what was that? Was that poisonous?' The snake had glided out of the situation as quickly as it could.

'Course it was ya fackin stupid pommie prick.'

'But I'm not a...'

'Ah fack, do I give a fack if yar fackin English or fackin Jockish. Yar still soft. Look at yar.' He turned to his audience. 'Did yars see him? Did yars see him? What a fackin idiot.'

All the faces closed in, curled in laughter. I couldn't bear to look down and see Beata.

I took off, past the smoko truck and stumbled, ankle deep in mud, over some rows, far enough that their laughter became only a rattle among the trees.

My sandwiches were scattered where they fell, trampled now by the crowd that came to laugh at Roy's goading and my cowardliness.

I wouldn't have screamed. I'm sure I wouldn't, if only I had been forewarned.

I hated it.

I pulled a couple of unripe bananas off a tree and forced them down before the lunch break was over.

*   *   *   *

Everyone else climbed up onto the flatbed of the ute and lined up along the benches. The only space left for me was standing on the rear step, holding on to the roof bars. I hoped my bruised back and jellied knees wouldn't give up on me and drop me on the freeway on the drive home.

My head was above the roof of the truck, separating me from all the faces and laughter, the manly banter.

The stringers were packing up and heading for their truck. I didn't watch.

As we trundled over the rutted track leading to the road, I caught a snip of conversation from the English guys at the back.

'Do you know what that snake was?'

'Do you?'

'Yeah, well, it looked like a brown snake... you know, it's a... what is it... a king brown.'

'Poisonous?'

'Shit, yeah. Deadly.'

'Poor fucker.'

*   *   *   *

We pulled up at the top of Butler Street.

Regular shouts went up. 'Roit, who's for the pub?'

'Quick pint then back to the hostel, yeah?'

'It's a schooner, ya cunt.'

The other ute was there, dropping off the women.

'C'mon, the girls're in.'

I got away sharp.

The little supermarket was fluorescent bright and cool, prickling my skin after the steaming fields. I was grimy and foul. The old woman I let served in front of me curled her nose. I picked up beer, bread and chocolate but lingered long enough to let the street clear.

As I passed the Top Pub someone stepped in, swinging its doors saloon-like. Roy was at the bar giving full benefit, "...Roy's the one that fackin knows how to take the..." Beata was standing next to him, propped against the high bar, elbow under her head. It was an impression of full attention.

Or it was full attention.

The door stopped swinging, holding their times inside.

I walked across town to the campsite, then picked between the tents to my hut. For my treat I could prepare a banana sandwich, have a tin of beer. If I had the energy I'd shower off the fields. Oh, and aye, though it was the last thing I felt like doing, I needed to scrub the banana sap out of my one good pair jeans.

*　　　*　　　*　　　*

CHAPTER 3

I slept well, but I usually did in Tully – heavy sleeps to get over heavy days and dreams full of bananas. That night though, my dreams were fraught and naughty, Beata featuring highly. The insistent electronic alarm burst in at five forty-five. My awakening was met by a pungent spermy musk. I woke to find Davy asleep curled up in the middle of my own foetal curl. Revulsion bucked me out of bed, and I fell back, through the net, taking the sleeping bag with me.

The smell hung on me. I checked myself, but I was dry, my shorts dry, I was clean. Picking myself up, it was clear that the rich saltiness was strongest over the bed, over Davy. Davy remained curled, my old t-shirt bunched around him, one corner balled in a fist. His breath had a slow, contented rhythm and a very wee snore. His moustache blew out in feathers then sucked back in. I couldn't bear the thought of waking him to check whether something unpleasant had happened in the night. In any case, the previous day had been a tough one. It was hard to believe after his spin in the washer, but I told myself, if nothing else that old fella is going to need another bath, and left him. I couldn't see what else to do – I had fifteen minutes to get to the pick up or I'd miss my day at work and most likely lose my place on the gang.

Suffering the last prickly tingles of distaste, I gathered up my work gear. As I clomped out in untied boots, my brain was hoping that he would still be there when I got back so that I could try to find out who or what he really was; while something visceral was wishing that he would be gone and I'd never have to see him again.

*   *   *   *

The gang gathered outside the bakery at the top of the town's short main street, bought their morning cakes and tea and hunched in surly bunches around the pavement.

I sat on the kerb on my own, munching on a cinnamon twist. I was shunted with a boot. 'Oi, Soft, move yer arse.' The ute had pulled up and most of the gang were already on.

They all referred to me as Soft Jock. In the real ocker parts of Australia, any Scot is called Jock, Jocky or Jocko. They'd started calling me Soft on my first day when I struggled and trembled under the fifty kilo bunches we had to carry.

I squeezed into the last small space before the tailgate swung up, pressing hard against my thigh.

There was a dank smell to the press of us – the creeping moisture in the air against unwashed bodies, badly laundered clothes or boots that hadn't been dried out properly. Some of the blokes nodded off, some took up murmured conversations, Aussie guys together, the English together. The rasp of the tyres was enough to let me phase out any talk. There didn't seem to be any point in telling anyone about Davy, and how could I?

About a mile outside of town the ute stopped at Roy's shack and honked. Every morning he came out at once like he was stood waiting with his hand on the doorknob.

I kept my head down pretending to sleep.

Roy said, 'Roit, you, pommie, hoppit.'

The guy sitting opposite me, Steve or Simon or Stuart maybe, was forced to get out of the truck to let Roy on. After the tailgate was up, that guy had to stand on the rear step and hang on to the roof for the rest of the journey.

Roy's knees pressed against mine. He jerked them. 'Oi! Oi, Soft.' Forcing me to look up. His shaven head and stubble blended. He looked pleased with himself.

'You bastards are a roit miserable lot. What's the matter with you cunts? Beersy, how's you mate? Tonto, ya still hoppin, ey? Silly bastard. How bout you, Prick?' Roy was the source of various nicknames in the crew. 'Hey Beersy. Beersy mate. Ya never guess who I've left at moi place.' Beersy down the other end was as thick-set as Roy was wiry. He always wore tight little footie shorts and a singlet that showed the tattooed tiger on his shoulder and the rolls of flesh at his gut. 'That Bronwyn slut. Ya know the one with the fackin big norks.'

'Na shit.'

'Na shit. She's back at the shack, facked senseless. Tellin ya that little bitch was fackin screamin an buckin like a fackin wounded croc. Tell ya what though, I can't be facked with all that writhin and squealin shit.'

Beersy beamed boyishly. 'Ow'd ya sort er then Roy?'

'Just fackin flipped her over and stuck it in her arse. Didn't stop her screamin, but it stopped me fackin listenin.'

Other blokes hoofed and huffed in appreciation.

He caught my glance. 'Whasammatter Soft? Ya don't think that's funny? You're a bit of a fackin queer anyway, incha mate? Wouldn't know a pair of bloody norks if they landed on ya fackin head.'

There was nothing I could say to stop him playing to his crowd.

'So you thought you'd crack on to that Swedish Sheila, did ya Soft. She wasn't havin none of it though, ey Soft, ey? Really gave you the flick, fa sure. Hey, you fellas remember that yesterday? Jeez that was funny. God ya were fackin screamin like a girl.' They all laughed.

After the laughs had died, Roy leaned over. 'Ya should realise that I'm poppin that bit of lolly. Ey? Diya not know I'm fackin given her the old fella, ey?' With his meaty breath in my face, he growled, 'So ya better leave er well enough alone, ey, ya soft bastard.'

We turned off the bitumen onto a rough road. Steve or Simon or Stuart Maybe clinging on tight as we rattled and hopped over the storm-channelled track.

Then Davy was there.

Literally.

Davy was there squeezed into the tiny space between Roy and Don. Roy was caught up in some rant, trying to out-lewd Don with his sexual fairytales. Davy was there winking up at me and giving me a thumbs-up. His beard was fluffing in the breeze. No one else reacted. They all just continued nodding off or droning on, and all I could do was stare. Davy winked again with a cheery nod, dead gallous. I failed to suppress my laugh.

'What's so fackin funny, Jocko?'

'Eh, what, sorry?'

And Davy was gone.

'I says what's so fackin funny about moi brother's woife?'

'W... w... well, you guys were laughing, weren't ye?'

A loud cackle came from the other end of the truck.

Roy snapped round. 'So who the fack's the funny bloke, ey?' The truck bumped and heaved on the track; heads bobbed.

Someone called back, 'What you talking about Roy?'

He squared up to me. 'Who's ya mate up there?' And the guffaws came again, loud and rolling. Roy leaned forward and shouted up the truck, 'Who the fack is laughin?'

'Fack's sakes Roy, what ya on about? Nobody's laughing.'

'Give it a fucking rest Roy.'

But I didn't get it. Why hadn't they heard?

And there he was again, round the back of Roy, hanging off the outside of the truck with my old t-shirt flapping and cracking in the breeze and his bottom poking out. His head was right by Roy's ear, face split in a leering grin. Davy sucked on one of his fingers and stuck it deep into Roy's ear.

'Ah fack! Don ya dirty bastard!'

'What?'

'What the fack d'you stick in my fackin ear ya dirty bastard?'

'What the fack you talkin about?'

'What the fack just went in my fackin ear?' Roy was screaming.

A voice came from behind me, Davy's low brogue shouting, 'Yer loosin it big man.'

'Ey?'

Roy's glare gave me the fear of God but Davy's voice came soft in my ear. 'Tell him tae gie it a break.'

'Eh… Give it a break Roy.'

'Tell him that he's workin too hard.'

'I think... You're working too hard, mate.'

Roy was getting confused. 'Soft, what the fack are you on about?'

So was I.

'Tell him yer jist a wee bit concerned.'

'I'm just a bit concerned for you Roy.'

'Aboot the state ae his health.'

'About the state of your health.'

'Tell him he shouldnae be stayin up aw nicht when he's got a hard day's work tae be daein.'

'Roy… you shouldn't really be staying up all night. You know, when you've got a hard day's work to do.'

'Soft, are you takin the piss?'

The ute pulled to a halt.

'Tell him no, yer jist a bitty worried that he isna fit for a day's workin after a night like he's had.'

The lads were starting to get up out their seats, hunching under the roof.

'No Roy, I'm just a bit worried for you. I mean, are you fit for a hard day's work after the wild night you've had?'

There were a few sniggers.

'Aye, an tell the ugly gowk tae mind his manners and no talk aboot wimmen like that.'

'And Roy…' He stopped as he was about to step down from the truck, '…would you…'

Roy screwed his eyes up as he waited for what I had to say.

Davy climbed down and gave me a wink as he walked away from the truck.

'Well, eh, you know, Roy... You can always have a wee rest if you... if ye find the strain is getting too much for you. I'm sure none of the lads here mind.'

Don slapped Roy on the back and another bloke said, 'Yeah Roy. Don't go straining yourself mate. You're hearing things.' The others laughed.

I was trembling. Why had Roy not smacked me in the face? I wanted to ask Davy how he'd done all that, but he was nowhere to be seen.

We started on a new field that morning. Night rains had left the ground super soft. Between the rows of trees, the troughs were a slurry of deep mud. I stumbled my way through most of the morning.

Within the first hour I was lagging behind. Old Graham kept a warning tally from the truck. 'You won't be on this gang much longer boy if ya don't put it up a gear.' It had been said so many times before that it blurred into the background like the smear of greenery, the bur of insects and the rattle of a sudden downpour.

After the rain, I didn't slip but sunk and stuck, having to pull each footstep away from the ground.

Twice when I went after a tree with Roy under it, he cut at the wrong angle so that the bunch went off to the side and I had to lurch after it, trying to stay upright. He cackled and shouted abuse as I lumbered off.

Occasionally I thought I caught glimpses of Davy tracking along beside me, a few metres off, or once sitting in a tree, peeling back the skin of a banana, but I couldn't give him attention for long against the fight to move, the deep aching in my back and thighs and the sharp pain at my knees from the number of jars and scrapes they took.

At lunch, I took my sandwiches and a cup of tea under an old passion fruit tree at the end of the field. Its bed was raised enough to be relatively dry under my bum, and its shade let me cool a little as I fanned myself with my cap. Several purple bulbs of passion fruit lay scattered around, some already squished or chewed by wildlife, many whole. I couldn't summon the effort to split the soft husks and suck out the pearly seeds. I closed my eyes and hoped the tea could vitalize my limbs.

'Wullie son, whit are ye daein this terrible job for?'

For the first time, Davy's face was level with mine. Deep tracks of worry lines wound across his shiny brow.

'Aw Davy, I wish I knew.'

'Don't yous youngsters come tae Australia for aw the action and adventure?'

'Aye we do, but… but well, it never really worked out like that.'

'I'm tellin ye son, ye cannae keep battlin awa like this.'

'It's got to be done.'

'Does it? Could ye no jist jack it and heid tae a beach?'

'I've done that, and it's not much fun on yer own. At least here I'm making a bit of money. I'm hopin I can head home with some.'

'Whit? Back tae Scotland?'

'Aye. My year's almost done.'

He fixed me with a look, eyes screwed up and half a smile, then his glance went to where the boys were slowly moving back to the field. 'Right ma boy, dinna fash yer beard.' Davy chucked me under the chin. 'Better the day, better the deed that's whit I awways say, an thur's nae better day than this.' He skipped off into the trees. The t-shirt I'd given him seemed to have shrunk, fitting him better and affording me the disturbing sight of scrotum drooping below the bottom seam.

I had not a clue what Davy meant, but no time to figure it out. I pushed up to my feet, pulled my cap back on and walked over to the smoko truck to drop off my cup. Roy's voice came out loud as he, Don, Beersy and Wobbo took their time climbing down. 'Ya don't wanna let these bastards think they can get away with it.'

The four English guys were waiting in the field. I let them pair off with a cutter and start, giving me a short lapse before the first bunch became available. Then I noticed Davy standing next to Beersy, waving me over. I trudged.

Roy shouted, 'Ya better move a bit faster than that ya fackin lazy bastard.'

I readied myself under the bunch. When it hit, it seemed like I'd got one of the lightest bunches ever. Beersy slapped the nanas in a signal for me to move off. Davy ran out in front, waving me to follow. The path he picked was clear and I followed as close I could. As I stepped up to the truck, Davy's hand was under the bunch and it lifted on with no effort at all.

Old Graham noticed the improvement in my pace. 'Keep at it Soft.'

As I jogged back I saw Davy standing by Wobbo. I took his bunch, this one not as light as the last, but far from heavy, and followed the wee man back to the truck again.

With Davy there, the afternoon progressed swiftly. He showed me which bunch to take and lead me by the easiest path to the truck. When the bunch turned out heavy, Davy got under it and helped shift the burden. My pace stayed good and the cutters started to call, 'Over here Soft.' 'Soft Jock, come on mate, ya ready for this one?'

Then Davy was stood next to Roy.

I realised that so far none of the afternoon's bunches had been Roy's.

'Soft bastard,' was what Roy said.

Then his bunch was on my back, and by god it was a heavy one. I waited for the stalk to be cut and for Davy's helping hand but when I heard the knife hit, the bunch suddenly got heavier. Roy's second blow had cut the trunk of the tree again, freeing it completely and leaving me under the weight of the bunch and the tree combined. My knees gave out and I collapsed under the lot.

'Told ya, ya soft bloody bastard.' Then he cut the stalk.

Lifting a full bunch on your own is seriously hard, and I knew I would get no help from the nasty nutter but Davy was with me. He pulled me up and tossed the bunch onto my back. 'On ye go Wullie.'

And we set off.

This time, it felt like he was holding me and the bunch from above, a seven-foot midget lifting me into flight. I can still picture Roy's gaping face as we toted the bunch lightly to the truck.

Roy waited with his machete crossed over his chest. 'Oi, Soft, over ere.' He waved away another humper. I could see that he had chosen the biggest bunch he could find.

I jogged over. 'Keep them coming Roy.'

When his knife hit, I saw a black something spring away from the tree. It bounced from the ground onto my chest at the same moment the bunch hit my back. A spider. A dirty great spindly-legged stripy banana spider as big as my palm leapt from the tree to the ground and up on to my chest. I jumped and let the bunch fall. With the back of my hand, I brushed the spider off. The touch of it gave me shivers.

Roy was buckled with laughter.

This time he helped me get the bunch onto my back. It was heavy and Davy didn't come to help my stagger over the yards to the truck.

'C'mon Soft, back over ere. What you fackin hangin about for? Scared of little fackin spiders, are ya?'

I got myself under the bunch and waited for the thump. I heard Roy's knife hit the tree, then Roy's scream. I spun round to see him doing a St Vitus dance, twitching and flicking at himself. A spider was on his neck, but he was swiping at his leg. Then I realised there was a spider on the top of his head, a spider on his chest, on his arm. Roy was covered in spiders.

His curses and thrashing had stopped the other guys working.

'Whassamatter wiv you, Roy?'

'Ants in yer pants?'

'Nah, he's got fackin spiders in em.'

'Ah hah hah hah.'

Above our heads, I spotted Davy hopping from tree to tree, a crazed little monkey, flicking spiders at Roy. Most of them hit, others landed on the ground then crawled or jumped at him. The blokes laughed.

I stepped closer. 'Roy. Roy, hold on. Stop jumpin. Hold on Roy, hold it.' I reached out and flicked a small spider from his shoulder, the touch making me tremble. Roy managed to grab the one out from his neck and hurl it away. I flicked another and between us we cleared them off. The spiders skittered into the undergrowth.

Beersy slapped Roy on the back. 'Jeez Roy, ya know they're harmless, don't ya?'

Don stood back in disgust. 'Jumpin around and squealin like a friggin girl.'

'Fack off you lot. There's nothin the fackin matter with me. Ga on, fack off. Get back to ya work.' He pulled himself to his full height, several inches over me, pinned his shoulders back but at the same time his eyes widened as he stared at me. He turned swiftly and paced away up the row.

Two of the English guys stopped by me. 'Nice work Jock.'

'How'd he get all them spiders on him?'

'I dunno.' Davy's musky scent dropped through the air. 'Must be his fragrance.'

'Ha, yeah, he don't half stink. Would've freaked me out though, all them spiders.'

'Yeah, it would've freaked anyone out.'

Someone else came over to cut the tree. The bunch turned out to be not nearly as heavy as I'd thought. In fact, for the rest of the day, it seemed like I was getting the easy part of the job. If I looked Davy would be there above me swinging through the trees or running next to me, but when I stopped moving he didn't come close enough to talk.

Roy gave me a wide berth.

*　　　*　　　*　　　*

We were heading back to the ute at five when Don stopped and dived into a bush. 'Ere, ya buggers, have a look at this.' He came out backwards, tugging at something. He leaned on both heels and pulled hard on the tail of a snake that emerged long and thick. Not deep brown, this one was striped white, black and tan. 'He's a fackin beaut. Lookit this lazy bastard, thinks he can have a kip while we're doing all the bloody work.' Seven foot of snake emerged, then Davy came out, sitting on the snake's back near to its head where it whipped and lashed. He was riding it like a cowboy, waving an imaginary Stetson and calling, 'Yeeeeehaw'.

The other fellas around joined us, laughing at the site of Don with a riled snake trying to whip round and get him.

Even with Davy fooling, the sight of it gave me the jitters.

Don started to pass the tail of the snake through his hands, hand over hand, slowly letting the snake smooth through, working further up its body. As he did so, the snake began to settle; its lashing eased and its head lowered to the ground. In the short gap between Don's hands and where the snake's head touched the ground, Davy slipped off.

Don said, 'Allroit, which one of you pommies wants to hold this big bastard then?'

The four other Brits backed off.

Davy pushed me forward. 'Yer awright, Wullie. Burnt bairns may dread the fire, but no you, ma lad. Go ahead.'

I stepped up.

Don said, 'Ya sure Soft. Didn think ya loik snakes much.'

Davy said, 'Go on yersel, Wullie.'

'Go on, I'll take it.'

And I held out my hands.

'Ya sure Soft? It'll know if yar afraid.'

Don let the weight of it softly fall into my hands. The skin was smooth like hard burnished leather. Its body glided through my hands; its muscles moved under the skin as though independent from it.

Davy stood beside me. 'Nae bother tae ma laddie.'

*   *   *   *

On the journey home, I was at the tailgate again. Roy was at the other end. Three of the English guys were bunched up near me – Mark, Paul and Gary they were, not Prick, Tonto or Shitbeak – and Steve again hung on the outside. They were in high spirits, but I feigned exhaustion and zoned out because I knew Davy was at my shoulder. I waited until we hit the tarmac and then under the drone I took my chance.

'Davy, what was going on today?'

'Och, I telt ye son, you done me a service and I will no soon forget it.'

'Noh, no. What I mean is… I mean, am I losing it?'

'Dinna be daft son.'

'But how can you… How come one minute, I'm squashed under a bunch of bananas and the next, you've picked me up and I'm… we're sprinting like we're carrying feathers? Or what about, I mean… there's you messing Roy up, and then… How come you're on my shoulder giving me the right things to say?'

'Och, it's jist a wee bitty magic fae the hameland. We canna let oor ain be treated the way they bampots were carryin on.'

'It was brilliant. You were…'

'Ach, Wullie, son, ye didna really need me. You could sort that Roy eejit onyday.'

'No Davy, I couldn't. One thing but. How is it that nobody else can see you? I mean, it seems like I'm the only one'

'Eh, have ye no seen me talkin tae other folk? I'm daein it aw the time.'

'No… Davy, I've not.'

'Ach, enough ae these blethers. Listen, there's something I've been meanin tae ask you. Whit's aw this aboot a Swedish lassie?'

*   *   *   *

CHAPTER 4

The ute pulled up in Tully and we all tumbled out.

Paul grabbed my arm. 'Hey Jock, we're all heading into Top. You coming for one?'

Gary joined him. 'C'mon Jock.'

Paul tipped his hand to his mouth. 'I bet you're gagging for a pint?'

I was, and Davy, grinning up into his cheeks, was rubbing his throat.

'OK, only it's William, not… That's my name, William.'

'Sure.'

'Cool Will, let's go.'

I had been in to the Top pub – further up the street than the Bottom pub – twice on a Friday, post work and apparently to see in the weekend with my workmates. I left alone after my first drink both times. And this was a Tuesday.

We launched through the double doors, Steve and Mark too, feeling like a posse. Beersy, Wobbo, Don and Roy came in behind us and together we took up a clump round the near end of the bar that filled the centre of the broad room. There was a scattering of other afterworkers around, a few with their drinks perched on the ledge that ran round the walls.

Davy scuttled in behind us. The return swing of the doors caught him in the back and sent him tumbling among our feet and up against the leg of a stool with a paralytic old drunk on it. Davy elaborately dusted himself off. His head did not even reach as high as the seat of the stool.

'You alright Davy?'

'Aye. I'm jist gonae get masel a drink.'

The drunk's head, hanging down on his chest, swung with the jostles as Davy stepped from rung to seat and up on to the bar with a nimbleness defying the age he looked.

Before he'd passed out, the old fella had obviously ordered a beer, which Davy grabbed and chinned in two gulps. I saw froth fly from his smacking lips. He gave me his wink and skipped over an ashtray and a wine glass to the next beer he found. And still no-one noticed.

I saw him. I would swear to you then and now that there was a tiny wee man moving around on top of the bar. I saw the glass he picked up. I saw the level of the beer drop and the splash as he left it. But yet, the guy whose beer it was didn't pay a blind bit of attention, nor did the chatting barmaid when Davy stepped over her arm. A man not much higher than my knee on the bar, stealing drinks and giving winks. My wee pal.

Paul caught my attention. 'Will, a beer for you?'

Orders were shouted and beers arrived. Conversation was scant: a couple of references to this afternoon's snake and to Roy's spiders, but he cursed down anyone that brought it up. We moved quickly from the first to our second schooner.

Davy was doing circuits, taking pegs out of any drink he could get hold of, except mine. He hopped, jumped, strode and teetered between glasses, bottles, drinkers and staff but managed to avoid banging into people or knocking things over. Every time he passed Roy's glass, he dropped something into it. I saw a couple of peanuts, then a matchstick. I stopped looking.

Two sips into my second schooner and I was bursting for a pee. Top was filling up and to get to the toilet I had to excuse myself past sweaty hairy bodies. In Sydney, the bars have signs reading, 'No Singlets or Thongs'. That would cut out most of Top's clientele – beefy arms and hairy toes to the fore. I tried not to press too close or tread too heavily.

Davy was perched on the metal trough next to me. A thick flow splashed down between his feet.

'It's braw in here, eh Wullie? Could dae wi a few wummin but.'

'Hey Davy, will ye leave Roy alone now. I think he's had enough.'

'Och, I'm jist messin aboot. Nae harm done.'

'Leave him though, eh? Hows about we just have another beer and shoot off back to the campsite.'

'I think we can manage that, son.' He sprung down to the floor. 'Aye, I like this. Braw n busy on a Tuesday. My kinda pub,' then he shot off between the legs.

Another field gang were piling in, forcing me to take the long route round three sides of the bar. Between bodies I caught glimpses of our team across the way, their shouts and laughter drowned out. There were two blonde women with them, talking to Paul and Gary. Davy was round there already, stood on the bar peering down on someone between Mark and Roy, someone shorter who leaned in such a way that her dark ponytail was caught between her back and the bar. It was Beata. Beata stuck in the middle of my picking gang. My tummy clenched; I couldn't face her again. I'd have to just sneak straight past to the door and get out. Quickly.

'Excuse me. Sorry, excuse me.'

Clumps of men barred the way. Some bloke leaned across passing a glass, another turned to look up at the TV, blocking me with broad shoulders.

'Sorry. Sorry, can I just get through?' A small gap and I had to brush between a bottom and a hip. Growls from huge homophobes.

At the bar corner I looked across; Roy was leaning in, too close to Beata, Beersy stood with him. I willed Mark to keep her attention, to get her away from that nasty piece.

I shunted more aggressively.

Davy was on the bartop calling over heads to me, 'Hey William, Beata's ower there.'

'I know, Davy, I know.'

'Ye better shift it, that Roy is giein her the glad eye.'

I reached the door, about to push it and flee.

'Hoi!' Davy shouted, 'Where ye goin, laddie?'

'I cannae...'

'Whit aboot Beata?' He was at my side, holding the corner of my shirt. 'Is she no the lassie yer after?'

'Yeah, but...'

'Is she no the one, the best one. The difference?'

I looked down, and the little man's cheeks were pushing up from under his beard. 'Go on, Wullie,' he said, 'I'll help ye oot.'

I squeezed past the backs of Paul and Gary, both engrossed in the girls they were chatting up, and came around Steve. Roy and Beersy had closed in on Beata. Mark was sulking away. I thought I saw Roy's hand on her arm, his face close to her ear.

'What do I do?'

'Get her ootae there Wullie.'

'But how?'

'Jist get a hold ae her. Say anyhin tae her n get her awa.'

'But how do I get her past Roy and Beersy?'

'Jist belt on in there son.'

I shouldered Beersy to one side, not too hard. 'Hey Beata. Hi. How are you?' And held out my hand.

She looked round hopefully. 'H...' But looked puzzled to see me.

Roy came quick. 'What the fack do you want, Soft Jock?'

Davy nudged the back of my leg. 'Jist sayin hello.'

'Just saying hello. How are you Beata?' I reached out my hand and took her wrist. She tensed. I scratched my brain for a route out. 'Eh... em... I was just talking to... Davy over there.' Her eyebrows knitted. I tried again, pulling lightly on the wrist. 'Davy, yeah, Davy wants to talk to you.' Roy's hand did not leave her other arm.

Beata looked past me, probably for a more familiar face. Davy had managed to get up on the bar behind her and was making tugging motions, but what could I do? I didn't want to be the worse of two evils. I tried to compose my expression, implore, but not let on to Roy. I wanted to appear trustworthy but probably looked as confused as she did. My resolve ebbed, but as I made to let go her voice came. 'Hello it's... The Cure t-shirt, right?'

'Yeah, that's right. Do you want to come over and say hello?'

'Sure, sure, that would be great.'

Roy sucked a tut through his teeth.

Beata stepped away from the bar. For a moment Roy held on. A hiss broke off into, 'Why'd ya wanna go off with that poofta?'

Beata turned on him. 'Let go.'

Red marks ringed her upper arm where he took his hand off. Beersy stepped back to let us through. As I led her out of the group, Mark looked gutted, but Paul gave me a wink and I got a playful prod that I thought was from Gary until I saw Davy hanging off Gary's belt hoops. My hold slipped from Beata's wrist onto her hand, sending electric tremors up my arm. We squeezed through the bodies to a small space in the corner. The crowd forced us into closeness; my timidity forced us into a moment with nothing but waiting in which she scanned our tight corner.

Finally she said, 'Who is Davy?'

'I'm sorry, I know you don't know me.' She would leave soon, I knew, but I wanted her to stay. 'I just thought you might... Well, I don't know what you think of Roy, but I thought it might be good to get away from that spot.'

'Yes, that guy... he's... not very pleasant, isn't he?'

'Yeah, well ... but I thought maybe you...'

'That Roy think I want to go with him. Aak, what a horrible idea. I hate the guys like him.'

'But, your friend, Emma, didn't him and Emma have a thing?'

'What? No! She cannot stand with him!'

I guessed that while she was chatting to me, she was also looking for an escape from this corner I had dragged her into. I needed Davy. Why wasn't he near?

I said, 'Sorry, it's just... Also, I just... I really wanted to say hi.'

'Hi.' She smiled, 'I'm sorry, I don't know what is your name.'

'It's William.'

'William? OK. Not Will or Bill?'

'Well, it could be... Bill... if you liked. I mean...'

'No, William is nice.'

She pushed away a loose strand of hair that had been playing off her top lip. 'Well, thank you William, but I'll...'

'Sorry, do you want to get back to your friends?'

She looked towards the bar.

I said, 'That's them with Paul and Gary, isn't it? They seem nice.'

'Yes. I guess also, Roy is still there.'

The clamour of the bar came between us, no music or even pokey machines, just the clash of loud male voices. She seemed reluctant to go but reluctant to stay. I needed to give her a reason. 'Would you like another drink? A beer or a wine or something?'

'No, I'm... Well OK, can I have a vodka coke please?'

'OK. Do you want to... I mean will you go back over to your friends?'

'It's OK, I will wait here.'

Behind the bar, Davy was standing by the optics, leaning over and apparently whispering in the barmaid's ear. She grinned and whooped at some joke. Davy threw his head back, laughing. When he saw me, he pointed her to come over for my order.

The wee man slipped down then climbed onto my side of the bar.

'Errs ma boy. So howzit goin?' He was slurring through a damp beard. Are ye gonnae be bringing her home wi ye the night?'

'Hardly. I don't even know what to say to her.'

'Whit dye mean? It cannae be that hard, she's ony a lassie.'

'That's it. That's the problem. I've no idea how to talk to a lassie.'

The barmaid came back. I paid and picked up the glasses. The whole time, Davy scrutinised me. 'OK, son, I'll see ye in a minute.'

I got back to Beata and we cheersed, clinked and drank. I wiped steam from my glass and watched bubbles rise through my beer. I took another long glug. Beata filled the pause. 'So why is it you are here in Top on Tuesday? It's not normally, is it?' Imperfect diction, with the almost perfect accent – the scoops and dips of the Scandy that make English more tuneful, more playful.

'Er... well... you know, a beer with the lads after work, and...'

'Do you like work with those guys?'

There was a loud bellowing from behind me and what sounded like two men having sex. I guessed someone was wrestling.

'Well, you know, that's the gang.'

I was so much in dread of silence that I could think of nothing to say. I cast around for something to spark a topic and noticed Davy down at hip level. Then his voice whispered to me, 'Jist ask her whit she's up tae. Ask her aboot her work n that.'

'So... how's the stringing? Is it... well... is it good work?'

'No, it is awful, but I really need the money, and I've met a lot of nice people here in Tully. Have you?'

'Oh, aye, well...'

Davy circled Beata and said, 'Ask her aboot her country.'

'So... you're Swedish, aren't you?'

'Yes. And you, I remember, you are Scottish?'

Davy used a stool to propel himself up onto the drinks ledge that ran round the wall. Head height now, he looked at Beata. 'Ask her aboot her travels. Go on son.'

'Have you been in Australia long?'

'Six months. Hopefully, after a month here I might be able to travel more.'

I was a bit unsettled by how fixedly Davy was staring at her, but he gave me the question, 'Where's she want tae go?'

'I might go up to Cairns. I'd love going into the rainforest, maybe go diving.'

He reached out and rested a hand on her shoulder. 'You wannae dae that too. Tell her ye think it would be grand tae dae that.'

She answered with a thrilled trill, 'Really it would. It must be wonderful under the reef.'

Davy turned to me with serious intent. 'Ask her if she wants another drink.'

Beata had another vodka.

Our conversation flowed through travels and family and dreams and careers. All the time Beata played with the carved bone that hung on a leather thong around her neck. As we became absorbed in our own little bit of space and time, Beata relaxed, leaning against the shelf, almost against the wee man. Davy's intensity lessened. He genially prompted our conversation while he twirled a lock of Beata's hair. It was the colour and lustre of wood stained under a dark reddish resin.

Still the advice came. 'Smile at her.'

I smiled.

'Touch her arm.'

I touched.

'Stand closer.'

'Whisper in her ear.'

'Ask her if she wants another drink.'

Then this little old man, this little Scots granpaw, leaned over and gently kissed the side of the beautiful girl's cheek.

My breath caught mid-whisper.

Beata pulled back to look at me. 'Are you OK?'

'I'm... I'm... fine. Fine. Are you OK?'

'I'm great, thanks.'

With an unflustered smile she went back to what she was telling me. I hardly heard. I was frightened and guiltily excited. I didn't want Davy to be there anymore. I didn't want to imagine what he was working on her, but I didn't want her to leave.

Davy, almost sweetly, ran his fingers down the side of her face and Beata stopped speaking to sigh. Her lips parted slightly.

I wanted to speak up and say to Davy, No, it's not good. It's not nice. Enough now!

But he turned, winked and then leaned in as if to give her a full kiss on the mouth. I reached out and pulled Davy off the shelf. He thumped to the floor.

Beata looked alarmed.

I said, 'Sorry. I'm sorry, I...'

Then she took my hand, pulled me closer and kissed me. My head reeled at the sweet taste of cola on her soft, wet lips.

When the kiss broke, I looked down. Davy, sat on the floor, had hurt in his eyes. I mouthed, sorry.

Beata touched my chin and tipped my face back towards her.

I could hear Davy struggling, as if with great effort to his old limbs, to get back on his feet. When he spoke, his voice was flat. 'Look intae her eyes, Wullie. Put your hand on her back and tell her how bonnie she is.'

My struggle became one of trying to ignore my surge of guilt, while trying to keep Beata close, talk to her nicely and hope that she was happy.

And she was, giggly and fun happy, and tipsy. When she took her turn to buy a drink, she said, 'It's not normally, I drink like this.'

Then Davy said, 'Ask if she wants tae go hame. Ask if ye can walk her.'

I walked Beata to her hostel. We stopped and kissed in doorways, under trees, against cars.

Davy was always somewhere near. 'Hold her hand. Tell her aboot yer family. Stop and kiss her again. Hold her tighter. Talk aboot the stars.'

To say goodbye, we kissed long and hard at the hostel door. Beata whispered, 'It's been nice getting to know you, William.' But it was me that had got to know her and the hot breath passion of our fumbles under the moth-whisked porchlight made me gasp and grasp out. 'Can I see you again tomorrow?'

'Yes. Yes please. I'd like that.'

We shared another deep kiss that Beata broke off. 'I better go, I must get up early.'

'Me too.'

I stepped to the door with her as she took her key to the lock then stepped inside.

Davy stopped the door swinging shut. 'Hoi, look my lad, there's no onybody aboot.'

The hostel was run by an old couple. They managed it in an overprotective, over-controlling way – strict rules to be adhered to, curfews and definitely no visitors at night, definitely no members of the opposite sex in the dorms. Usually a night porter sat next to the entrance until midnight when the shutters came down.

Davy grabbed my hand, 'C'mon son.'

'No, I...'

I was inside and Beata turned at the bottom of the stairs.

I said, 'Beata, I...'

'Come quickly, William.' She reached out for my hand. 'Quick!'

Davy said, 'Ya dancer!'

We snuck up the two darkened flights of stairs, holding hands, stepping softly, shushing and giggling. Someone's soft-soled feet skiffed across the first floor corridor. We sped up the second flight and lightly bundled to her door.

As we stepped inside, I heard Davy's feet skittering across the linoleum floor.

Beata flick the switch to the bare overhead bulb – I got a flash of the whole girlthing cluttered room, a single bed and a double bunk at the walls – but she clicked it off again just as quickly. 'Too bright.' I made no move while she stepped away and scuffed and bumped to the window to twist the blind and let in the moonlight. In it, her profile was a vision of blue skin and black flickers of hair. We met in the middle of the room.

I couldn't help being conscious of Davy. It was uncomfortable to think of an old man in the room with us, somewhere. His voice whispered out. 'Wullie, my laddie, now's yer chance. Take it jist a wee bitty further, y'ken?'

I ran my hand up under her t-shirt.

'William, no.' She gently stroked my arm away. 'Just lie down with me.'

We kicked off our shoes and climbed into her bed.

The half light of the room reduced us to hushed whispers. I was filthy, banana field raw, she must have been too, but we clung close, skin on skin at our arms and legs, face and lips. It felt like something childish, sneaking into a dorm room, kissing and cuddling, and we giggled at our daring. Beata told me a story of a school trip and midnight feasts. I realised how drunk she was as her words slurred and her tale trailed off whenever sleep tried to take her.

And then the door sprang open. The light burst on above us.

I rolled over, tumbling off the narrow space of the single bed and knocking Davy off. I hadn't realised he was perched at our feet.

Two blonde women came in, Beata's friends, Emma and Suzie.

Emma's mouth hung in surprise, 'Hey... What... What's he doing in here?'

Beata lifted her head, 'Hey Em. Sorry, William's just... He's just...' She was face down, her t-shirt scrunched up her slender brown back. It was hard to believe; the thought of it, the thrill of just that sight. But already, under a bright light, there was a nagging doubt – it must have been the drink that had weakened her judgement or... or Davy.

The wee man's face was folded over, giving angry eyes at the intruders.

I said, 'Yeah, I'm... I'm just...'

'He's just leaving.' Emma's voice was edged with annoyance. 'Isn't he?'

Davy shook his head, 'NO! No yer not, son. Tell her tae sling it.'

'Eh, ah, no, I'm...'

She barked, 'You're leaving! You shouldn't be in here, you'll get... You'll get someone in trouble.'

Beata propped herself up on an elbow and tugged her t-shirt down. 'Hey Suze.'

Suzie said, 'Hi Bee.'

'Don't worry, Emma. He's just going.'

'You better be bloody careful that no-one sees you.'

Davy huffed and puffed and tutted, but Beata beckoned me over. She took my hand and pulled me to her for a kiss. 'Goodnight. I'll see you tomorrow, OK.'

As I bounced home, Davy and I didn't have to talk. We just gave each other a look, because we both knew.

*　　　*　　　*　　　*

CHAPTER 5

When my alarm screeched out next morning, Davy wasn't there. A lingering musk hung around the hut, but no sign of the wee man. The fridge was lying open with contents tipped out onto the floor. The last of the beer had been drunk and the can scrunched and discarded by the door.

I didn't have time to fret. I was heavy-headed and needing to get to the pick up.

The ute was already in when I got there.

'Hi Paul. Morning Gary. What's going on? Why've you not left?' As I spoke, the truck jerked and started to roll.

'We were just waiting for you.'

Gary leaned towards me, conspiratorially. 'So Will, Beata eh?'

'Eh erm, well… it's…'

Paul picked it up. 'Yes mate, you dirty devil you. I can't help but notice you haven't had a change of clothes since yesterday.'

'Or a wash you dirty bastard. You've not been home, have ya? I don't think Emma would be too pleased at having an extra roommate.'

I couldn't help but laugh. 'Aye, she didn't seem too chuffed when…'

'Oooooh, so you were at it then. Nice one.' Little gleeful Gary.

'Fuck's sakes, we're not allowed anywhere near that hostel with Suzie and Em, and this fly bastard is right in there. That was a pretty smooth move you made on Beata last night. We could all take tips from you, mate.'

'How was she then?' Gary looked like he actually expected me to answer that.

Paul added, 'You not worried about Roy?' A point I hadn't thought of. I might have been fly, but Roy was still a hardman. He had plenty of dirty tricks for a normal day – things to wind me up, humiliate me – but what about when I'd taken a woman from under his nose? There was the potential that he could do something really nasty, violent, even dangerous out in the field where no one could see.

When we pulled up at Roy's shack, I watched for his burst through the door, for his brash angry bark. The truck hooted, but Roy didn't appear. The horn went a second time and still no Roy.

Beersy spoke up. 'Filthy bastard must've been at it again. Ere, let me past. I'll go get him.'

We shifted our knees out the way as the big man jostled through, and watched him step up and rap on Roy's door. After a moment, he pushed it open, stuck his head inside and then stepped right in. In the minutes that elapsed everyone watched the door. Beersy came back out and waved to the driver, signalling that all was cool, but still no Roy. The row shuffled up to let Beersy back onto the truck and he sat next to me.

Roy stepped out and slammed the door shut. The whole shack shook. In his few steps to the van I saw a bit of gauze taped to his scalp in a big cartoonish cross of sticking plaster and bruises on his face. Steve shifted in his seat, getting ready for the order to move, but Roy lifted the tailgate shut, stepped onto the back ledge and banged on the roof. When Roy stood up his chest and head were hidden by the roof. We could see bruising and some deep grazes on his arms and legs. As the truck pulled away, I thought I heard him briefly cry out.

Beersy raised his eyebrows and puckered his lips in a whistle.

Steve asked, 'What's the score with Roy then?'

Paul and Gary bunched closer in.

Beersy glanced up Roy's way before he began. 'Well, sfar as I can get it, Roy was caught shaggin his fackin sisternlaw.'

'You're kiddin. What, actually on the job?'

'Na mate, I don't reckon. I reckon it was his brother found out somehow. Somebdy told him and he came after ole Roy last noit.'

'Looks like he gave Roy quite a kickin.'

'Yey. I think he must've gone at him with a fackin bat or somethin. Roy's not wantin to talk too much abaht it. Says he'll get the bastard back loik.'

I asked, 'Dye think he will?'

'You ever met Roy's brother?'

'No.'

'Jeez, he's a bad sort, he is. Makes Roy look like a fackin angel. A fackin midget angel n all. He's a huge bastard that Rodge.'

'Rodge? Roy and Rodger?'

'Yey, that's roit.'

The truck rattled and banged through the rest of the journey. We pulled up at the bottom of the sloping hill of an unplanted field. Roy stepped down and walked off up the hill following a furrow.

Old Graham came round the back of the ute and told us, 'Roit you lot, yar not pickin tday, yar plantin. See up top the field there, we've got a whole bunch saplings that need plantin out. I want each of you pommie fellas to pair up with one of these lads and they'll show you what ta do.'

As I walked up the field, Davy was next to me, stepping double time to keep up. He had somehow acquired a flat cap.

'Davy, hey. Where did you get to?'

'Aw, ye ken how it is, laddie. A wee bitty this needin done, a wee bitty that. I'm no much ae a sleeper anyhow.'

'But Davy, you weren't on the truck. How'd you get out here?'

'So onyway, you must be pretty pleased about yon Swedish lass.'

'Oh, I can't wait for tonight.'

'Aye, she's michty bonnie, michty bonnie.'

He'd also acquired a pair of flannel shorts and black round-toed shoes that looked as if they had been stolen from some wee boy on his way to school. He had a boy's cap perched on his head to match. The shorts hung almost to his ankles, my filthy old t-shirt tucked into them.

'You know, Davy, I think I need to say thank you for last night.'

'No me, lad, no me. It's aw yer ain daein.'

Talking to Davy slowed my walk down and by the time I reached the stacked plants there was only one of the Aussie guys left to pair up with – Roy. He stood at the top of the first row but had been bypassed by the others. Davy just shrugged and waved me on. Roy thrust a spade at me and said nothing. The bruising was mostly down the left side of his face, and it was bad: one swollen eye, the ear cauliflowered. His silence worried me. He must have been packed full of anger and frustration after his brother's attack and the most likely outlet for it all was here paired up with him.

Davy said, 'Aye well, that big bully deserves aw he gets.' I think he was trying to reassure me. 'C'mon Wullie, get started. I'll hing aboot an make sure Roy doesnae get up tae anyhin.'

The others had already started and I could see that in each pair, the pom was on the row, digging a hole, while the Aussie carried over the saplings to drop in and then both trod down the earth to firm it into the ground.

I shoved my spade in at the top of the row and felt the soft mulch and earth give against it. It was quick and easy to square out a hole about a foot deep. A ragged panting told me that Roy was there next to me with the sapling, but he didn't drop it into the hole, just left it next to me. The plant had a loosely tied bag around its base that had to be removed before it could be put into the earth. Roy moved off showing a bit of a limp. Roy had left me to undo the bag, drop the sapling in, scrape around some top earth and then tread it down. At this rate, I thought, Roy would be leaving me with stacks of plants as I struggled to get all the bits at my end carried out. The others were already two or three plants in, working methodically with start-of-the-day focus. Roy was trying to play with my head. As Davy helped me to tread down the earth, I expected Roy to be there with the second plant before we'd finished. He wasn't. He was still stood next to the stack, breathing in short, shallow gulps and holding on to his left side. I took my chance and quickly dug out the second hole. Roy didn't change position. I didn't want to badger him, but I thought he must have been waiting for me.

'Ready Roy.'

He hissed through his teeth, picked up a plant with his right hand as his left clutched his ribs. His face screwed up in pain. Each step seemed to take an effort of concentration on where his foot should fall. Davy stepped behind and poked Roy sharply in the back, causing him to wince and stumble. The wee man laughed. I shook my head and frowned him away. Roy's ten steps came slowly and he dropped the plant at my feet, drawing in a suck of air as he righted himself, panting as he walked back up.

I had long got the second sapling planted when Roy hirpled over with the third.

'Roy, you have a go at the diggin. I'll carry the plants.' I handed him the spade, then got on with unwrapping the sapling and planting it. Roy watched, barely balancing the spade, its tip pivoting against the ground.

I left him and went for the next plant. The short saplings were not that heavy, even with the clod of earth at the bottom. Sure, after carrying ten or twenty they would begin to weigh, but this first made an easy job. Roy had barely turned a spadeful of soil. He was awkwardly balanced, his left foot up on the spade head, but that side of his body was tensed up, pulling him over. He dropped his foot and tried to prise out a small clot of soil using only his right hand on the handle. Davy gave him a push that sent him tipping, stumbling to keep his balance. Roy gasped and moaned.

I stepped forward and grabbed the spade. To try to stop him falling, my other hand took his arm, his left.

'Ah, ya stupid cunt!' He shook my hand off and finally fell.

I left him to it, dug out the hole. Davy helped me plant the tree.

Under my breath I told Davy, 'Leave off him. He's in some state.'

'Like I say, he deserves it, and plenty more.'

I couldn't see his expression under the brim of his cap.

Moans and curses accompanied Roy's efforts to get back on his feet. He was silent when he came to stand next to me.

'Look Roy, which bit is better for you, the carryin or the diggin?'

With a rough grumble, he pulled himself up to as much of his height as he could, stamped his right foot then tried to stride manfully back to the plants. He hobbled. He grabbed one plant in each hand, jerked them away from the ground and immediately yelled out. He folded, crumpling down on top of the saplings.

Davy barked out in laughter.

The open field offered no cover, nothing to muffle Roy's cry, nothing to hide the sight of him in a suffering pile. The rest of the gang stopped, looked or started to come over.

I got to him first.

'Roy, are you alright, man?'

'Get the fack away. Fack off.'

Beersy joined us. 'Get up ya silly bastard.' He held out a hand but Roy stayed down, his arms wrapped tight around his ribs. For an instant when he looked at Beersy, the anguish of a hurt little boy was in Roy's face. He quickly turned away.

Don asked, 'Roy, ya orright mate?'

The rest came up and looked.

Old Graham took charge. 'Roit, get back on with it you lot. Get back to yar rows.'

I moved a bit away and watched Graham hunch down over Roy.

Davy tugged on my hand. 'Ha ha ha. Did ye see the look on eejit's face? Doesnae think he's so tough now, y'ken? That's rare that is.'

'Davy, stop. That's just not nice.' I couldn't help feel sorry for Roy. Too much pain. Too much humiliation.

Davy hunched his little shoulders, apologetically, but they were jiggling as he chortled.

Roy's voice raised. 'The fack I am.'

Graham shouted back, 'Well I'm taking yar as far as the bloody door an droppin yar off, then ya can do what the fack ya loik.' He stood up and called, 'Beersy, come an help me get Roy dahn to the ute.' Then to the rest of us, 'Roit, while I'm gone, keep at it, roit?'

We watched the slow progress of the three of them down the field – Graham and Beersy each under one of Roy's arms. It must have hurt a lot to be carried like that.

When Beersy got back, Don asked, 'Is he alroit, ey?'

'Ah fack mate, could be betta. Graham says I'm in charge, so betta crack on, ey?'

We kept working. Not having a gaffer gave us the chance to mess about a bit and take a few more breaks, but we still kept on. Old Graham had been working with Paul. With him away, the two of us worked together. The sun was broken by scattered clouds, giving moments of sun blast and moments of shade. We got a touch of breeze and there were occasional scatterings of rain as well. We sweat but got cooled. The work was monotonous, but we weren't picking bananas.

Davy suggested I start up a game of twenty questions with Paul, a way of passing the time. Before long, most of the gang were playing, shouting their questions across the field. After a few goes, I guiltily took Davy's idea of the next person to guess.

I asked, 'Who am I?'

'Male or female?'

'Male.'

'Alive or dead.'

'Alive, barely.'

Laughs and quizzical blurts. 'Are you famous?'

'Oh aye. In Tully. Infamous soon.'

'Australian or British?'

'Australian.'

'In Australia?'

'In Australia, currently travelling rapidly south.' More laughs as they caught on.

The last couple of questions were:

'Have you been hit on the head by Wily Coyote?'

'Have you got a walk like Long John Silver?'

When Graham pulled back up in the ute, we hadn't got much further up the field, but we were working. The gang was an odd number now and Old Graham was happy to take up the role he did best – supervising while the rest of us did the labour. Not long after he got back we had a lazy long lunch; he seemed to think that we had been working extra hard or that the job was extra tough, so we needed more of a break. Really the day turned out to be pretty good craic. Paul and I motored on fine, taking turns at digging or carrying. All of the pairs kept pretty much level throughout the day as we worked from one set of rows to the other. A bit of banter flew around, not the usual nasty shouts and jeers, more the jokes and teasing of a bunch of mates working together.

And Davy hung about, giving me quips and jokes to come back with when I needed them, just sunning himself or messing when I didn't. I think I saw him kicking at plants in some of the other rows, but by three in the afternoon the whole field was planted out, and Graham let us knock off early.

At the end of it all, the gang stood at the bottom of the field surveying our work.

'Shit,' said Mark, 'I didn't think we'd nearly get all of that done.'

Don leant on Mark's shoulder. 'Let's hope they don't all get washed away in the next big rain.'

*   *   *   *

I wanted to go to the hostel and find Beata, but she wouldn't be back from work yet, so I stopped by the Post Office to see if any mail had come in for me, Poste Restante.

Dear Willie

It's been a long time since I heard from you. I hope your alright son. I know you have been going off to have your adventures and all the rest but it would be nice if you could get in touch from time to time I haven't heard from you and its inevetible that I worry. I have hardly seen Helen these days because she is so busy with her work all the time she has not even called me for more than a week and there is nobody around hear much that I would give the time of day too. You know that the McGourlays moved just about two months ago now and without Meg around to talk to its like I don't get to see anyone these days. The health visitor comes in but she's a miserable old soul I cant say that it does me much good when she comes in. Only you really can manage things the right way around hear anyone else just gets in the way. I wish I could do it myself but you know what its been like ever since your father but I don't want to just complain about me. Anyway I was feeling better yesterday and I managed to get out in the car for the messages and today I knew that I would be able to write this letter to you just as long as my hands last.

I hope your enjoying yourself. It is so great for you, my own boy, doing these amazing things but I am really glad that your going to be coming back to us soon. You must be really missing your home and all of your things that you have hear and your friends. I have kept your room right for you and I will wait untill you get back before we put up the Christmas decorations because I know that you enjoy to do that so much each year.

How are Timothy and Alan tell them I said hello and I am sure their mothers are missing them too.

Lots of love from your

MumXXX

I sat on the bench outside the Post Office with Davy standing at my shoulder. 'Timothy and Alan,' then he put on a posh voice, 'Who are Timothy and Alan?'

'Oh, Tim and Al. That's ... They're some ... friends of mine. Well, they're the guys that I came over to Australia with.'

'From Scotland?'

'Aye.'

'Well that's braw, lads frae the hameland. We'll be hookin up wi them, will we no?'

'Jeez.' I shook my head. 'I hope not.'

'Aw, right. Bad sorts are they?'

'Ach, well ... They were my friends. Or I thought they were. I've known them since school. That's why we travelled over her together.'

'But they were holdin ye back, so ye ventured oot on yer ain? Bold lad.'

'No, it was just ... As soon as we got here they were, like, everybody's pal, running around like nutters, just like... not like they were at home at all. They spent all their time just smokin dope and partyin and ...'

Davy flicked my ear.

'Ow. What was that for?'

'Numpty.' A bony finger poked at me. 'Sounds like they boys were daein exactly whit you should be.'

'Thank you very much. I'm quite happy doing things my way.'

'Whit way? Talkin tae naebody, keepin yer heid doon, huvin a shite time?'

'Davy!'

Standing on the bench next to me, he came up near to my head height. His old man's face was concealed under all that white beard, but he sounded gruff. 'Ye need tae get oot ae that. Is that no how ye've got me aroon?'

'I'm not sure,' I said. 'Why is that?'

He snatched the letter out of my hand and probed it with his pointing finger. 'Yer maw doesnae exactly sound like a ray o light.'

'Hey.' I grabbed it back. 'Watch it. She's just not very well is all.'

'Aw bless.'

I scrutinised him. He just kept reading.

'Ever since yer father,' he said, 'There's a michty strange thing tae say, is it no? Ever since yer father whit? Ever since he last took her tae his bed?'

'What's with you? That's my mum, don't talk like that.'

'Whit? Whit's the deal?'

'Dad's dead.'

'Aw ya wee pet lamb.' He stroked my head. 'So whit happened tae the auld fella then?'

'Don't do that.' I pushed the hand away. 'An overdose. Sleeping tablets and whisky.'

'In the hoose?'

'No.' It tumbled out. 'He said he was down in London on business, but mum got a call saying he'd been found dead in a hotel in some wee seaside town in Ayrshire.'

'Aye, aye. A wee hideaway. So why's she bringing that up noo?'

'You know, one of my uncles, Urquhart, said on the day of the cremation that Dad had always been licentious and libidinous. Imagine saying that in front of a nine year old on the day his dad's buried.'

'Sounds like a good man, your paw. Dinna ken aboot yon Urquhart though.'

'He's dead too, not long after dad. Cirrhosis of the liver.'

'Crivvens, but you're frae good stock, eh? Come away ower the pub.'

Top was in sight of the post office.

'No, let's get back and freshen up.'

There was time yet to grab a bit of shopping, head back to the campsite, get washed and changed and put my best on. I tucked the letter back into its envelope and crammed it in a pocket. 'C'mon Davy, let's get a shift on.'

My hut was still turned upside down and still smelled vaguely of Davy. It had only been, what, not even two days since that morning. That seemed hard to believe. Hadn't Davy been around ages already?

In the enclosed space I began to wonder if the smell was a remainder or if Davy was still rank. 'Right, Davy, here's a towel. I think the pair of us need to get in the showers quick and have a good scrub.'

His lip curled, hand pulled away from the towel. 'Och, I dinnae think that's necessary.'

'It is. Come on now.'

I persuaded him into the cubicle next to mine in the shower block. I had to reach in and turn the knob for him.

The showers were good and hot and powerful.

'Here, Wullie, hae ye got that bar o soap there?'

A wet gnarled hand appeared under the wall of the cubicle, fingers twiddling.

'Here ye go.'

'So son, ye jist goannae get up the hostel an get the knickers aff her?'

'What? Davy, did you just say...?'

'Oh, eh, awfy sorry son, no, whit I meant y'see is are ye just away up there and tell her whit a bonnie lass she is.'

'Erm, well, right...'

'Ye should say ye've fair fell for her.'

'But I don't want to take it too fast, Davy. I'm going up there to talk, see if she's still interested. I mean, she was pretty drunk last night. She probably hardly remembers anything about it.'

'Dinna be daft son. Ye won her ower proper.'

'Hardly. I tell ye though Davy, it was so great. I've hardly even talked to a girl as nice as Beata before. Even if nothing else comes of it, last night was...'

Under the shower, doubts started to creep in about whether Beata would want to see me again. I closed my eyes and her face flashed across my memory. I suddenly realised I wouldn't have the guts to just rock up and talk to her. Sure we had talked for ages the night before, but we hadn't had much sober conversation. What if she regretted what had happened as much as I was blown away by it?

Davy sat up on the sink next to mine while I shaved, the little hand towel I'd given him wrapped around his waist.

I said, 'I don't think I'll know what to say to her.'

'Ach, ye dinna need tae worry aboot that, laddie. Ye ken that I'll be aboot tae gie ye wee pointers.'

'Will ye Davy? I think I'll need that. Just at the start, like. See later but, will you just leave us to it?'

'Aye, I will that Wullie. I will that.'

*   *   *   *

During the day, anyone could walk in and out of the hostel. For a while we hung out in the lounge area, where we could see everyone arriving.

Davy was wearing a t-shirt and a pair of shorts not unlike my own. After our shower, he had shot off, butt naked, across the campsite and came back wearing them. I asked where he got them. 'Frae the bins oan the other side ae the camp. Honest.' The t-shirt had Poo-shooter written on it and a cartoon of a grinning dog shooting poo from its puckered anus.

Feeling twitchy, I decided we'd better check Beata's room. I took the steps three at a time.

I stopped at her door, hand hovering, ready to knock.

'Go on son, rap as hard as ye can.'

'It's not that easy, Davy.'

'Aye it is. Here.' Davy battered three times on the door. I jumped and felt like running. Chappy like we played as kids, knock-door-run. An unbeckoned smile was on my lips when the door opened.

Beata did not return the smile. 'Hallo. It's you. Yes?'

'Hi Beata, I…'

And Davy had cleared off.

Beata frowned. She let the door fall open as she walked back into the room. I stepped in and closed the door.

Beata sat down on her bed. I scrabbled around for something to say, something bright and sunny, something funny. Nothing came. I wanted Davy there to make sure I didn't say the wrong thing. Then I noticed her backpack propped against the bed, looking packed full. There were a few things – a book, sunglasses, a camera, a diary and a pen – scattered over the bed.

I said, 'What's going on?'

She picked up the diary and stuffed it into the top of her pack, not looking at me. 'I have to leave the hostel.'

'Wh… What?

'Fi fan! Förbannat! Are you stupid? I pack up my bag because I have to leave the hostel.'

'But… Have you had some kind of argument with Emma, or…'

'Ntt shhhh… no. Not that. I… I lose my job too.'

'Oh, what? What on earth's happened?'

'This morning, I sleep. I sleep a very long time. I was so damn asleep I didn't wake up until after ten. Stekare, I am. It was horrible when I realised the time, and I knew I had to try to call the farm, but I was still so sleepy.'

Her look blamed me. 'I thought to better take a shower before I call them.' An image of her naked in the shower flashed unbidden through my mind. 'But still it was really hard. It took so long to wake up properly this morning, I almost cried. I couldn't believe and then when I went down to phone the farm Mr Dougal stopped me and told me I have to leave the hostel.'

'What?'

'Yes, he says he knows that I have a man in the room last night.'

'Shit.' She didn't need to give me a look for the blame to land heavily.

'Someone has told him.'

'Who?'

'I don't know who. I don't care because it is worse than that, Mr Dougal he told me that he phoned the farm to tell them and…'

'He can't do that.'

'He can. You know, the Dougals arranged the job for me. They do for lots of people, but then they use it, you know? Bloody kukhuvud! And when he tell the farm, then they say that I not turn up for work today and together they decide that I lose my job.'

'What?! They can't do that. Well, they can do that, but it doesn't matter. Just go to another farm, getting a packing job or something.'

'No. Bloody Dougal says he make sure that I can't work for any farm. That I broke the biggest rule so he will make sure that I don't work for any farm in this bloody town!'

'What? No, but…he can't…' But in a town like Tully it was only too likely. And all of this was my fault.

Beata sat down again. I crossed the room, sat and put my arm around her.

Just as I asked, 'What are you going to do?' the door burst open.

Em and Suzie bounced in. They were in the middle of a loud conversation, but cut themselves short when they saw Beata with her face in her hands.

Emma shot me a glare. 'What's he been doing?'

Beata looked up confused. 'No, no. It's not him. Em, I've lost my job.'

'I know, I know sweetheart. Dwight came asking for you, and I said you were sick, that you'd probably make it in for lunch if you could get a lift. But he came back later, said someone told him you were in the pub last night getting pissed and that's why you couldn't make it in today. He was pretty mad, said that's why you can't come back. I did tell him that you're not a drinker, that you don't get pissed, but he wasn't having any of it.' She pointed at me again. 'And I've already told him that he shouldn't be in here.'

Beata told them about the conversation with Mr Dougal.

Em was furious. 'What bastard went and told them? Who would know?'

Suzie sat down and put an arm around Beata. 'What you gonna do Beet?'

'I don't know. I don't want to go, but I guess I have to.'

'Why don't you go to Innisfail, get work on a farm there?'

'Oh I don't know. I don't know. I thought maybe Cairns or… I can't leave tonight anyway because there are no more busses.'

I heard a tap at the window and looked round. Davy was hanging on the outside ledge pressing a scrap of cardboard to the glass. On it he had written in a scrawling hand,

Get her to stay at your hut.

Suzie said, 'Oh Beata, what're you going to do tonight? Won't Dougal let you stay one more night?'

'No. He said I could stay long enough to talk to you, but then I have to go.'

I blurted, 'Come and stay with me.' All three heads spun. 'I've got a hut at the campsite, there's quite a lot of room in there, and if it's just for one night…'

Beata's face softened. Before she could reply, Emma cut in. 'You can't trust this dickhead. It's his fault you lost your job in the first place.'

'That's not fair.' It was.

'Course it is. You got her pissed and then snuck in here. It's your fault she lost her job and your fault she's getting kicked out.'

There was another rap at the window. This time his sign read,

Tell her to shove it up her hole.

I said, 'Yeah, you're probably right.' Then to Beata. 'And I'm really sorry. I guess the best I can do is try to help out now. If you're stuck for the night, then you're welcome to come and stay in my hut. There's enough room and I'll give you the bed tonight.'

Em stepped between me and Beata. 'The dirty bastard's just trying to get into your pants. Don't trust him.'

I crouched in front of Beata. 'I'm sorry. I really am, and I know that you won't be interested in me after what's happened. I really mean it that if you come and stay with me, you can have the bed and I'll sleep on the floor. I can stretch out my sleeping bag down there and it'll be fine.'

'Thanks William. That's really nice of you, and it's probably a good idea.' She stood up, face to face with Em. 'In fact, it's probably my only option. There's no other hostel in town, and I've got to sleep somewhere.'

'Yeah maybe, but I don't trust this guy.'

'Yes, but I do.'

Beata gathered the stuff that was scattered on her bed and put it into her day pack. The three of us watched silently. I picked up her backpack and we headed for the door.

Suzie said, 'Leave us a note tomorrow. Tell us what you're planning.'

Davy was at the window, grinning, waving and holding a sign that read, YA BEAUTY!!!

*   *   *   *

CHAPTER 6

I slid some rubble out the way with my foot, put her rucksack down then took her daypack and nestled that together with the bigger bag – a little gathering of Beata in a mess of me. The daypack tipped over.

'I'm really sorry about the mess of the place. I wasn't really expecting… And that smells not … Well, it's not …' I slid open the side windows and turned the fan on.

Davy followed us in and backed away into the corner next to the bunch of bananas.

I pushed the seat towards Beata. She studied my clutter and picked a book up off the floor. I nudged my journal under the bed then busied myself putting the kettle on and rinsing out a couple of cups, all the time stealing glances at the beautiful Swede sitting in my hut. 'Tea OK?'

'Is this good?' She was holding up A Confederacy of Dunces.

'Yes, brilliant. Really really funny. Do you read much?'

'In English, no. I could show you some very funny Swedish books.'

Beata flicked through the book and then through the leaves of my CD pack. Her hair was tied back in bunches, exposing the taught lines of her neck and shoulder as she stretched across the table.

'Can I put some music on?'

She managed to pick out the only new CD among my dated selection – a compilation of Aussie bands. The tinny speakers crackled on grunge guitars and coughed the bass kicks. I turned the Walkman down after bringing over the mugs of tea.

'Thanks, that's lovely. And thank you again for letting me stay. This is really kind.'

'I'm sorry it's such a mess.'

'Don't worry, it's normally. You saw our room at the hostel.'

I took the rotting bananas and put them outside the door. Davy watched me move round the room, squatting on his haunches. As Beata and I talked, I filled a plastic bag with dirty laundry, stacked dishes in the sink and scuffed litter into a pile.

'Beata, I hope you're not too angry with me. It's my fault that you got kicked out of the hostel, isn't it? And your job.'

'No it's not. It's those stupid men Dougal and Dwight. They think they are so important running this little town and really they are only pathetic. Nobody important is in Tully. It makes me angry. Who they think they are, telling us how to live our life?'

Tea sloshed from her mug, some spilling onto the book. 'Sorry, sorry.' She wiped it against her shorts.

'But, are you ready to leave?'

'Aff, no. Not really.' She placed the book on the table and cupped her hands around the mug. 'It's not… I am OK to travel on my own, it is only I enjoy to be here with friends. It is always better to travel together with friends, and I thought maybe I would with Emma and Suzie. They would leave quite soon. I still need also maybe a few weeks more money. I think then I better afford to travel. So no, not really ready yet.' She stopped staring into her cup and looked at me. 'And too I would like to know you more.'

'I…' There was nothing I wanted more than to get to know her. I looked to Davy and he winked. But all I could think to ask was, 'So you think you'll go to Cairns?'

'Ah… I was wanting to go there anyway. I only… Perhaps maybe I should go to Innisfail. I get more banana work and then after meet up. It's only… you know, a new place and trying to find work again and…' Davy was wiggling his eyebrows and jerking a thumb towards Beata. 'Aff, William, I wish it was easy.'

She sighed then asked me where the toilet was. From the door, I pointed out the block on the other side of the campsite.

As soon as she'd gone, Davy jumped up and grabbed my wrist. 'Whit ye waitin fae?'

'What d'ye mean?'

'Well, are ye no gonnae tell her that ye'll go wey her?'

'What, to the toilet?'

'Naw, ya numpty. Go wey her when she leaves Tully. Heid aff wherever she's goin.'

'What? No, I can't. I'm workin and…' There was nothing to keep me in Tully. 'She'll not want me to.'

'Ye willnae ken till ye ask her, laddie.'

'D'ye think? Do you really think I could?'

Davy had sketched out the whole deal by the time Beata returned.

I said, 'You know, I was planning on leaving soon too.'

'Really? That's great. Maybe then if I go to Innisfail, we can meet again soon. Will you go north?'

'Yes but, well, what I was thinking was...'

Davy said, 'Ye jist need her tae hang aboot fae wan day.'

'If you could hang on for another day, then I could leave with you.'

Beata's eyes and mine held for a moment before she responded. 'No, William, you have work and...'

He was getting excited. 'Ach, tae hell wi that. We're talkin love action here.'

I said, 'That doesn't matter. I've been here long enough. Really. And I've saved up enough money already. I'm not sure even why I'm still here. It would be no problem for me to leave with you, and I think it would be great. Don't you?'

'But don't you need to tell them before? You can't just walk out.'

'I ...'

Davy kept me up on it. 'Ye'll jist ditch it the morra.'

'If I go in and tell them tomorrow that I'm leaving, they can't really do anything about it, can they?'

'They can take your pay.'

'Aye, will they?'

'I don't think they would. They're pretty decent. And in any case, I got paid last Friday. If they hold out, then I'd only be three days short. And it's not like they would miss me or anything.'

'But you have your friends here, those guys that you work with.'

'Jings, they eejits?'

'I don't really know any of them very well. I arrived here on my own and I only started to get to know them, well... yesterday. It would be good to have someone to travel on with for a while, wouldn't it? Like you said, and we are going the same way.'

'But do you want to go to Innisfail?'

'Rightio son, this is the clincher. Don't mess it up. Cairns, rainforests, pubs, shacked up thegether.'

'No, I won't. I mean ... What I was thinking was, why don't we both go up to Cairns? I want to go to Cairns. I thought I'd maybe do a rainforest trek or learn how to dive or ... maybe... I'm not sure. And I think you could get some work there, in a bar or a restaurant. I've heard that women backpackers can get jobs from there on ranches and nanny or... if you got stuck, I can help you.'

'No, you can't do that but, maybe... yes, this would be great, William. I think you are right, why not? I can get to Cairns and then we see what happens. Right?'

'Right.'

Davy was clapping. 'Ho, ho. Here we go, son!'

'Thank you William. I felt some like I was being left alone, you know. I think, yes, I am really happy that we can go together.'

She stood up, put her arms around my neck and kissed me.

My wee pal tugged on my shorts and made a rude gesture with an upraised fist.

Beata sat again and I pushed the mozzie net back to sit on the bed. Davy got up beside me. Beata and I talked about what our plans could be, and got excited about the cool things we could do in Cairns.

I explained to her that I only had a month left on my working visa, and I was rueing the fact as I told her, but it did mean a month that we could spend together having fun, hanging out, sharing a room and... I couldn't help thinking that she would be my girlfriend for that time and I felt sad already about the day that I would have to say goodbye.

'And what will you do after your visa runs out?'

'I need to go back to Scotland. My mum's not that well, and I said to her I would be back after a year.'

She gave me a sympathetic look then began to tell me about her mum and dad, her two sisters and the dog back in Alnö. I was happy to let her talk, the details of my family life wouldn't make such interesting listening.

I made cheese sandwiches and we had a can of beer each out of the little fridge. I slipped a beer and a butty over to Davy.

It was late before we realised and then it was time to go to bed.

I took my sleeping bag and spread it out on the floor. Beata unclipped hers from backpack and lay it on the bed. I began to bundle some clothes in a towel to make a pillow, but Beata said, 'No, that is too unfair. I take your bed and your pillow? Here.' She put the pillow at the head end of my sleeping bag.

I quickly stripped down to my boxers and sat on the floor, wriggling into my bag. Beata turned her back to me as she took her trousers off. Her knickers showed below the hemline of her t-shirt. Davy came to stand next to me head. 'Och, boy. That's some fuckin sight, that is?'

I turned to him, shocked, but he was staring fixedly at her. 'So, are we sneakin in there once she's dropped off?'

'Davy, mate, just get yourself down to sleep... somewhere... In the... I dunno, maybe...'

'Nae bother, son. I'll just finish my beer then I'll make masel scarce.'

I plumped the pillow as best I could then lay down, sliding further into the bag.

Beata said, 'Shall I switch off the light?' then stepped over my legs.

'Sppttt.' Davy spluttered beer all down his front.

The moon shining through the un-curtained side window silhouetted Beata climbing through the mozzie net and lying out on the bed.

I sensed Davy move away, thought I heard the screen and door quietly slide open then closed again. I felt bad, like I'd banished the wee man, but it couldn't be right for him to sleep on the bed with her, and apart from there where else was there? I didn't worry for his well-being. He would probably end with a better nest than me.

I lay uncomfortable, from the floor and from the silence, my need to say something, to bring her presence across the small dark room. Then Beata said, 'You know, William, it is not often I feel so comfortable with someone. I think that's good, with you.'

And slowly, she began to talk, about herself, about her plans for the future, how she hoped to go to Asia, to backpack and work if she could; she wondered whether to go from Hong Kong up into China. Lying in the dark, she told me how she was deeply in love with her own country and her family, but said at that moment she wanted most of all to explore and experience as much as she could and to share with friends, new friends, interesting people, nice guys. I said, 'Yes,' and 'Ah-hum' and let her move gently on, to India, to Indonesia, Thailand. She wasn't brought up religious, but she was interested in Hinduism, Buddhism, Islam, had faith in all faiths, and doubts in them all. Listening to her made me wonder if I should create a new persona for myself – a life that would be worth regaling her with – but I contented myself enjoying her lilting tones as tiredness took me and I drifted towards sleep.

The last thing she said to me that night was, 'Thank you William. You are a very kind person.'

*　　　*　　　*　　　*

I slept fitfully. In nightmares I did things, unspeakable things, to Beata. I woke anxiously but always relieved for her to be sleeping comfortably a few feet away. The only sound was the whirring of the fan panning round the room.

Then I woke to hear Beata's breathing coming shallow and rapid.

I sat up, panicked that she was in a fever, hoping it was merely a bad dream that I could wake her from. In pale blue light, I saw Beata asleep on her back, her limbs fallen flat, her face tensed. Her chest heaved under Davy. Davy was sitting on her chest, rising and falling with her breaths. He was naked and staring intently into Beata's face. Her t-shirt had been pushed up under her chin. Davy's legs were splayed either side of her breasts and his penis lay across her sternum, his testicles bulging on either side. The light caught him, and he looked up suddenly. His cheeks began to rise in a grin. I shunted my sleeping bag off and leapt to my feet, raising a fist. Davy started and slipped down the back of the bed in one fluid movement like a cat chased from the table. Beata let out a long sigh, turned and curled onto her side, tugging her t-shirt back down. Her face, touched by the light, relaxed as the air left her. I got onto my knees and looked under the bed. The light didn't reach there, but there was no movement, no scuffle, no Davy.

PART II: CAIRNS

CHAPTER 7

Davy sat cross-legged on his bed, doling out advice like a withered buddha. 'Errs only the wan true way.' Withered and corrupted. 'If the lassie's no giein it oot, ye gottae take it.'

'I'm not like that.' I perched at the edge of our bed, Beata sleeping soundly behind me. 'That's wrong. It's ... nasty. And I don't need you tellin me to do it.'

'Fuck's sake. A wee finger ner did a lassie ony herm.'

'Davy.'

'Whit?'

'Stay away from her.'

'Whit d'ye mean? I done nothing.'

I tried to keep my voice down but insistent. 'Stay away from her, Davy, or I swear to God, ...'

'Aye, whit?'

'Just ...'

Davy laughed at me, noiselessly. I could see it shaking in his belly; his head bounced a little. 'Anyhow, fuck her.' He shook his head, then glared at me with a wicked flash in his eyes. 'Whit aboot yon lassie last night, that Orla? Fuckin lovely big jugs oan it, eh?' He weighed his hands in front of his chest. 'An she's well up fur your cock. When we gonnae get a bittae that?'

'I'm not interested.'

'Aye, mair fool you. Whit's the point ae me helping ye oot, if yer no gonnae take a shag when yer gied it on a plate?'

'That's not what it's about.'

'Who says it isnae. It's whit that Orla's aw aboot.'

'I don't want her. I'm with Beata.'

'Aye fuckin Scandy's no giein ye yer hole, but, is she? Unless, ye knaw, ye let me loosen her up a bit.' He wiggled two fingers in front of his nose.

I sprang from my bed and grabbed him by the neck. 'Do not touch her. Don't even think about her.'

Davy sneered. 'Calm it.' His backhanded push sent me staggering back to my bed. His bottom lip pouted out. 'It's no fair, but. I gottae get a bit ae action.'

'Leave her alone.'

Davy dropped down off his bed, crossed to ours, climbed up and put an arm around my shoulder. He said quietly into my ear, 'I tell ye whit, son, I'll dae ye a deal. Hows aboot you get a wee bit ae action somewhere else, an I'll lea yer fuckin tight-holed virgin alane.'

'What d'ye mean?''

'An aud fella like me doesnae get much, y'knaw. I dinnae even get tae see it much. So, if you …'

'You want to watch me have sex with some other girl?'

'Aye, well? Scandy'll ner need tae knaw. Fuckin, I kin set it up fur ye. Aw you need tae dae is get yer dick oot. Soon's we're back fae oor wee holiday, I'm oan the case.'

Beata's breathing stopped for a moment, disturbed in her sleep, then returned in sibilant waves. There was some promise in the thought of keeping Davy away from Beata; if he would leave her alone, leave us alone... And yes, the thought of sex. I stumbled on a memory from the bar the night before, a girl close to me, her lips parted waiting for a kiss.

It was Davy luring me in. All of it.

I said, 'You're not coming.'

'Whit?'

'I don't know what you've been tryin to do... to her... but I just, I want to go to Port Douglas with Beata. Alone.'

'Whit?'

'I don't want you around for a while.'

'Whit?' Davy jumped down off the bed. 'Look pal, ye widnae huv goat anywhere near that lassie if it wurnae fur me.'

'I want to do it for myself.'

Davy stepped towards me, his eyes narrow, his jaw set. He pointed a long knobbled finger in my face. 'Ye kin go fuck yersel if ye hink yer gonnae get any mair help fae me.'

'I'm not telling you to go away for good, just...'

'Any kind ae man wid be able tae play away frae hame an make sure the bird's nane the wiser.'

'That's not what I want to do.'

'Aye, but it's whit yer auld man widdae done.'

'Who?'

'Yer auld fella. Yer da.'

'My … What d'you know about my dad?"

'Fuck aff oan yer wee holiday, son. Gwon.'

He turned away and walked towards the door.

'Davy, what d'ye mean about my dad?'

'Huv a nice wan, aye?'

His long middle finger stretched up at me, just before he slammed the door shut.

'Davy!' I felt my stomach clench and my teeth grit, 'Ach, ya wee …' My fist was waving at the door. '… bastard.'

I watched Beata in her sleep again, as I had done in the campsite hut, on the bus from Tully to Cairns, here in this room, watching her, watching over her, watching that Davy is not there, on her, near her, harming her. Her lips curled in a touch of a smile, breathing smoothly: perfect serenity. Doubt clawed me. What was it that Davy did to me? To her? What if I didn't have that wee man around to bolster my feeble attractions...?

$*$ $*$ $*$ $*$

Not long after we arrived in Cairns, Davy and I had gone to the post office so that I could send a letter to my mum, a few words of reassurance, yes I was coming home, yes I would be there for her company before too long. I couldn't say what I was feeling, Mum, I've met this girl and, Mum, I want to stay with her forever, wherever she goes, be her companion for life, I'll bring her back to meet you some day, Mum, but for now we'll just be travelling. Together.

I was standing reading the letter through a second time when a woman with a lot of carefully arranged curly blonde hair approached me.

'Is this the poste restante?' She had a strong Irish accent.

'Whoof.' Davy bumped into my leg as he backed away, looking up at the terrace of her bosom.

'Em...' She also had long dark lashes over sharp blue eyes and a lot of teeth in her smile. '...aye, it is, the main post office, yeah.'

'Aw great, tanks. Is it just this counter here?' There was a long queue.

'Well, you'd be best to check the list on the window outside. It shows if you've got anything to collect.'

'Where's that then?'

'Eh, well...'

'Wullie, son, yon lass needs a bit ae special guidance.' He got a hand behind my knee and pushed me forward.

I said, 'Why don't I show you?'

'Aw, that's really kind of you.'

I took her out the main door and showed her where, on the big windows at the front, there were long rows of printouts with an alphabetical list of people who had mail to collect. Mine wasn't up there. No-one yet knew I was there. Davy pressed his head against the glass to get a better look as she ran a finger through the list. Her shoulders and back were covered in dark freckles, the kind that join further together the more they are in the sun.

'Ho, that's brilliant. It says here there's three for me. Aw, tanks a lot.'

I stepped aside to let her back to the door.

Davy said, 'No no no no, wait son, wait. Dinnae let her just walk aff. Why dint ye...'

Orla stopped mid-step and said, 'Here, are you not in Joe's hostel?'

'Aye, that's right.'

'We saw yous arriving yesterday. You and a dark-haired girl?'

'Yeah, that's right. That's my... That's Beata.'

'And you're a Scot, are ye not? What's your name?'

'William.'

'I'm Orla. Nice to meet you.'

'And you.'

She shook my hand in a fast grip.

'Och here, nice wan, Wullie. Ye almost let slip there, but ye've got this wan oan the line, eh?'

Orla said, 'Here, me and a few others are going to the Woolpack tonight. D'ye know it?'

'No, what's that?'

'It's a bar. They do a ten-dollar meal with a pitcher of beer. It's usually pretty good craic, if you fancy joining us.'

'Sounds great.'

'Well, tanks again and we'll come and give you and yer girl a shout when we're off out. What room yees in?'

'203.'

'Great. See ya.'

I slid my sunglasses down over my eyes and couldn't help a quick glance at her backside as she returned into the building. She had very short shorts. I was kind of shocked as well. An attractive woman had just approached me and asked me to go out with her and her mates. That never happens.

Davy nudged my thigh. 'She's a bit ae awright, eh William?'

'She seemed nice, aye.'

'By jings, too right. Ken whit they say aboot they fiery redheided Irish girls, eh?'

'She's not a redhead.'

'Ach, ye dinnae ken that, mibbe she dyes it. There's only wan way to find oot but, eh?' Nudge and a wink. 'Anyhow, ye ken whit they say?'

'No Davy, I don't. What do they say?'

'Aboot they fiery Irish birds, eh? Fuckin bang like the heidboards in a hoor-hoose.' He sniggered.

'Davy!'

I looked down on him. His shoulders shoogled with laughter. The top of his bald head was worryingly red, flaking at the sides next to where his white hair hung sparsely and lankly. In fact, even the hair of his beard seemed to have thinned, straggling in clumps rather than the powder puff it has first seemed. Perhaps he could be doing with another spin in a washer. The narrowness of his beard made his nose seem more prominent, beak like.

I said, 'What's with you and the swearing? Do you have to keep talking like that?'

He kept on, 'Real wild yins like, the Irish. Fuck aye. lovely big arse on her an aw. Not like that skinny Scandy bird. Bit ae flesh on that wan. Ye gonnae chase that young lass, William?'

'No. I'm sticking with Beata.'

'Aye, but wouldnae matter if she didnae find oot, eh?'

*   *   *   *

She was lying on her tummy, propped on her elbows along our double bed, her journal in front of her and a pen waving in her left hand, a guidebook folded back next to her. There was another, single bed on the other side of the room. Davy had slept there, but at the moment the contents of Beata's pack were spread out on it. Davy pushed a space and flopped out. 'Oof, exhaustin that.' A pile of folded clothes tipped to the floor.

I dropped the shopping bags by the door and flexed my fingers. The plastic had dug into them during the hot walk from the centre of town.

I said, 'You got far with the sorting then?'

'Aff.' She looked over her shoulder at the mess. 'No. But I did go for a swim.'

'Really? They have a pool here?'

'No, but I spoke to the girl at reception and she told that there is the big outdoor pool along the road.'

'On this road? I didn't see anything.'

'The other way, out of town. It is only five minutes.'

I dropped the bags and pressed my fingers into the back of my neck. 'Oof, I could do with a swim. I'm so stiff and sore.'

Davy muttered, 'Aye, cause yer no gettin any.'

'Too long on the farm.' Beata jumped up. 'Come here.' She stood behind me and stuck her thumbs into the muscles above my shoulder blades. An intensely satisfying pain shot through them. 'Aff, it's so tight, like ropes. I think you should let me give you a massage.'

'Wahey.' Davy picked up a bottle of massage oil lying next to him. 'A bit ae lubrication, eh?'

I tried to ignore him. 'Sounds... great. I could really do with it.'

'Sure, but let's have lunch first. I'm bloody starving.' She grabbed one of the bags. 'Argh, bananas!' The bunch flew at me. 'How could you?'

'Believe it or not, I'm addicted to the things. A couple a slices of bread, some peanut butter, and wham – what a sandwich.'

'Ech. I'll have cheese and ... yes, chocolate spread.'

After lunch, Beata got me to lie face down on our bed, stripped save for a towel across my bum. Davy was puckering, but Beata's clothes stayed on. She pulled out small bottles of oils and scents that she mixed in a tiny bowl. She told me about the qualities of the oils that she was using, how the marjoram would soothe my muscles and the lavender would help me relax.

The banana farm work had left my back tense and sore. Aches spread when I slept at night so that I usually woke up tighter than when I had lain down. Beata said to me, 'Your back is very muscled.' I had never been conscious of a developed muscle anywhere on my body.

She started in slow sweeping motions, pressing from the base of my spine to my neck and out across my shoulders. Washes of sensation flushed through my muscles and burst in my skull. She began to focus on the space between my shoulder blades. I felt her hands come up against the tight knots of sinew, but she delved into them, separating and softening. Again, the pain was intense and pleasurable.

As Beata used her strong fingers, she talked about energy flows, chi and blockages. She said that the tensions in my muscles could reflect tensions in my mind and maybe I needed to let go of some fears or worries before I could properly relax in my body.

I turned my head to the side and found Davy a little too close. He screwed up his face and tapped a finger to his temple. I didn't know if Beata was a bit batty with this hippy stuff, but I didn't care when she pressed her thumbs into the base of my neck and my head felt like it lifted two inches.

Beata spent a long time working round the muscles of my shoulders and arms, travelling down my spine and spreading out the muscles across the back of my ribs. It was just as she was working into my lower back, pushing the towel a little lower across my buttocks that there was a knock at the door.

I had zoned out into a sublime place, but I managed to mumble, 'Just ignore it.'

'Aye, we're jist getting tae the good bit.'

But Beata went to the door. I spread the towel a bit wider. Davy was at my ear. 'Aw pal, hows aboot this. When she gits back, jist whip the towel aff, flip ower an show her whit ye've got.'

'Davy, do you have to keep talking like that?'

Beata said hello and I recognised the voice that replied, 'Hey, hello in there. Can I have a word?' I turned my head as the door swung open to reveal the Irish girl, Orla. 'Aw hey, didn know I was disturbin somehin. Sorry bout that.' She was dressed in a pair of shorts and a black bikini top. The small triangles of material were pulled tight across her chest.

Davy groped his two hands in front of his own chest. 'See the…?'

I frowned at him.

Orla said, 'I just came up t see if yeez fancied a game a volleyball. But I guess yer busy.' Her eyes travelled on me. 'Anyhow, I was wantin to tell ye that we're meeting tonight at six, down at the reception. See yeez there, aye?'

Beata looked unsure, but said, 'Thank you.'

As the door closed Orla said, 'Have fun yous two.'

Beata came round and sat on the side of the bed. My head was turned away from her. Davy had slipped over to the side I was facing, still too close to my face.

Beata asked, 'How do you know this girl?'

Davy looked worried.

'Eh, I, ah … met her today. Erm, down at the post office.'

'You just bump into her?'

He ran an imaginary zip across his lips

'Aye … yes, … pretty much.'

'She's Irish, isn't it?'

'Y … yeah. I .. I think so.'

'I like the Irish. I was with some Irish boys in Byron Bay, surfers. Very funny guys.'

Davy wiped imaginary sweat from his forehead.

Beata laid a warm hand across my back. 'So, what do you think of my massage?'

'Oh, it was great. Thank you.'

Davy blurted, 'Right son, we're back oan.'

'Do you think it help?' A finger played across one of the muscles she'd been working on.

'If ye play this right, ye might get a bittae action. Jist ask her tae get her hauns back doon there.'

I turned my head so that I could see Beata. She smiled gently. Her hand slid softly up my back. There had been no malevolence or jealousy in her questions; she had simply wanted to know. She was beautiful.

'Right boy, get it up a gear.'

I pushed the towel back down to the top of my buttocks. 'I was so enjoying that. It's doing a power of good. And this bit, could you just …'

'That's it son. When her haun's on yer arse, whip aroon and gie her somehin tae massage.'

'What?' She tugged on the towel. 'Maybe you are hoping for a little bit more.' I could feel all of my left buttock being exposed to the air. There was a light touch of fingers on its skin.

Davy's eyebrows wiggled

Beata said, 'Hmm.'

Then her hand cracked down on my backside in a ringing slap. The noise bounced off the whitewashed walls and the pain seared through me. I jumped from the bed, grabbing for the towel, but it slipped out of reach. I chased Beata, stark naked and hollering, 'Right! I'll get you.' She squealed, ran round the room, vaulted the bed and dived into the bathroom, sliding the concertina door across.

I shouted, 'This door'll never hold you. I'll get you.'

'Eeeh, sorry. I just could not … not …' She lost herself in a fit of giggles.

I inspected the red handprint glowing on my backside and laughed.

Blood pumped and twitched through me. In a giddy moment of exhilaration, I breathed to myself, 'Oh, I think you're great.'

Davy walked round me, looking and inspecting my nudity. 'Is that it?'

I went to pull some shorts on, and Beata gingerly slid the door across. I jumped at her. Beata squealed again, but when I got hold of her, I kissed her and said, 'This is nice, isn't it?'

She pushed the fringe away from my forehead with a fingertip and said, 'Yes, you're right. It is,' then kissed me again. 'Hey, you want to do something fun?'

'Sure.'

Beata grabbed the guidebook from Davy's bed and then dived flat out across ours. 'I was reading about a place called Port Douglas.'

I lay out next to her and saw the name printed above a block of text.

'And it says it has a very beautiful beaches. It's not so far, look.' Her fingertip traced the short line between Cairns and Port Douglas on the map. 'I thought maybe we could go.'

'Well, sure, I …'

'Tomorrow?'

'Great.'

'And we hitchhike.'

'Eh, …'

Davy was at the window, pushing back the curtain to look down at the volleyball court. 'We no playin?'

*   *   *   *

'This here's Brando. That's Harry, Barbara and Troy, and this is Paula.'

Brando was hairy, apart from his head, Harry a muscled sportsboy. Barbara and Troy were wrapped right round each other and Paula looked worryingly demented.

'Hi. Hi.'

We shook hands or waved at each other. Everyone was smiling like kindergarten teachers. It already looked like an interesting evening. Orla took charge and hustled us through reception.

'Let's rock.'

As we stepped out of the hostel, a minibus pulled up. The logo on the side was 'Oz Adventure' next to an Aussie map with a backpack slung over it. The side door opened and two empty VB cans rolled out followed by a throng of backpackers with loud British voices, all looking sunburnt and eighteen, hanging off each other. Davy scampered from behind me, between the legs of the backpackers and up to the bus. He leaned inside and took a long, hard sniff.

'Herr we go again,' said Orla. 'Another crowd of gappers all filling the gap with beer and shaggin.'

'Here's to that,' shouted Harry, throwing an arm round Orla's neck and pulling her down towards the ground.

Everyone else called, 'Wahey!' and I couldn't help joining in, buzzing on instant camaraderie.

Orla pushed Harry away and swung a kick at him that missed.

As we barrelled up the road, I found a hop in my step – I skipped down off the pavement and back up again, bouncing round Beata, who grinned back at me, but took my arm and slowed me down. Orla kept pace with us and talked to Beata about Swedish friends she had, told me how she thought Glasgow was a brilliant place to get drunk in. Harry came round and grabbed onto her a few times trying to get her into the play. She flicked him off. Before we reached the town centre she was on Beata's other arm.

The others were messing about, getting ahead or behind us and Davy was high on it He ran round between the feet of our new gang, laughing at their jokes, tripping up Harry and Brando and slapping my arse whenever he came flying past.

The Woolpack was just off the central square. A street door led straight into a black lined staircase. Chalkboards on the way up showed the menu of burgers, steaks and battered fish. Orla tapped one on the way past, Backpacker Special $10 meal and a pitcher. 'That's us.' It was a dimly lit bar, no outside windows, just neon signs and a couple of bare bulbs hanging from the corrugated roof. An array of disco lights hung at various points unlit, and back in the gloom it looked like there might be a stage. All of the furniture was rough hewn out of heavy pieces of wood, varnished but scuffed and tarnished. There was something familiar and welcoming about the place's lack of pretension. The eight of us got round a long table with a bench running either side. The tabletop looked like it had been sectioned out of a particularly unhappy stump of tree and the benches were high, leaving our feet dangling like kids' at a grownup table. The orders were easy, everyone was on steak and chips or fish and chips, except Beata who was forced into that pub veggie staple of lasagne. 'I've eaten so many bloody lasagne in this country.' The others laughed it up by piling all their limp salads on her plate when the dishes arrived. Everyone ordered a pitcher of beer.

Beata and I sat next to each other at one end of a row, bunched up tight so that our hips were pressed. She was left-handed and I'm right so our elbows kept bumping as we ate. When she put her fork down to talk to Orla, she put her hand on my leg, ran it across the flesh at my knee.

Davy sat under the table, grabbing all the falling chips.

Orla and her friends taught English. They worked in a couple of different small language schools. Apparently, most of their students were young Japanese who took a fortnight or a month or maybe two to come to Cairns, do the tourist stuff and try to improve their English; other nationalities as well, Europeans, South Americans. Teaching seemed far more of a proper job than what I would expect backpackers staying in a hostel to hold down, but they made it sound like it was a blast. Classes took up their mornings. Their afternoons were spent on excursions with the students – bungee jumping, white water rafting, scuba diving – or just dossing about when they were meant to be preparing.

I asked Orla, 'How can the schools put up with you if you're just skiving off all the time?'

'Ach, it's easy enough to do the teaching. They don't mind as long as you keep them busy and they're having fun.'

Harry leaned in confidentially. 'And I'll tell you what mate, some of those Japanese girls can get a bit friendly, if you know what I mean.'

'Whit?' Davy looked up from between my legs. 'Dis that mean he's havin his way wi wee lassies? Dirty bastard.'

I asked Harry, 'But aren't your students... I mean... aren't they like, schoolchildren?'

'Nooooo mate. What do you think I am? They've all left school. Late teens, early twenties. Totally legit and fuckin nice.'

Davy stood up, leaned on my knee and looked at Harry. 'If that ugly bam kin get some, kin you no? Ask him whit thur like oan the job.'

I asked, 'But aren't there communication difficulties? I mean, if their English isn't very good.'

'Not usually a problem. Just keep their mouths busy.' He rolled his tongue against his cheek and pumped his fist to his mouth.

I made a note to avoid Harry, but Davy was laughing and slapping my leg.

I realised Beata wasn't next to me. 'Where's Beata?'

'Over there.' Orla pointed a couple of tables away where Beata was sat next to a woman with white blonde hair falling down her back. 'I think she met some other Scandy girl. They're rattling away in hurdy gurdy anyway.'

I wasn't sure what to do. I still had a bit of my meal, but I wanted to be next to Beata, find out who she was meeting. I turned again to see if she was looking my way.

Orla asked, 'So, you really like Beata do you?'

'She's great, yeah. She's... It's easy, y'know?'

'How long have yous been together?'

'Oh, not long. We only met properly in the last week.'

'Really?'

I sat back round to finish my meal. Orla rested her elbows on the table and raised her glass. 'Cheers.'

Beer was getting slopped into everyone's glasses out of the pitchers. It was hard to keep a tally. You just bought another pitcher when yours was done. With all that unaccounted for beer, Davy was happy, always with a glass in his hand. He gave me a fright when he slipped on a spill and fell off the tabletop. I looked under and he was happily hanging onto Orla's leg. When I came back up, she was eyeing me.

I went over to say hi to Beata.

'Hej William, this is Astrid. She's Swedish. We were just talking about horse riding. It is something I love very much, and Astrid too. She says that it is great to go horse riding in the rainforest.'

Astrid said, 'Yeah, there are heaps of good places to go riding. I think Beata n me are gonna take a trek. Right?' She had an Australian accent.

'Right. Oh, it's so exciting. It's such a long time I have not been on a horse.'

They continued to talk about horses, in English at first. Pretty soon the disco lights came on, the music got louder and they drifted back into Swedish.

Orla, Paula, Barbara and Troy jumped up onto the small dancefloor and started flinging themselves around. The beat was cheesy techno, dreadful high-pitched versions of old pop classics. Because I had removed myself from the group, I felt a bit awkward about getting up with them. My dancing sucked anyway. I got my pitcher from the other table and topped up Beata and Astrid's glasses, then my own. Theirs sat untouched as they blethered away. I kept refilling mine and watched the crowd on the dancefloor. Orla and Brando were bumping their bums against each other and Paula hopped up and down on the spot punching her hands above her head. I spotted Harry at the far side of the floor. He was holding on to a timber pillar talking to a short woman, but his glance kept flitting to Orla.

Davy was swinging like a gibbon from the light rigging; his teeth and eyes flashed blue, green, red. I downed my beer and found a jug to refill myself.

A steady stream of people was coming up the stairs from the street. Some of the bar staff came out and took away the benches at the sides of the dancefloor. The first person to make the move up to tabletop dancing was Orla, to a cheer from the crowd. She hitched her t-shirt up at the front and tied it under her breasts, then hoiked her g-string up over her hipster jeans. She popped the top button to reveal a bit more of the black lace, a wee bit of bum crack showed at the back. She had to hold on to the roof to steady herself and stop her head from banging off it. A few other people followed her example and climbed up. The bar staff clapped and cheered them on.

Suddenly, I felt Davy land on my back, his arms round my neck, piggy-backing. 'Hoi hoi, livenin up in here, eh? This is whit we wahnt. Gonnae get up there an shake yer thing big lad?'

'Not likely.'

'Aye, much better stayin doon here an gettin an eyeful, intit?'

But the next track was Nirvana's Smells Like Teen Spirit. As the first chords crunched in, the whole dancefloor began to jump and slam in a moshpit. Davy shouted, 'Slamdance!' and I couldn't help but throw myself in. I pulled him off my back and tossed him in the air. He came down with a, 'Hey hey,' but I don't know where he landed. Suddenly, I was hit in the back, sending me tumbling forward. Orla had jumped off the bench onto me, clamping her legs round my hips and grabbing my shoulders. I nearly fell off my feet. Orla shouted, 'Hoo hoo', and slapped my chest. 'Go on, William.'

Davy repeated her. 'Gwon son!' And I bounded round the dancefloor.

The dj went into another noisy guitar tune. Orla slipped down to the floor, grabbed my arm and slammed against me, getting us messed up in the melee. She pounded the floor with her bare feet and punched the air. Then Davy was on Orla's back. He punched his fist in time with her, his other hand hung tight on to the collar of her t-shirt, pulling it even tighter under her breasts. Every time I banged up against them, Davy shouted, 'C'mon the William. Mon!' I was stoked, excited. Harry was in there too, slamming against us. Orla gave him a big two handed push that sent him flying against a group of women standing at the edge.

I had to break away, bending double and holding onto knees to catch my breath.

'That Orla wan is a cracker.' Davy was in my face. 'She'll gie ye a braw time, ma lad.' He pushed my face around. 'Err she is. Gwon.'

Orla was standing close behind. She laughed, holding her hands on her hips. Her breath heaving.

Davy pushed me towards her, but my foot caught, and I tipped forward landing nose-first in her cleavage.

'Oh hey, big boy, easy does it.'

'Oh jings, I'm sor...'

But she was grinning at me, broadly, loving it. 'If you want to play, just ask.'

'Right, William. It's like this, ditch the Scandy and get yer hauns oan Orla.'

He pushed me towards her again and I ended up close – we were almost in each other's arms.

She rubbed against me. 'I know you're with that other lass, but if you,' she whispered close to my ear, 'you know.'

'Brilliant, Willie. Step in an gie her a snog.'

I looked over to Beata; she was still engrossed with her Swedish friend.

'Yer lassie willnae knaw.'

Orla lowered her head, looked at me through her lashes. Her lips plumped and parted.

'Jump around!' Harry grabbed Orla's shoulder. 'Jump around! Come on.'

A big bouncing hip-hop track had started to play, Jump Around. Heads were bobbing all over the bar. Orla's hand slipped down and squeezed a bum cheek before she jumped away with Harry.

'Bollocks. That fuckin Harry's for it.'

I was left with a guilt in my gut, like I really had kissed Orla and cheated on Beata. And yet, the dancing, the slamming and the flirting, it was exhilarating. Energy twitched through me, and as I looked again at Beata, I knew that she was where it should be directed. I bounced over to her.

She smiled. 'William, you're having fun.'

'Really really.'

Davy was at my side. ''Mon then lad, let's see if yer Scandy is up tae it.'

I took her hand. 'Come on. Let's dance.'

'No. I'm fine.'

Astrid was watching our exchange.

I took both Beata's hands, pulled her onto her feet. 'Come ooooon.'

She came up into my arms. Her proximity reminded me of the closeness just shared with Orla. Again a spasm of guilt but a frisson of excitement too. It felt warm and vital. As I leaned forward to kiss her, my hand was on her bottom. Davy took my fingers and pushed them down, squeezing round the curve of her backside.

'Hey.' Beata nudged my arm away with her elbow.

Davy pulled my hand onto her thigh. 'Keep at it son, she'll gie it up.'

I leaned in again, pouting for a kiss. Our hands pulled her leg against mine, trying to wrap it around me. I pressed my excitement against her.

'William, no.' She was wide-eyed, startled. 'Whoa. I think you are a bit drunk.' And then composure slipped back. 'But you were wanting to dance, so let's dance.' She pecked me a kiss on the lips and pulled me to the dancefloor.

'Tight bitch.'

We danced facing each other, but separate, giving us room to jump. My guilt fell away at the sight of her letting go, enjoying the hop and the silliness that was going around. Orla and Harry were wresting in the middle of the floor, standing and twisting around each other, trying to trip the other up. Paula was tickling Harry. Troy, Barbara and Brando were shouting them on. Davy was doing a little can-can of excitement next to the wrestlers, trying to get in close to Orla's body when she veered toward the floor.

When the music segued back into cheesy pop, all of our crowd gathered around the table and gulped beer. Beata wrapped her arms tight around me from behind, ignoring the sweat on my back. All of our pitchers were coming to an end.

'Listen,' said Orla, 'who's up for heading to End of the World?'

'What's that?'

'It's a nightclub. A bit bigger than this. We usually end up there.'

'Sure.'

Everyone else was up for it, except Beata. 'I'm tired. I think I prefer to go back.'

I said, 'Aw, c'mon Beata.'

'No, you go. You are having fun.'

Davy stood on the bench. His arm was linked through Orla's. 'Noh, Willie, she's right. Yer making pals, huvin a rer aul time. Let's party.'

'But ... But, no, I can't let her walk home on her own.'

'Yer part ae this mad crowd noo. Wur gettin pished.'

'I can be okay, William. It's maybe more fun for you to go with these guys.'

'Hink aboot it. Ye widnae've been daein this a couplae weeks ago.'

Before I'd met Davy, I'd never have found myself in this situation. It felt good, really good, to be meeting new and interesting people, even better to feel that I was new and interesting to them.

'C'moan, lissen tae yer wee pal. This is whit it's aw aboot. And ye might get tae fuck big tits here.' And with a lick of his lips, he prodded a bony finger into Orla's right breast.

*   *   *   *

Davy grumbled on the way home. 'Nae fuckin use. Should be huvin the craic. Should be jumpin yon Orla's bones. Cannae score in a barrel ae fannies, you. Fuckin feckless wee shite. Useless bastard.' He was drunk and stumbling. I was too, but Beata held my arm and rested her head against my shoulder. She talked animatedly about the chance of going horse riding with Astrid, and the chance of having another night out with our new friends. She squeezed my arm a bit tighter.

When we got back to our room, Beata began to undress. Davy's tongue flopped out. 'Thshee's gonnae thuck ye!'

Standing in her bra and pants, Beata said, 'Aff that bar stinked. I'm going to take a shower. Here.' She picked up a bag of rubbish. 'This stink too. Can you drop it to the bin?'

As I left the room, I got a flash of bare backside. Beata was stepping out of her underwear.

'C'mon, shift it Willie, shift it. Get back up there an get an eyeful. C'mon, jist drap the bag here.'

Back in the room, the door through to the bathroom was open, and I could see Beata's form through the shower curtain.

'Kit aff Willie, jump in there, she's gaggin for it.'

'She's havin a wash.'

'Aye, but she's nuddy in there.'

'Do you mean … Can I? I don't think I could.'

I undressed and approached the shower. My hand hovered at the curtain. Beata showed no reaction.

'She's fuckin nuddy behin there. Let's see it.'

I pulled back the curtain. Beata was holding the shower over her head, washing shampoo from her hair. The bubbles were flowing over her shoulders and breasts, down her stomach.

'Oofya.'

I stepped into the cubicle and touched her gently on her side.

She screamed and nearly hit me with the shower.

'Hey. It's me.'

'Faan. William, what are you doing?'

'I …'

'Ye jist needed a wash an aw.'

'I just thought I should have a wash as well.'

She didn't make any motion to cover herself.

Davy said, 'Take the shower aff her. Sprinkle it on her hair.'

'Here. Let me help.' I let the water fall over her head. She kept her eyes closed, both her hands working though her hair. I stepped nearer. Our bodies touched from chest down to feet. I kissed her forehead, getting my face wet letting her face fall against the crook of my neck. She kissed me there and said, 'Mm, that's nice.'

Beata took the shower from me and sprayed it against my chest. 'You stink, you know. So a wash is a good idea.'

I squirted some soap in her free hand and she ran her hand over my wet skin. I put soap in my hands and began to rub them over her.

I was painfully erect. There was no doubt that Beata was aware of that as I touched against her. I could no longer see Davy, wasn't aware of where he was, but agreed with him when he said, 'Thurs nae doot aboot it, son. She knaws whur this is goin.' And I followed his instruction. 'Get yer hauns oan her bits.' I rubbed soap over her breasts, used the shower to wash it off, then bent to put my lips to them. She said, 'No,' but my blood was coursing and tension had to be released.

'Go fur her fanny.'

I reached between her legs.

'No, William.'

'Open her up son.'

But Beata said, 'You can't just ... like that. Ow. Please, ...' She pulled my hand away.

'Fuck her Willie. Dinnae lissen tae her. Jist push her against the waw and gie her wan.'

I mumbled, 'I'm sorry I ...'

'Get yer dick in her.'

I pulled her closer, let my erection press against her belly, tried to kiss her.

'OK.' She turned the shower in my face. 'Back off.' And then sprayed it on my willy. 'You're too hot.' Suddenly the water was cold and it shocked through me, battering against my raging hot groin. I yelped. Davy hollered like he'd been caught in the blast.

Beata squealed too and stepped back, pushing the curtain back trying to get away from the cold spray. We wrestled for the showerhead, water spraying around the room and then Beata shut it off.

We looked at each other, dripping and bedraggled. My tumescence had subsided. The guilt crept in.

Beata said, 'Ha, well, now that was a different kind of shower.'

We dried and dressed silently, though she used her towel to rub water off my back and allowed me to dry her.

Sitting on the bed in shorts and t-shirt, a towel wrapped around her head, Beata put a hand on my knee. 'I'm sorry William. I know that you must want to ... And I do too. I really do. But you were just too ... aggressive.' I knew I had pushed it too far. I had let the situation get the better of me, the drink, or ... Davy. But there was no anger in her voice. 'I do want to be with you, but not like that. You were just a bit like a monster, not ... William. And I want to be with William. He's the good guy.'

Davy was sulking. He'd climbed, still wet, under the sheet on his bed, knocking more of Beata's belongings to the floor, a black look over his face.

I felt shame, a blackness inside. It seemed absurd that she was trying to cheer me up. 'Come on.' She chucked me under the chin. 'Let's plan for tomorrow.'

*   *   *   *

CHAPTER 8

Beata's face was crossed by a length of hair that fell from her fringe. I pushed the strand away.

Beata stirred. 'Hmmm are you getting up already? What time is it?'

'Nearly half nine.'

'Aff? No. Really? But aren't we going to Port Douglas?'

'Sure, sure. If you want to.'

She sat up and put her arms round my neck from behind, running a hand across my chest. 'Good morning you. Did you sleep OK?'

'Hmm.' I held a hand to her face. 'Are you OK? You seemed a bit... unsettled in the night.'

'No, I'm fine. I have a very very good sleep. Too good.' She stretched and rubbed her eyes. 'Slow head. Come on, we better go if we want to go.'

We set off to hitch, standing under Jolly Joe – a huge roadside statue of a backpacker outside the hostel, taller than the buildings. Jolly Joe was permanently hitching a lift, his thumb raised to the traffic heading out of town. Someone had managed to climb up and write across his outstretched arm, ANYWHERE. We mimicked his pose.

It took us two rides to get to Port Douglas – a manic teenage redneck in a souped up jalopy, then a long-haul driver in a mammoth artic. We trundled swiftly past a continuous stretch of deserted beach, save for occasional housing and mangroves. Still, it was gone three o'clock by the time we reached the town.

Throughout the day, both of us kept conversation to a minimum – not taciturn, or uncomfortable, but easily, happily quiet in each other's company, and not keeping to ourselves: when the redneck cussed, we shared a grin; when we walked, we held hands; when the road lead nowhere, we sped up, running and laughing under our packs until the beach appeared suddenly from behind a bush; when the high-pitched squall of children got too much, we swam out into the sea, beyond the other bathers, where the hubbub hushed away.

Under the water the plops and slops of the ocean filled my ears. The blurred vision of Beata swam below my salt-stung eyes; a glistening flickered in her wake. The current she created buffeted against my belly. She came up with handfuls of wet sand darted through with chunks of coral and tiny whorled shells. 'Little lives and universe that slip through our fingers.'

'It's amazing to think of all that life out there.'

'I think we should scuba together. You and me. Let's make that our next plan.'

When I opened my mouth to reply, she slapped a sandy hand on top of my head and pushed me under, filling me with seawater. I came up coughing and she laughed. I dived back under to grab her legs, which kicked and wriggled and we came up entwined, struggling to keep our joint weight afloat, treading towards a depth where we could land.

We bought overpriced fruit from a beach vendor – cool, dripping wet slices of mango and watermelon – and slurped. We jumped back into the sea to wash off the sticky juice then stretched out on our towels letting the sun dry us off. My skin tightened and tingled as the salt crystallised on my back then the heat drew beads of sweat that trickled down the length of my spine and pooled.

I reached over and took Beata's hand. 'Can we just stay here?'

'Hmm. We can.'

We lay. We dozed. We swam some more.

The sun dropped behind trees at the end of the beach, denying us its last flourish, but the sky burst out in a wide seam of deep orange that gave way to yellow and paler into white above us. Every colour – of the sand, of our towels, of the trees and umbrellas, sunsuits and Beata's skin – took on a new vibrancy, an electric sunburst of joy at daylight's last fling. We held each other and looked out to the gentle pull of the ocean, sitting out the dying of the day. In the East, it was already dark, speckled through with stars. A few thin strips of cloud gathered around the low moon.

*   *   *   *

'Som smackar mycket gott.'

'Pardon?'

'It's good, isn't it?'

'Hits the spot.'

'Pardon?'

I took a swig of my beer then cut off another chunk of thick omelette, knocking a chip onto the formica. Beata grabbed it with her fork and crammed it into her mouth.

'Hey, eat yer own chips.'

'What chips?' Her omelette was alone on its plate.

'You must be a chip fan.'

'Chipaholic.'

Beata took a paper napkin from the tin holder and wiped ketchup from her mouth. 'You know, you have insisted on that I tell you about me, but I think I know little about you.'

'That's cause there's not much to tell. I'm pretty dull. Surprised you've stuck around as long as you have.'

'That's not true. You are a very sweet guy. Good fun.'

'Then I've got you fooled. Ha ha har, you'll never know that really I'm – Super Dull!'

'Dull means boring, right? You are all this way in Australia. Don't you think that is exciting?'

'Are you excited?'

'Yes. It's exciting to be here. Exciting to hitchhike. Exciting to go in a place where I never seen before.'

'It's exciting to be here with you.'

'You see? Sweet guy.' She reached over and spiked three chips, one after another, onto her fork. 'But you have been in Australia for a long time. Did you not have lots of excitement?'

I finished chewing my chunk of omelette before answering. 'Yeeaahno, not really. I had a rubbish job in Sydney. Then I had a rubbish time travelling up the coast. I spent all my money, and I ended up stuck in Tully.'

She shook her head. 'But you must have had fun on the coast. Did you go to Airlie Beach or to Fraser Island?'

'I did all those things. It was just, well…' I didn't want to expose myself, but couldn't find it in me to lie. 'I came to Australia with some friends and travelled with them, but… we didn't get on well. After a while I kinda got the impression that they had never liked me much, even before we left Scotland.'

'Then why would they travel with you?'

'I don't know, maybe they felt they had to because we'd known each other so long or because our families know each other or… something.' I knew it sounded lame. I had managed to reveal myself as a social cretin and an equivocator.

But Beata just shook her head and smiled again. While she ate the rest of my chips, her gaze stayed on me, lashes batting over dark brown irises, gentle but unemotional. Still, I felt comforted by her gaze – there was no sign of judgement or displeasure in her. I felt like I was being accepted.

I sliced up the last chunks of my omelette and ate them dipped in ketchup and washed down with chugs of beer.

After the food was gone and beer nearly drained, Beata asked, 'Do you have a brother or sister?'

'I've got a sister, but we don't get on all that well.' She raised her eyebrows, so I said. 'Yep, another failed relationship.'

'Aff, brother and sister don't ever get on well. But never so serious.'

'Yeah, I dunno. I don't think she likes me much.'

She reached across the table and gently smacked the back of my hand. 'I think you worry too much. You don't know what your sister think.'

'I do. She says I'm too much like my dad.'

'She doesn't like your dad?'

'Dad's dead. He died when I was eight.' Beata took hold of my hand and I could see the sympathy, but I didn't want it, it wasn't necessary. 'It's just daft. She doesn't even know what dad was like really, but … well … Dad betrayed us. He made a right mess of it, really.'

'Are you like your father?'

'What?'

'Is that some worry for you?'

'No, I …' I was willing her not to think that, not to see into me and work it out, work out what Davy had wanted me to believe. I couldn't go into that.

I think Beata understood. 'It must be very difficult without a father.'

'No. We were OK.'

'Did it make you closer with your mother?'

I drew my hand away and turned side-on, pressing my back to the wall and stretching my legs along the bench. I drained the last of my beer. Beata watched.

I said, 'I got a letter from mum a few days ago.'

'That's good.'

'Well, yeah but, she just made me feel guilty that I haven't written to her for ages or spoken to her or…'

'But it is nice to hear from family.'

'… and it got me thinking about the fact that pretty soon, I'm going to have to go back to Scotland.'

Beata's face pinched in a frown. 'You sound as maybe you don't want to go back.'

'It's just, I feel like I'm only starting to do something with my time. It's almost a year already and everything I've done up till now has been a disaster. No, not a disaster, just… pointless. But right now, I feel like it's finally starting to happen. Life is changing. I think maybe, I could change. When I left home, I really thought that I was going out to become better, a new person, someone who takes chances and lives an exciting life. If I go back now, I'll be giving it all up without really having changed at all.'

'I think is as much important to stay close with family as make good your life, you know?'

'Sure, yes, of course I agree. It's just, my mum, you know, she's pretty hard work. Dealing with her can be quite a depressing experience.'

'Do you not think then that it is your mum who is depressed?'

'Sure. I mean, it is. She is. She's in counselling.'

'Then don't you feel bad that you don't speak to her for so long time?' Her voice betrayed a touch of irritation.

'Well, no, I mean I'm going back. I'm going back for her sake.'

'But it's not so hard to do, to make her a phone call. It will cost a little money but to call is very easy.'

'I guess.' I knew that Beata was leaning across the table, trying to close the gap, but I couldn't look her in the face. Instead, I pulled out my wallet and flipped it open. 'I've even got a phonecard. I'm not sure how much is left on it but.'

'You should use it to call your mum.'

'I guess you're right. When we get back to Cairns, I'll…'

'No, I think now. You should call your mum now.'

'No, it's…'

She leant right across and laid a hand on my shoulder. 'Why not? We can ask the waitress where is a phonebox and you can call.'

'No, but I'm…'

'Is easy. We'll do it and then when it's finished you'll be glad.'

*   *   *   *

'Hello?' Mum's voice, small and worried.

'Hi, Mum. It's me, William.'

There was a pause. 'What?' A long delay on the line. 'Oh, William! Willie. How are you? Son, ah son. How are ye?' She was shouting into the phone.

'I got your letter mum. I just thought I'd give you a call and tell ye I'm fine. I don't have much credit so I won't be able to talk for long.'

'Oh Willie. I'm so glad ye've phoned. I was worried.'

'There's no need to worry Mum, I'm fine.'

'I saw Timothy's mother, and she said that ye weren't with him anymore, that ye'd gone off somewhere, and then I was so worried because there was no way for me tae know where ye were. I almost called the embassy. I might've called the Australian police, but I asked yer sister an she just said not tae worry, that ye'd be fine, but there was no way for me tae know.'

'Mum, I'm fine. I'm great in fact. I've met a really nice girl, a Swedish girl, called Beata.' Beata was holding onto my arm. I stared at the rapidly depleting numbers. 'I'm travelling with her now. We're staying thegether here in Cairns.'

'Oh.'

'Well, we're in a place called Port Douglas now, but we're back in Cairns tomorrow. We're just visiting for a day because it's a good place tae come to for the beach and for the swimming an that and it's…'

'You're where?'

'We're in… Cairns. We're in Cairns.'

'Well… you're in Cairns now. Well, ye said ye were going there. Did ye get my letter?'

'Yes. Are ye OK mum?'

'Me? Yes, I'm… well yes I'm OK. I wouldn't want you worryin about me.'

'Are ye gettin out much?'

'No, not much.'

'Are ye…' There was a far off sound on the line of someone else's conversation, like interference on a radio. 'Is Helen OK?'

'She's fine, as far as I know. She said she's caught up in some big business that keeps taking her to London. She's been up and down a lot. Last time she was in she was… och, I'm no sure, anyway she was helpin me get the winter covers out…'

'Mum. Mum, ma money's…'

'…and she was sayin that I'm gonnae have tae cut…'

The credit clicked to zero and Mum was gone.

I hung up the receiver and Beata took my hand. 'OK?'

'Aye. Yes… she's OK, it's just…. Ach. She's fine.'

Beata squeezed my arm. I pulled her away from the box and said again, 'She's fine.' I tried my best to smile.

We found a shop and bought a few cans of beer and some chocolate, then headed down to the beach. We took off our shoes, tied them to our packs and walked barefoot along the breakwater. Clouds had gathered, the stars gone, but there was a strong glow from a high moon and enough light for us to pick our way. We came across a washed up log, sat and cracked open a couple of cans.

The timbre of Mum's voice stayed with me, giving animation to an image of her face. I could so easily picture her delight when I appeared again on her doorstep, but I could also see the joy slipping away as we returned to the mundane circuit of our lives. Ours was a house with few words, little sound and little activity. All it had was the effort it took to get Mum through each day.

I could make out the edges of Beata's features, the crescent lines of light touching her cheeks, the curves of her chin, nose and forehead and I imagined what life could be if I were to go with her, if we were to strive together to discover whatever it was that she was wanted to find. Even if there was nothing there, a journey with her seemed far more than a life sitting still in front of the television next to Mum.

I said, 'Beata?'

She turned. 'Hmm.'

'I'd like to stay with you.'

'I like to stay with you too. This is nice.'

'No, I mean, I want to go with you, travelling. I want to stay with you. It's just … It's so good being with you. I feel … good. Ah! I don't know a better way to say it. When I'm with you, it feels alright … being me, I guess. It's stupid. It's just … Ah! I don't really know what I'm saying.'

'I do. And it's nice.' She kissed my cheek. 'It's easy with you, William.' She sounded surprised. 'You know, in Tully, Emma wanted me to think that you were a monster, that all you want was molest and dump me. She was right.'

'What?'

'I think sometimes you are a monster. Or, it is you have the monster in you. Like last night in that bar. There's an excitement that make you act weird. But sometimes that is exciting too, or fun, like when you save me from that Roy man, you were my hero.' She squeezed my arm and kissed my cheek again.

'Ha. Hardly, I just …'

'But, I think the good thing is that you have control on it. You don't let it get you over. I think you know when it get you too bad, like maybe when you drink too much. And most of the time, like now, you are gentle, and quiet – a different person. Maybe that's why I like you. I get to go out with two person. I'm a … What am I, a bi-married, or a double-…'

'A bigamist?'

'Yes?'

'You think it's bigamy?'

'Sure.'

'Well I think it's big of you too.'

'Uh?' She screwed up her face. Though I don't think she got it, my toothy grin must have told her it was a joke. 'Aff, you.' She rolled around to lean on top of me and started tickling with fast hands scrabbling around my armpits, my neck and legs. I tickled back and we slipped off the log, scrabbling in a sandy flurry. When it settled, we got back up and held each other tightly.

I knew she was right. There were two, me and Davy. But she was right too, that I could control him. Right then, I really thought so, that I was the one in charge, that I made the decisions. I believed it could only work out right. Davy was the strength that could pull me up and push me through, and I could steer the course.

And there it was, that moment, my happiest. I felt in control, in a good place. And Beata held me.

Beata broke the silence. 'You see the glow in the sky in that direction?'

'Yes.'

'You think it must be Cairns, isn't it?'

'Right.'

'But look out there.' She pointed out to sea. 'You see still on the horizon there is a glow a little also. Only a little. But you wonder that can't be correct because the sun, it set over that side, over behind the trees, right? And too in the light, you can see... aff, I don't know how you say... it's like waves in the air, you know, the air is moving.'

'It's shimmering.'

'Shimmering, that's a good word. What do you think that is?'

'It's the heat. The heat from the day coming up off the land.'

'But out in the sea also?'

'Well, yeah. I mean, we're on the land, so isn't it coming up from around us?'

'I don't know.'

I watched the sky, the air, saw the glows shimmering like a dark heat wave.

'You know,' she said, 'I think the earth is very powerful here. Or maybe no, it is powerful everywhere but out here you are able to see it much more.' She spoke in low resonant tones, a tender range. 'Have you been into the desert? To Australia's middle? Everything feels so strong there. The energy, the power that the land has. It is easy to understand why the aboriginal have so many myth and story about the desert, about creation, how life started and grew. So strong.'

I looked and I saw that shimmer in everything – in the sea, each glowing breaker, in the treetops that swayed and rustled, in the sand, in the grains that gathered in folds, in the log that supported us. 'I guess, I know... I'm...'

'Here.' Beata wrapped her arms around one of mine. 'You feel the touch, the warmth, the feeling between our bodies? This is the energy, the power that combines us, that tells us to know that we are with a person who is alive, who has life and in our touch it is sharing just like we are sharing with all that energy from the land when we sit here. We do not have to ask it to happen, or let it to happen, it is only being close, with people, with the land and we are sharing.'

Beata's arms clasped tighter; her fingers squeezed against the cotton of my shirt. I felt the chill that blew against my face and my legs, but the warmth from those pressing fingers spread out to every reach of my body.

She continued, 'The aboriginal walk across the whole desert and they know where to find the water, where is the food. They say the land talk to them and they sing to the land when they walk.'

'Do you want to sing and walk?'

'We could sing when we walk.'

'Jings, you're not going to suggest we walk back to Cairns?'

'Hey, you want adventure and excitement. Maybe we should walk off into the desert.'

She prodded me in the ribs and I gave her a tickle that ended in a kiss.

'So, William the adventurer, do you know where we are going to sleep?'

We had planned to sleep out on the beach – a balmy night, getting up with the dawn, rousing ourselves in the ocean. We hadn't planned on the strengthening wind that was whipping up sand along this length of exposed coast or the clouds gathering thicker and lower.

We headed back to town, looking into gardens, hoping to find a bit of secluded shelter or perhaps a bit of park that could offer us soft ground and thick bushes. What we eventually found was a building under construction, close to completion but open to the world, with no doors or anything to stop us sneaking in. There was a lot less clutter upstairs, a lot of dust and dirt, but hardly any tools or scraps. Wind blew in through the empty window frames but one corner was windowless and better sheltered.

Beata scraped away a flurry of dust with her boot. 'I think we can put our bags onto here.'

'Looks really comfortable.'

'Will I go to the beach and bring some sand to put down?'

We rolled out our bags and lay next to each other. Beata pulled her bag up to her nose, her hands gripped the top edge. 'This is funny, isn't it?'

'Stupid, yes.'

I shunted closer, so that I could feel her body up against mine through the down. Her fingers came round and took mine.

I said, 'I'm really, really sorry that I am going to have to say goodbye to you. It doesn't seem like we will have very long together at all.'

'You know, I am hoping that one year later I will be in Sweden. You can come to visit me there.'

'That would be great. It's just, I think, maybe, you know... a chance like this doesn't come along very often, to meet someone that you like so much and someone that you know you could happily travel with. It's such an unlucky coincidence that I meet you now when all of that is about to stop for me.'

'Coincidence is a stupid idea. It is an excuse. Nothing happens for no reason. There is some very good reason that me and you we become friends at this time. You know, we will maybe be friends always, or maybe tomorrow something will make us go apart, but this, what we do now, it will have effect on the rest of our life, and maybe sometime we will think back and remember what it was like to lie here in the dark talking like this.'

'I know I will.'

'With this uncomfortable floor and the noisy wind.'

'And that strange scuttling.'

'You mean that noise? Yes, what is that? Is it something alive, do you think?'

'Something coming to get us.'

'But you can protect me. You will be my hero?'

She reached her arm out and touched my face. I put mine inside her sleeping bag to hold her. Then we kissed and tried to get close to each other. We laughed at the ridiculousness of having two thick bags between us.

'This is the ultimate sex protection, no?'

We unzipped the sides of our bags and slipped our limbs through to each other's skin.

'William, do you have any?'

'Any what?'

'Sex protection... condom.'

We had packed in a hurry and really I hadn't taken it as a possibility. And now it was a need.

'I could go back to the shop, get some.'

'No, don't. It's late. We can wait. There's still some weeks before you go. There is still lots of things for us to do.'

So we held each other and kissed. We touched and fumbled, and Beata didn't push my hands away. Between the touch of fingers, of lips, of tongue, along the contact of our legs, of our chests, our hips, our groins pressing together, I tried to feel that flow of energy Beata had talked of. I imagined I could feel my sensations heighten, my life-force sharing. But to clasp and writhe on the boards meant to have a hip or an elbow or a shoulder pressed painfully. Our sleeping bags slipped away and we were exposed to wood and wind.

Eventually Beata said, 'Let's sleep now.'

We rolled apart and zipped ourselves back up into separate shells. I lay there aroused, intense and feeling alone, like a roadside accident under the orange glow of streetlight that permeated the room. Slowly, my excited buzz gave over to the nagging of tiredness and sagging eyes, but the floor remained hard, the building draughty and night noises continued to disturb me. Towards morning, I dosed fitfully while somewhere far off, perhaps out at sea, over the vast and vibrant reef, thunder rolled.

*   *   *   *

CHAPTER 9

And then it was finished. She was gone. Beata left me, and so she should. I deserved it.

Two days after Port Douglas, Beata was pushing a note under my door to say that she wanted me to bring all her belongings to her. It didn't matter anymore what I wanted. I wasn't going to get it. And what Beata had wanted, that didn't matter. She stepped away. Cut her losses.

I managed all her stuff into her bags. I managed not to go into her diary – I wouldn't have been able to understand it, but I could have seen how often she'd written my name – and I met her in a restaurant across the road from Joe's Hostel.

She was such a cool cat. She wanted her belongings back, but she wanted to talk too. 'Your face was so like a unhappy puppy when we drove away, and you were standing in the rain. I couldn't get it out of my head. But no. You are a dog, only not a puppy, isn't it?' But she was smiling when she said it. 'I think you understand that the thing for me is the trust. I have to trust. And it is easy to give, I think. Right from when we meet, I trust you. But if trust go, I cannot get it back. I cannot be with that person anymore.'

She expressed sadness because she thought I was a really nice person and she had thought that we would be able to have such a good time together. She told me of her hope that I would have been able to come and visit her in Sweden. She knew I would like it, still thought I should go, but not to get in touch with her.

I hardly spoke.

*   *   *   *

The bright sun of the day before had lapsed into an overcast gloom when we left Port Douglas. The air felt dense, oppressive, and in the walk to the highway we quickly grew short of breath. The sweaty film on our skin was blown by a cold wind coming in off the sea. It was like having a winter chill or flu – hot and cold sweats. We both complained of aching hips and backs from our night spent on the wooden floor.

At the highway, we found a bus stop, local rather than the pricey tourist bus that ran from Port Douglas. We waited at the stop and thumbed for a lift, whichever came first – bus or hitch. There wasn't a flicker of attention from any passing driver and an hour passed before the first bus came. We hadn't prepared supplies and were peckish when we got on the bus, but buoyed by the idea that the journey would fly past. We hadn't considered that local buses take local routes, go by local time. It detoured, bypassed, stopped, exchanged drivers and waited through the questioning of pensive travellers checking destinations with the driver.

The bus eventually dropped us on the Cook Highway not far from Joe's, but our first urge was to hit the nearest diner and pig out, eating away the hunger and drowning the frustration in strong tea.

Throughout the morning we had talked little, but it wasn't with any awkwardness. We had grown comfortable enough with each other to be silent together. I was amazed that this could have happened in a week. I sent out another little thank you to Davy, and was struck by the fact that I had managed a very successful day without him. It was reassuring. I was getting control. I wanted to share with him how nice things had been, how I was feeling and how open Beata and I had become to each other. Whatever argument we'd had would pale next to that.

When we made our way to Joe's, the clouds hung heavy and a smir of rain began to fall.

The woman at reception stopped us. 'You guys in 203, ey? Here's ya Bill.' She waved it at us. 'And a message for ya.'

ASTRID RANG

CALL HER

4692 1306

Orla walked through from the courtyard, catching me off guard. A little shock of guilt. I told myself I didn't deserve that sudden pang.

'Hey. Alright guys? Where ye bin? The pair a yous been having fun? Looks like you just missed the rain there, eh?'

Beata replied, 'Hallo. It's... Orla, isn't it? We're just now back from Port Douglas. It is lovely up there. And yes, but it's already a little raining.'

'Hi Orla. How you doin?'

'Aw, hey, that's cool. I hear it's lovely up there. Here, yous wanna come out later? I'm meeting up with a bunch of ma students. They're out diving. I woulda gone with them, but I got a bloody ear infection last time I went out. I'm gonna catch up with them after though.'

'Where're you meeting them?' I didn't have any intention of going. The idea of being out in a big group paled against staying in with Beata, but it seemed rude not to ask.

'We're meeting in the Fox and Hound. You know it?'

'No.'

'Well, you know...'

'Sorry,' Beata cut in, 'I will call Astrid.'

'Sure.'

'Right, it's not far...' I turned side on to Orla so that I could watch Beata as she moved over to the pay phone, dug out a coin from her money belt, put it into the slot and began to talk with a push of that long flick of hair that fell in front of her face. Recognising the reflex action made me feel like I really knew this woman, that I had become part of her life. No-one could compare.

She was still talking when Orla finished up. 'That's cool then. I'll see you down there. Later, yeah? Nice one. See ya.' She pointed at Beata. 'Say bye, yeah?'

I went over to Beata and listened to her Swedish babble. When she hung up, she had a big smile on.

'Astrid is going for one day horse trekking in the rainforest and I can go.'

'That's great.'

'So great. So, I am going to go to stay at Astrid's house tonight.'

'What?'

'We go tomorrow. You want to go out to the pub with these other guys, and I don't. Astrid and me have to leave early in the morning and also Astrid's husband is gone, so we can have a girls' night. A Swedish girls' night. That's great, isn't it?'

'But, no. I'm not... Can't I come with you?'

'Hah. I bet you like to have a Swedish girls' night. But it is good for us to talk and it would be boring for you.'

'But does it have to be tonight? I thought maybe that you and I could...'

'It have to be. Her husband come back the day after tomorrow and then him and she are going to Sydney.'

'I guess that makes sense.'

'Oh William, don't look so sad, it is only for one day. I will be back tomorrow night and then Astrid is gone for some time. Why not we go to the room and plan now what we do together the next day after?'

But Beata busied herself sorting through her sandy clothes from Port Douglas, and getting clean things to take with her, fussing over what would be appropriate for getting on a horse. I hung around, collected up her and my dirty things for a wash, tried and failed to pick some music to put on, flicked through Beata's guidebook aimlessly.

We showered, separately. With complete lack of inhibition, Beata stripped in front of me for her wash, startling me with sudden pink flesh that disappeared into the bathroom. Afterwards, she came out to rub moisturiser on her skin in front of the mirror, in front of me. I had intended to jump in the shower straight after her, but I dithered around in my boxer shorts, pretending to look for something. There was a tightening in my chest that shortened my breath. Beata caught the refection of me watching and laughed.

She said, 'So, you will go to the pub tonight?'

'No, I don't think so. I don't fancy it much.'

'I'm sure you will later.'

She ran the cream along the length of her legs. The muscles on her thighs stood out and her breasts hung in the triangular space between arm, leg and body.

I kept the shower cold.

We stopped again in reception to pay our bill. As we were sorting the travellers' cheques, the room grew dark. Outside it looked like night had fallen. A loud clap of thunder came, and then a rising hiss that built until a rattle of heavy raindrops battered against the glass panels on the front door.

The receptionist leant forward on the desk, peering out at the rain. 'Thank Christ. That's the wet finally started. The day's felt preggars, ya not think? Like it's bin waiting ta pop.'

'Know what you mean.'

We waited until Astrid's car pulled up outside. I held my brolly over Beata's head as the raindrops bounced off the pavement. Astrid was beckoning, so Beata gave me a quick kiss, said, 'Have fun,' and jumped in.

'Yeah, you...' the car door shut, '...too.' The wheels rolled away through flowing wet sheets. I stood watching, letting myself feel mournful. They were quickly out of sight, but I stood and stared up the road. The rain turned everything distant into a blur of shadows. At the end of the block, a figure was lurking among the signboards outside the corner shop. The shape stepped further into the pavement and turned in my direction. The person was barely taller than the fire-hydrant he stood next to.

*   *   *   *

Beata had come back because the rain was forecast to last, they had decided not to go riding, and she wanted to spend the night with me. Who knows? Maybe that would have been the night. Instead she turned on her heel and went straight back to Astrid's.

I was too blown away to move. I have known ever since that I should have run after her, naked in the rain if I had to. I should have gone. It wouldn't have made any difference, but I should have.

Beata left, and Orla stayed.

Orla said, 'Well there's no need for me to go back to my room then,' and she tried to pull me close, to snuggle in. I couldn't touch her. I rolled off, turned my back and faced my thoughts. When I knew she was asleep, I got out of our bed and climbed into Davy's. I lay awake, staring at the wall. Later I heard Orla begin to breathe heavily and to toss and turn. I ignored her until she gasped and gave a small cry. I sat up. Davy was sitting on her chest between her splayed breasts. His knees were pulled up either side of his head, his hands flat over Orla's breastbone, his obscene tackle draped, swollen. He drooled and stared fixedly at her as she writhed and groaned in something like sexual ecstasy, her arms over her head, her legs kicking and twisting in the sheet. Then Davy turned to me, grinned and winked.

I pulled the pillow over my head.

Beata's words from the first night we lay together in my hut came back to me, 'Thank you William. You are a very kind person.' She was wrong. I had deceived her all along.

We had deceived her.

*　　　*　　　*　　　*

'I can't believe what ye made me do.'

'Whit?'

'What you made me do. You bloody well pushed me into it. All along, you pushed and pushed.'

'Ur ye sure yer awright son? See when ye banged yer heid last night, d'ye think ye fucked up yer brains? Cause I didnae make ye dae anyhin. Ye shagged her on yer ain. Looked like ye were huvin a rer aul time an aw, right up till the frigid Scandy bitch walked in.'

'Don't.'

'Ye see the look on her puss but.'

'Bloody don't. You wouldn't let it alone. Shag her, shag her, shag her. Go on, shag her, get yer hons on her big Irish tits. Are ye happy now?'

'Happy for you son. Ye got yer end away.'

'Christ. That is not all there is. But it is for you, isn't it? What were you doin to Orla last night? What are you Davy?'

'I told ye. I'm jist yer wee…'

'Pal? Yer ma pal? What kind of fuckin pal are you? That was the best thing I've ever had. That was …'

'Pffft. That wis fuck aw. That wis a fuckin tight-holed usin cow that jist wahnted you followin her aroon like a beagle.'

'No. Davy, aargh! You don't get it. I … I'm sure I …'

'I tell ye whit, but. I'll be keepin ma promise.'

'What have you ever promised?'

'I said, if ye shagged some other bird, I'd lea yer Scandy bitch alane. Well errs fuck aw chance ae us gettin near that cunt again, is thur? Haw haw hurr hurr.'

Orla roused. She stretched her arms over her head, yawned then saw me on the other bed.

'Why ye over there? C'mere and give me a cuddle.' She pulled away the sheet, revealing all of her naked form. Davy puckered his lips and said, 'Oof.' With both his feet, he pushed my backside until I slipped off the bed. I stepped over and sat on the edge next to Orla. She said, 'That was so nice what ye did for me last night. It was so weird though, I felt like I was still asleep the whole time, like it was a dream.'

*　　　*　　　*　　　*

It was still lashing down with rain. Orla tried to hold the umbrella over us while holding me up. I got wet again, but the rain was at least a little refreshing and would wash some of the beer off. She fizzed away in anger. 'Who's that prick think he is? Fuckin smart arse. He'll fuckin get it. Got it comin...' Her voice and the sound of the rain fazed into a background static against my struggle to keep the contents of my stomach down and my feet propelling forward. My stumbles and occasional tip towards the pavement brought ejaculations of sympathy from Orla. 'Aw William, ye alright there? Come on now. Yer doin fine.'

The comic meanderings of our walk eventually overtook her anger and she laughed at me. 'You're a right sorry state, so ye are.'

'This is dead kinda you. Sorry I'm... sorry I...' I was careening along the edge of the kerb, feeling my flip-flops running its lip. Davy was next to me, on the roadside striding through the gutter, laughing and barking, 'Hoi, hoi.' He gave me a push that sent me out of the path of the fire-hydrant and against Orla, shoving her over into a hedge.

'Hey, William, calm down would ye? We're nearly home.'

I bumped against Jolly Joe and ricocheted towards the door. I think there may still have been someone at the desk, but Orla dragged me through to the stairs as quick as I would go.

'Can ye manage these William? Yer no that bad are ye?'

I pulled myself up. 'Nae bother.' And stuck my foot out for the stairs. I caught the first one awkwardly and stumbled up the next few in succession. The momentum got me up to the first landing, and we both laughed at my efforts.

'I'm sorry Orla. I'm a bit oof... ya know a bit...'

'I know ye are. I know. It's ma fault.'

We put our arms around each other and took the second short set of stairs. Orla propped me against the door to my room. 'Ye got the key

William? Where is it? In yer pocket?' She went in, jiggling her hand amongst my loose change. 'Ooh, there we go.'

As I tumbled backwards into the room, I grabbed hold of Orla, draggin her in with me. We tumbled and I made the bed my goal, pulling Orla with me all the way. We fell back, side by side, feet hanging over the edge.

'Ha ha ha. Oh William, yer something else.'

The room spun, and my head throbbed, but lying down I began to feel just a touch more together. 'Aw thanks Orla. I think I definitely needed to get out of there. They're lucky they don't have my guts decorating the walls.'

'We all are. Ye feeling a bit better now?'

'Aye. Yeah, thanks. It's good to be home.'

'I'm totally soaking. Have ye got a towel?'

'Aye.' I waved a hand in the direction of bathroom. She came back out rubbing her hair, arms and down her legs.

'How about you?'

'Uh.' She rubbed the towel over my legs, pulled my flip-flops off and rubbed my feet dry, then threw the towel at my head. I had a go at drying my face and arms.

'Have you got a t-shirt I can put on?'

'Aye.' I waved in the direction of my pack. She rummaged around.

'Do you mind if I borrow this one?'

And there was her chest, unbuttoned from the shirt she was wearing and let fall from her bra. She leant over me to grab the towel and rubbed it around her top half standing next to the bed. Her breasts shook. She pulled the t-shirt on, then slipped her shorts off with a flash of buttocks. She rubbed her bottom with the towel looking at me sprawled out on the bed, looking at her.

'Look at the state o you. I can't leave ye lying wet all over yer bed. Here, take yer t-shirt off.'

She climbed on to the bed, straddled over me and started tugging up my t-shirt

'No, I can do that myself.'

'Sure, let me help you.'

As I twisted to grab the corners, she pulled the wet material up over my head so that my arms were caught up in it, then left me to struggle the rest of the way out.

'And here.' She pulled at my shorts. By the time I had managed to disentangle myself from the t-shirt, she had them off too.

I had on white boxers. They were wet through.

'Your poor little fella must be frozen in there.'

I chuckled. Then was shut up by the feel of her hand inside the fly of my pants. She wrapped her fingers around my flaccid, cold, damp penis. It instinctively twitched with a pump of blood.

'Aw, the poor wee thing. I can feel he wants to say hello.'

My breath came short. I wanted to say, 'Orla, no.' But she gripped a little firmer and pulled gently.

'Come on, ye can't keep these on.'

Orla grabbed both sides of my boxers and tugged. Stepping off the bed, she pulled them right off then jumped back, straddling me. I could feel the damp material of her underwear against my thigh. She pressed down onto it and brought her face in close to my chest, looking up at me.

'Orla, you know, I think this is…'

She slipped down and put my penis in her mouth. The wet warmth shocked me. All my muscles clamped ridged. I was still soft but the strong pushing of her tongue rapidly aroused me. I raised my head and saw a mass of damp blonde hair swirling around my crotch. It gently stroked across my lower belly, my thighs and my groin. She moaned and gasped. I dropped my head back and let out a breath that had been held for far too long.

Davy was in there with us. At first I could hear him stumbling around and banging into stuff, his breathing laboured from too much booze or too much excitement. But when Orla started having sex with me, I heard that rasping, wheezing breath draw close, falling into a steady hiss as if pulled through his teeth.

I lay anticipating my guilt like an ejaculation, knowing that I wanted Beata, that I was betraying her, but my determination slipped away with the strokes of Orla's hair, her hand, her mouth and I let myself go. I sat up and lifted Orla's head. I guided her up the bed, pushed her over and pulled her knickers off.

She said, 'Yes. Yes. Come on.'

I knelt in front of her. My willie stood up, pointing past my bent knees between her spread legs. 'I better find a condom.' The momentary halt started the wilt, and I began to form the thought, I swear, that I would stay off the bed, not go back, but she grabbed me.

'No, it's OK.'

She pulled me on top of her. Her fingers closed around me again and guided me into her.

'I…'

The warmth spread from my centre throughout my whole body. A gentle pressure squeezed like a hug. I felt a shimmer of elation like I had achieved something I had been striving a long time for. Slowly, I gave myself over to the sensations: the throbs of happiness pulsing up my intestine; the shockwaves of energy that coursed my limbs and made them cling and clench; the need to move deeper and deeper.

I closed my eyes and saw Beata. Something animalistic took over, something that drove me wild, aggressive, something that had me saying, 'Yes. Right. Fuckin. Right. Here. Here it is. Take it.'

Orla's legs clamped around my buttocks and she shouted, 'Holy fucking Jesus, yes, yes!'

The smell of sex filled me, overwhelmed me. I opened my eyes and Davy was there, crouching next to Orla's lolling head. She looked up at me with a slack-mouthed smile. He looked into me with a leer of joy and triumph, his eyes shining, showing the reflection of my own face, every muscle in it taught. I stopped my thrust, shocked at the vision of how far I had let myself go, disgusted at me and at Davy, this thing, my life.

Orla screamed, 'Holy Mary mother of God.'

Then the door opened and Beata walked in.

*   *   *   *

I kept on the room at Joe's, paying the extra and living around the space that Beata had left, wanting to be conscious of her absence. I needed to see her, but couldn't find her. It was pointless trawling the backpacker hostels; I knew she was staying with Astrid. I didn't know where. So, I kept out and about in the town during the day, and always at night in the bars. As I wandered, I worked the case I would plead. Drunkenness. A fit of madness. Fear that she was too good for me. A self destructive impulse. None of it stood, but I thought I could let it all flood out, wear her down until she realised how contrite I was, and that I wouldn't let it happen again. I couldn't betray her. I wouldn't let my opportunity pass me by a second time.

Slowly, though, Orla began to fill the space.

It felt safer keeping someone else around. I was cosseted. I was weak enough to want the cotton wool of a social set. It let me feel wanted and just a little alive, more than I would have if I deserted them to live again with only my own company, and Davy's.

And of course, there was sex. I had a sex life, and Orla was an attractive woman. Another first. I was pained by guilt each time, and sorrow but at the same time I was carried away in the impossibility of my situation, a life implausible. I fantasised that my partner was dark haired and elfin, that the husky voice of passion was swooping low in the skirls of Scandinavian.

Davy thrived. He was ebullient, jokey and fun. His beard had all but fallen away, exposing the thin beakiness of his face, but his complexion was ruddy, his cheeks often lifted in a grin. And he cursed, by Christ he cursed, though he did it for the laughs, not the jibes. I saw that I could live with him best when I lost my qualms about the thin moral sinews that bound our daily habits.

When she wasn't working, Orla came around. Most nights we went out to a bar. Orla and her friends often brought along groups of the foreign students they taught. Davy loved the collections of young Japanese or Argentinian or Greek or French women we found ourselves among. These nights ended in my room, in sex and in Orla staying over. She was good at getting up and out to work. I slept late, wallowing in my hangover, and by the time I had recovered, freshening up with a coffee in town, Orla was finishing work.

I didn't bother trying to find a job, there didn't seem to be much point in the few weeks that I had left in the country. I just filled my time. I went on some of their school excursions: diving, river rafting; I did a bungee jump; I even went on a horseback trek through the rainforest. The problem was that filling my time rapidly diminished my money – the savings I had put together to take back with me. On the day I went to buy my ticket for Sydney to connect with my flight home, I went into the bank for funds and discovered that I was going back with practically nothing. I was left with the prospect of landing back at my mum's with no funds to get myself out again – nothing for a deposit on a flat, nothing for a car, hardly anything even to get myself out to the pub. I definitely would have to get a job as soon as I got back, but I had no idea what that was going to be. It sank in that I had never done anything much like a real job.

Orla was soon to be leaving Australia as well. Harry had gone already to Korea. A student of his was opening up a language school and needed a manager, a Director of Studies, to help set it up. Harry had put himself forward, despite having been a teacher barely more than a few months and, Orla told me, was a poor one at that. He was the kind of man that got into it for the opportunity to crack on to young foreign girls. Davy's kind of man. A week after he left Cairns, Harry started sending emails to all his teacher chums, trying to persuade them to come and work for him at 'his' school in Pusan.

Orla said to me, 'The thing is William, why don't you come as well?'

'What? No, I've gotta go back to Scotland.'

'Doesn't sound much like ye want to though, does it? And ye said yerself that yer goin back skint. Come to Korea. It sounds like the money there is gonna be decent. You can do six month and go back with the money that you've blown here. I doubt if there's gonna be that much to spend yer money on there, so you should have no bother saving some.'

'But I'm not a teacher.'

'Ah fuck, that doesn't matter. It's not that hard, and I can help ye out – tell ye what ye can do with yer students and that. Anyway, it doesn't sound much like they care whether they get teachers or not. They just want warm bodies. Native speakers that can stand up and pretend they know something about English. I bet if ye contact Harry, he'll give ye a job.'

'No, I don't think so Orla. I mean, I totally admire you guys for just upping sticks and heading off into a foreign country, but I don't think I have the guts. I mean, are you not really scared of... just... going.'

'Ah no. It's not that scary, and it's not like we've not done it before. I was a year in Turkey, Paula was in Spain, ye know? That's what being an English teacher's all about. Ye just go to a place and see what it's like. If it works out no good then ye get the hell out. It's usually a bit freaky when ye first arrive and ye don't know anyhin, but ye get over that quick enough.'

'Well, Jeez, good luck to ye. I wish I could do it, but I'll stick to Scotland.'

'Back to yer mammy.'

'Aye.'

The thought of travelling with Beata had sent my blood racing. It had seemed like a near-impossible dream that I didn't deserve but I'd be a fool to miss. There was nothing about my relationship with Orla or my new friends that said I had to cling, that I would go anywhere with them through thick and thin. I'd returned to the longing for a life I recognised, with little excitement, no adventure, but full of what I knew best, safe from the opportunity to mess up.

Davy thought otherwise. 'Whit the fuck ur ye hinkin?'

'What d'ye mean?'

'Whit the fuck ur ye oan aboot goin back tae Scotland fur?'

''Cause that's what I'm doin. That's what I was always doin.'

'And fur why?'

'It's home. My family are there. Because…'

''Cause of yer sick maw.'

'Yeah. Because ma mum's sick n she needs me.'

'An whit aboot you?'

'What?'

'Whit is it you need? I mean, whit the fuck is there fur you in Scotland? Fuck all, that's whit. It's a fuckin cold, dark, shitty country.'

'But you're Scottish. You love the country. Yer always bangin on about being a real Scot.'

'Aye, I love the country – oan biscuit tins, bottles ae whisky an oan the telly when the Hoops ur playin in Europe. I'm fucked if I wannae go back tae the fuckin place, shitehole that it is. It's fuckin brilliant bein a Scot – and the best way tae be wan is somewhere else, livin life, y'knaw? The craic is aw oot there, son, across the watter. Ye should be gettin oan a plane an heidin tae Hongky Kongky wi Orla.'

'I'm not gonna do that.'

'I tell ye whit, though, how's aboot we invite some old pals alang wey us,' he winked, 'Bring alang a bit ae the hame country, ye knaw? Ye wilnae feel sae hamesick then.'

'What are you on about, Davy?'

'Ne'er mind aboot that the noo. C'mon William.' He gave me a nudge and a wink. 'Nippon hus gottae be crawlin wey chinky fanny gaggin for a big Scots sausage.'

'Nippon is Japan, Davy'

'Who gives a fuck? Aw I knaw is, if ye go back tae fuckin Scotland, yer ne'er gonnae get a chance tae find oot. An yer ne'er gonnae get yer chance fur that wee change yer after.'

'I'm not looking to change.'

Then whit the fuck am I daein here?'

* * * *

I had an email from Paul – Paul from the Tully gang. Him, Suzie, Emma and Gary had all arrived in Cairns and were staying in some other hostel. He said he wanted to catch up and made no mention of Beata. I arranged to hook up with them mostly so that I could garner some news on Beata – I had an outside hope that they might invite her along at the same time. We arranged to meet at a café. I sat at a table outside with a coffee and saw them approach, four abreast, Paul and Suzie with arms around each other, Gary and Emma on either side of them.

Paul broke off and strode up to me with his hand out, 'Mate, good to see ya. How the hell's it going?'

'Yeah, good to see you too. You alright?'

They sat round the table, again, Gary and Emma sat on the outside of the other couple. I got the impression that not all was well in the world of Gary and Emma. They barely spoke to each other, hardly even looked at each other. Meanwhile, Paul and Suzie helped each other with their coffees, splitting sugar packs for each other, breaking off bits of cake, sharing.

Paul talked animatedly about leaving Tully and the heavy session they had as a send off that ended with all of the Aussie lot in a big brawl in Top. It seems that Roy had used the chance to get one over on his brother, and it had left both of them in hospital this time. He added quietly, 'We never found out what kind of condition he was in before we left.'

Suzie sighed.

When Emma asked, 'Who are you here in Cairns with now?' Gary cut over her asking, 'So, you fucked off Beata then?'

Emma and Suzie both tutted.

'I... eh... Well, have you guys seen her?'

'Suzie and Em have, but no sign of you, eh? So what happened? You shag some other bird?'

I asked Suzie, 'How's she doing?'

'Great. She's staying in a lovely flat owned by some Swedish girl and her husband.'

'And she told you about...'

'She told me all that in an email before we came up. She...'

Gary butted in. 'So who's this other bird then?'

'Eh? Aw... So, what's she up to Suzie?'

'Not a lot. I think she's been horse riding. You know she's leaving in a few days for Bali?'

'That soon?'

'Yeah, she decided that there was nothing in Cairns to hang on for and brought her flight forward. She's really excited about it. Her big adventure.'

'But, when you saw her. Did you… well, did you tell her you were coming to meet me?'

Emma replied, 'No, we didn't talk about you at all.'

*   *   *   *

'The thing is Mum, that I can get experience being a teacher as well. You know I was thinking about doing teacher training after I get back, and this will be a good way to get some experience, you know? I can find out whether I like it or not. And anyhow, if I'm going to do teacher training, it won't start until October. This way, I can do six months in Korea and come back with the experience and a bit of extra money.'

'But… I thought you were coming home Willie.'

'It's the experience mum, it'll be invaluable. It means I won't be going to it raw when I go to college, and it means that I don't have to spend the next few months just working in a bar in Glasgow or something.'

'But yer coming tae stay with me, are ye not?'

'Mum, I'm telling ye, I'm going to go and live in Korea. Just for a few months, and then I'll come back and start the teacher training, and I'll be back living with you for a while.'

'But when will that be?'

'If I do six months, then I'll be back in the summer. That'll be nice, won't it? Maybe we can have a wee holiday or something?'

'Could we go over to Ireland and see yer Aunt Rose?'

'Aye, we could do that.'

There was the silence of thought before Mum said, 'But… I don't know anything about Korea.'

'Neither do I Mum.'

'So, why are ye going?'

'For the work. Just for a few months.'

'I hope it's safe Willie. Will it be safe?'

'Perfectly safe.'

'Ye can't speak the language.'

'Apparently it doesn't matter for the teaching. I'm sure I'll pick up some, enough, you know, to do ma shopping, go to restaurants and that. I'll buy a book when I get there. I'm really going to try to learn.'

'Aye, I'm sure.'

'So, ye'll be alright, won't ye mum? I mean it's just gonna be a few months, not much longer really, and well, Helen's there if you really need someone to…'

'Och, I'll be awright. Ye don't have to worry aboot me. It's just, I was so lookin forward to seeing ye.'

'I know mum. It won't be long.'

* * * *

PART III: HONG KONG

CHAPTER 10

We gathered at a jetty in Central just after noon on Saturday, nursing hangovers from the statutory Friday night session that had only finished a few hours earlier. All the same, we had stacked the pier side with beers, bottles of spirits and mixers. Some of the wise had brought food for the eight-hour trip – breadsticks, packets of crisps, cheese that could melt in the heat.

Davy cracked through three cans while we waited, determined to stay drunk, and I couldn't help joining him. We'd had a great night and this had the makings of a blast of a day – sunshine, friends, booze, and, as Davy pointed out, 'Err's some mighty fine fanny alang wey us the day.' The wee man whistled the Blue Peter theme and I danced the hornpipe, anticipating our nautical jaunt and bringing up the laughs in our crowd as we waited to stumble onto a boat.

I had genuinely expected a junk – the traditional, wooden-sailed Chinese craft you see in the postcards – not the modern pleasure craft that picked us up. The boat had a wide sitting-out area at back, covered, good to keep off the sun, but open-sided to let the sea air blast away the head-fog. The roof was an open deck with mats for those brave enough to sunlounge. More than twenty of us piled onboard and there was room for more.

The Chinese couple who ran the boat asked us where we wanted to go. No-one knew. Sammy had a barked conversation with them in Cantonese, drawing a big circle with her hands in the air in front of her. The pilot shrugged and kicked the motor in.

I asked, 'Where did you tell them to go?'

'Around.'

In the harbour, among the ferries, tankers and ocean liners, we had to clutch on to our belongings and each other to stop everything sliding off the side and to hang on to our guts to stop the remains of Friday night slipping out as well. Folk were starting slow, Lucozade and painkillers, but as the boat moved further out and the waves calmed, we passed round the beers and everyone perked up.

We moored somewhere off Lantau Island, next to a beach. Most of the lads did the macho thing, jumping off the boat and swimming ashore. I was about to join them when Davy said, 'Naw, naw. Why dint ye go upstairs and lie in the sun.'

Tim and Al were up there, skinning up.

'I know what you're after. I don't think so.'

'Naw, naw. Up ye go.'

'I'll just fall asleep. I wanna go for swim.'

'Naw, ya dozy twat. Go up and take a look.'

I climbed the steps and stuck my head through to the top deck. Apart from my stoner friends, it was occupied with girls laying around in bikinis, some of them topless. 'Ah, right ye are. A spot of sunbathing, eh?'

'Dark glasses oan, boy.'

Davy and I held court among the ladies until the rest of the lads swam back. Then Davy's idea was to show off, be the first to jump off the top of the boat. 'Dive,' he said, 'Dive in proper like. It's way more mental. Cool as fuck.' I cracked off the water in a belly flop sending sheets of pain across the front of my body. The screams and laughter of everyone on the boat were muffled by the ocean above me. I broke the surface, forcing a big grin onto my face. 'I meant that. Honest.'

Davy shouted from the boat. 'That's ma lad.'

Several of the girls elegantly dove from the roof, hitting the water with a quiet shriff.

The excursion became a party. Tim's stereo was hung up from the wooden slats in the roof, happy house cranked up to distortion. The girls danced in their bikinis, the boys gleefully bumbled around them. Everyone smoked dope and did shots of tequila, shouting and hopping.

There was a little toilet cubicle on the boat, below deck, down in the hull. As I flushed it, I heard the splash of someone jumping off the boat into the water right next to me.

Just as I came out of the loo, Sammy stepped out of one of the cabins. 'William, come in here.'

Al was there with his head bent over a little side cabinet. He had a rolled up note at his nose. Davy was already up on the bed, watching what Al was doing. 'Ya fuckin beauty.'

Al came away with a long sniff and an expression of dazed, wide-eyed confusion. He held the rolled note out to me.

Davy bounced on the bed, jitterbugging with excitement. 'Go on, son, go on. Git it doon ye. Go on son, noo's yer chance. Bet it's fuckin brilliant.'

Al left me and Sammy down there. She cut up another couple of lines. Davy was bouncing off the walls, springing on the bunk and crawling round the shelves. As I came up from my second line, he gave me a wink and clicked the lock shut on the cabin's door.

I screwed Sammy before we went back upstairs – sex between mates, the heat of the moment, a release for the energies pent up by the sun, the company and the cocaine. The cabin was at the front of the boat, in the prow. Its walls narrowed in the direction I was shunting Sammy's head. Davy perched at the top of the bed, tucked in where the walls nipped together, watching us and masturbating rapidly. Davy's release spattered on the wooden walls and bedsheets as I climaxed inside Sammy.

I jumped into the sea afterwards to wash away the clinging sex. As I climbed back on deck, Davy said, 'Right, where's that wee doll Lorna? Ye no hink it's her turn doon below.'

When Lorna and I came back up on deck and I pressed the wrap of coke into Sammy's palm, she didn't look at me or say anything.

The couple who ran the boat didn't speak English. Sammy kept her distance from them, probably not wanting to get involved in their complaints. They were none too happy at the mashed up mess the lot of us had become, the boat too. Empty cans rolled across the deck with the sway of the sea. Food slipped off the table and got squashed into the deck by dancing feet. Some young guy slipped and cracked his head, spilling blood. Then, when some paper got set on fire and scorched the decking, the pilot shouted, 'Now go. Now go.' He started the motor and stood grim faced, waiting for any swimmers to get back on board. Some insane drunken cow shouted at him about doing what we told him because we were paying for the boat. More people jumped in the sea.

Davy got my attention, 'See yon there.' He pointed across the channel, through the haze to where I could vaguely make out the humps of another island. 'Is that no Lamma?' Three tall chimney stacks rose up from it. 'Has that no got pubs on it?'

'Aye, I think you might be right.'

He started repeating, 'Lamma, Lamma, Lamma.'

It went up as a chant, 'Lamma, Lamma, Lamma.'

Lamma was out of the pilot's way and you could see that all he wanted to do was finish and go home.

Davy snatched a wad of money out of my hand – I had gone round the boat and collected the money to pay for the hire. He waved the cash in the pilot's face. 'No Lamma. No money.' He held the money out and then whipped it away. 'No Lamma. No money.'

The pilot fumed. He started yelling Cantonese, spit flying off his lips. His wife stood solid and silent next to him.

Sammy told me, 'He says he'll take us.'

As we clambered off the boat onto the pier, he continued shouting. His wife shook her head and tutted as each of us slipped and stumbled from the boat to the steps. The same insane drunken cow shouted abuse at them as they revved the engine and pulled away from the pier.

I had heard about Lamma, it was one of the islands with no cars, no proper roads and no high-rise. People liked it because it was quiet. We brought the noise. I guess I was aware of the village we wandered into, something Mediterranean about it, terraces, a bay, open air eating, but I was more interested in the laughs and the loud and rowdy bundle of us as we staggered up the narrow street. Davy was fixated on the backsides of the hotpant-clad young woman that tumbled ahead of us. There was a seafood restaurant, and food fights, an argument over the bill and more drinking outside a pub. I got split up from Sammy and before I knew it, everyone else had gone for the last ferry to Central. Davy and I clocked on to a woman and staying seemed like none too bad an idea. Lamma felt busy. The pub was packed, and it seemed to me everyone was friendly. There were lots of chats to strangers, and other things, unsure things, maybe a moment or two with a lassie. Lamma was a blur.

A movement happened. And I remembered, this flat, it was in the Ghetto – someone called it that – a bundle of wee streets, lanes, blocks we skirted round, stairs I climbed, girl on my arm while Davy sang Show Me the Way to Go Home, and I didn't even notice we were there till the person in front disappeared into a doorway I fumbled to find, and then it was noise and people, the jumping and the dancing, then grappling and grasping, tongues and arms and sex. I'm sure. There must have been sex.

*   *   *   *

CHAPTER 11

I was woken by a vibration on my chest. Davy's snores rattled against my ribcage. He was curled naked and asleep, his weight, abominably large for such a tiny form, forcing my breath short. The room was dark shadowed, and yet a burning red ached my eyes. I was aware of another naked body pressed against mine. We were on our backs, squashed together – a single bed. The smell was there – Davy's musky reek of sex – but a stench of stale beer, cigarettes and dope pervaded. My stomach lurched and I knew I was going to hurl. Davy slipped, still asleep, onto the bed. He rolled against the flesh of the woman, wrapping his limbs around her arm.

Painful spasms gripped my gut as I scrabbled for my shorts and t-shirt. A sarong hung over the bedroom's window as a makeshift curtain, and the glow of the day was eking at its edges, setting the red and orange pattern ablaze and ochring the skin on the bed. I didn't know who the dark-haired woman was. She was deeply asleep, prostrate and immobile. Her breasts splayed across her chest, falling into her armpits. I didn't remember getting up close to that bosom. As I backed out of the door, drawing it gently closed, she rolled onto her side and pulled Davy close, hugging him like a teddy bear.

The room I had stepped into was blindingly bright. Daylight. As carefully as my urgent need allowed, I picked my bare feet through the spilled beer, broken glass and tipped ashtrays to the bathroom and puked a thin stream of alcoholic vomit through mouth and nose. My throat and sinuses burned. The unsettled bile left me hanging over the toilet for minutes more, sure that it would start again.

I needed something to wash away the taste. I skirted round an armchair with some bloke asleep in it to get to the kitchen. Any cup or glass was dirty, encrusted with the dried remains of wine or mixed drinks, so I put my head under the faucet and took a long swig. The water tasted metallic, but it removed the paste from my tongue.

The kitchen was so narrow that when I opened the fridge door it touched the opposite wall. After some rummaging it gave up one solitary can of beer. The tin was wet and cold; the beer fizzed on my tongue and flushed a momentary wellbeing through my body. It felt enough to get me down to a taxi, home and into my own bed. I smelled bad, and thought how much I would look like a Jakey to the taxi driver, drinking and stinking at that time in the morning.

On the far wall of the living room there were patio doors, large unblinded windows opening onto a balcony. It wasn't peculiar that I couldn't remember seeing a balcony, or even whose flat it was. Apart from the armchair bloke there was a woman asleep on a pile of cushions on the floor. Her bare legs, tanned but stubbly, were stretched out across the cold tiles, but there was nothing to hand to lay over her, except, Davy would tell me, myself. One of my flip-flops was jammed under the cushion she was using as a pillow. I tugged it out without waking her, and slipped both onto my feet. I opened the door carefully, not wanting to wake anybody.

The flat opened into a stairwell, no sign of a lift, presumably one of those old buildings where you struggled up five flights, sweating like a mental-case, to reach the apartment. It was a surprise that just one flight took me to ground level.

I stepped out into humidity and sunshine and reached for my sunglasses; I found them gone. The greenness of the blur in front of me solidified into a view of low lying dense foliage. The noise coming out of it, crickets and flies and frogs, made it sound like I was in the middle of a swamp. I didn't know where the hell I was, but it wasn't Central. I looked back at the building I had come out of. It was only three storeys, maybe one flat on each. All I could see beyond the swamp was a short hillside with two terraces of similar buildings – three-storey, white-tiled, with balconies at front, antennae or washing hanging off the outside and all around palms and banana trees. There was no sign of roads, pylons or anything that would have told me I was in the city.

Then I noticed, rising beyond the hill, the snub tops of three industrial chimney stacks and it came back to me.

Lamma.

The air was green – damp and rancid, smelling of stagnant water. Heat shimmered off the swamp.

A gritted slope led up between bushes and I followed it. The path was surrounded by small apartment blocks, almost identical. I walked, hoping my luck would lead me to a thoroughfare and a way off the island. My own bed had become a distant target.

I built up a sweat and drained the beer.

Occasionally, I came up against a ditch too deep to cross, or a dead end. I about-turned or squeezed round the side of a building and continuously hoped that another person might pass, someone I could ask directions. A cat slinked round a balcony and a couple of stringy dogs tussled.

I came to a set of steps going up between two buildings and thought I had seen them before, passed them already. I was turning circles. I decided to try the stairs, gain a bit of height – enough to see where the main part of the village was or, with real luck, a glimpse of the sea to make my bearing. I threw my empty can on a bin bag, wiped sweat from my brow and set on up.

I stepped onto a path and immediately had to step back. A vehicle careened past. People grinned, shook their heads and walked away. The sound of the engine brapped into the distance, folded away behind the bodies walking the path. Suddenly, people, and suddenly cars. But there were no cars on Lamma; I knew that.

Another truck came past, barely slowing, forcing everyone to jump to the side of the path. The driver gunned it round the corner and disappeared, no hint of concern. The vehicle didn't really qualify as a car. It had one seat perched at the front and about a meter of flatbed on the back. The engine sounded nothing more than a souped-up mower. Everyone regained the path and continued as if nothing had happened – a flow of people, a talking, shifting, blocking mass. They were mostly Chinese – adults carrying cooler boxes or deck chairs, kids with plastic buckets. I was almost unable to move. I blundered towards the first group. 'Excuse me, sorry, excuse me. Which way is the ferry?'

'Follow the path.' She pointed behind them, opposite to the way they were going, opposite the majority.

I picked my way through, bumping and excusing myself, until I came to a store hung with beach goods: the rubber rings, bucket and spades, kites, cheap sunglasses and all the other tat you find at beachside stores anywhere. I'd dropped into someone else's holiday – not the right place for me at all.

The shop was quiet and cool, a haven. A haven that sold cold water. With the last note in my pocket, I bought a large bottle. I checked with the store guy, 'Which way is the ferry?'

'This way, this way.'

She hadn't lied.

I stopped on the front step, slightly raised from the passing crowd. Aircon cool blew on my back. A few Westerners went by, relaxed dudes, taking their time, letting other groups pass. That put me right off. I needed to find the ferry.

And then I saw her.

I thought I saw her.

A woman walked past, flowing hair and flowing skirt, classic hippy. That wasn't her. But in the face, I was sure.

I set off.

She was going the way I needed to go, swaying in and out of the crowds. Her purple skirt swished as she stepped round a group of tourists. She stopped to let some children pass, turning to watch them with an indulgent smile and I saw.

My insides knotted.

At a bottleneck, I lost her. She slunk through and I got clogged. When I got past, she'd gone. I broke into a jog. I couldn't let her disappear. There was a pub on the right, raised a level above the main path. Early drinkers looked down on passing heads. I couldn't see her among them and pushed on. A restaurant with seating out front didn't include her, a wire mesh fence separated an empty square of concrete, restaurants on the other side, she wasn't there. I came to a stretch where the path widened for more restaurants and grocery shops. The throng spread out, but she was nowhere.

I'd started to recognised where I was, back in the village, near the pub I'd been in when I lost all my friends. Between buildings on my left, I could see the sea and the ferry pier. And then the loose flowing brown swing of her hair disappeared around the back of the building. The sign out front said Deli Lamma.

An old woman selling veg had baskets spread on the ground and I had to sidle round. The sun glinted off the sea. A thick smoggy haze hung, making any other islands invisible.

At the back of the Deli, there was a terrace over the seawall crowded with young drinking Westerners. She wasn't among them. From this spot, the bay curved around, and it would be simple to make a path across the backs of the restaurants and shops to the pier. She wasn't on that route; she had gone inside. I squeezed across the terrace. A few faces looked up, hoping to see a friend. The back entrance led into a narrow corridor. I stepped past the open door of the kitchen, where a roar and sizzle went up from a flaming cooker, then it was cool and dim among the seats, and hardly occupied.

She was sitting immediately inside the bar talking to some guy. I walked past. If she looked up she would have seen me. They were sat tight together. I was followed to my seat by a Filipino waitress so I ordered a coffee and took a menu. I didn't know if I had enough money to pay.

They smiled, and touched, a hand on an arm, a pat on a shoulder. Their whole posture ached of intimacy. I needed to leave. She was involved. She wouldn't want to see me. She had a world that didn't include me. I was someone forgotten, a moment, a mistake.

Another woman approached who they both greeted with kisses and hugs. When she joined the table, they all shared in that same close physicality, talking with heads leaned in, small intimate contacts passed. This was just their way. It was camaraderie and ease, Sunday morning breakfast, catching up with people that meant something to you.

She was tanned, her hair longer. She was a little plumper, filled out around the cheeks, her arms less defined, but it suited her. There were a couple of worn friendship bands on her right wrist, and round her neck was the leather thong and the carved bone. Her eyes flashed with the same crazy brilliance.

I drank my coffee, unnoticed and unable to stop watching, but trying not to conspicuously stare. Indecision slipped into ennui and the dilemma of staying or leaving, approaching or giving up, melted into a stupor. I was in a serious hangover, one that left me shattered and confused. My limbs ached and my stomach grumbled. My head was thick with everything that had gone into me in the past thirty-six hours.

And then she stood up. I heard her say goodbye, and she was heading for the door. An uplifting, rosy patchouli air hung where she'd flowed past.

I had to go.

Now.

I had to pursue. I needed to pay. I stood and dragged in my pocket for coins, grabbed the menu to see how much coffee cost, tried to throw the right change on the table. The waitress was approaching. I could hear the door swinging shut.

I turned, and she was there.

She had dallied to talk some man, a friend. The door had brought him in. And now I was stuck, hovering. The couple she had been with noticed. The waitress scooped up my coins and said, 'Thank you.'

I had come into view of myself in a mirror. I looked older. Pale and drawn, thinner. She hadn't known who I was.

I couldn't sit down; I was seen; it would look weird. If I left out the back of the restaurant now, I may never see her gain.

I approached and stood behind her.

She was animated and her friend listened intently, grinning broadly. I just stood there; I couldn't stop her mid flow. Her accent still scooped and dipped.

The guy noticed me and broke from her eye line. Her sentence trailed off, 'Sue asked if we would want to be part of it, but I wasn't sure if… if it was…' She had noticed her friend's distraction and the lingering presence.

I said, 'I'm sorry, I just… erm… Excuse me. Hi.'

'Hello?' She looked confused at being interrupted, but open to it.

I said, 'It's funny, I thought … I recognised you from over there… It is you, isn't it?'

Her smile didn't falter. She wanted to be friendly, though she didn't know what I was talking about. Then the twitch of a frown and, I'm very glad to say, her cheeks lifted with a smile. 'William?'

'Hi Beata.'

*　　　*　　　*　　　*

CHAPTER 12

She shook her head in wonder, voicelessly wowing at the great surprise of running into each other. 'Of all the places in the world, here! I thought maybe one day I would visit Scotland and just by chance there you would be in the street, but here?'

I blurted, 'I remember we said once we would maybe meet in Sweden.' Our lost plans; our shared goals, dropped.

'Hmm. Yes, I remember.' Her look was chastising, but good-humoured.

I hoped a cheeky grin from me could help my misdemeanour to fade.

Beata said, 'Come on, let's sit.' Then, once we were positioned on opposite sides of small wooden space, 'You look like you had quite a night last night.'

Her appearance was quite the opposite, like she'd had a good night's sleep and some early morning exercise to perk up the day. I wondered if her evenings ever involved the amount of abuse I had given myself, but I couldn't lie. 'I did. That's how I ended up here, really.'

'You didn't plan on to come to Lamma?'

'I didn't really know I had.'

She looked fixedly at me for a moment. 'You like to drink. It's a Scottish thing, isn't it? Or maybe a British thing.' Her smile was teasing. 'I don't think that is all you like if you stay up all night.'

'I didn't say I stayed up all night. I did get some sleep.'

Red eyed, mumbling and smelly: I was there in front of her as evidence of the way I lived my life. Beata was still curious to know more, wanting to know about how I had ended up in there, and what I had made of myself. The full truth wouldn't have helped, I felt, and so I told her just enough of how my life had turned from Cairns to Korea and to Hong Kong so that Beata could take my experiences as full, vivid and enlivening.

'It must be amazing to live in a culture so different to your own. I mean, to live there really, to work and experience their life. That is something quite different, isn't it?'

'It was definitely different. Way, way different.'

She was wide-eyed, excited; how great it must have been for me.

Then she asked, 'But what about Orla, is she here in Hong Kong?'

'Ah, well… you know… Orla and I are not together any more. When I went to Korea…'

'She didn't go?'

'No, I mean, we're not here together in Hong Kong.'

'Oh dear. I thought maybe you were become boyfriend and girlfriend. I saw you together a lot in Cairns.

'You…' I hadn't seen her once in my final weeks in Australia. 'But …' I had ached to catch sight of her, to talk. 'But then why didn't ye…?' There was so much I could have offloaded on Beata then, spewed out all that gut-aching, selfish angst and pity.

I said, 'What I mean is, Orla and me, we didn't leave together, from Korea. We just… kinda… went different ways in the end.'

'That's a shame. You should tell her how much a good place Hong Kong is, and maybe she would come.'

'You're right, maybe. If I got in touch with her… Maybe.'

'What about Scotland? I remember you said you would go back, wasn't it? Is your mother feeling better?'

'Ye…ah… well, nnn…'

Before I could respond, a tall, older guy, grey haired and wiry, stepped into the restaurant and said hello to Beata. He was pulling a dog on a string, a fat thing with a large body and disproportionately short legs. The waitress chased them both out, saying to go around the back, not in the restaurant.

The hair that played over her pixie face was longer than before. She pushed it away.

When he left, I said, 'What about you? Are you still thinking about going back to Sweden? You said you would.'

'Yes, I know, I am going to, but… I'm not sure when. For sure I will go back for holiday, maybe in a short time.' She tucked her chair a little tighter under the table to let someone pass. Our legs touched.

Beata had been in Hong Kong for weeks, and on Lamma from her first day – a travelling friend had told her it was the only place to stay. Her times had been in Bali and Thailand, Cambodia, a chunk spent in Laos and even a short stay in Burma. She was brimming with it, full of the buzz and joy. She said it had been a growing experience, learning and making more of herself, but really, she was no different. The spirited, broad-minded, openhearted, funny person that I had known in Australia smiled at me across the table with her eyes blazing brown.

Our conversation was often interrupted by the door of the Deli Lamma opening and some head sticking through saying, 'Hey, Beata. How you doing?' or 'Hi sweetie, I thought you were heading to the beach.' Bodies drifted through the restaurant on their way to the terrace, stopping to chew the fat, dropping me out of the loop, though Beata was kind enough to introduce me with, 'This is an old friend of mine.' I was flattered, a friend, and part of a past that none of those new-timers knew anything about.

Beata's friends looked fresh-faced, like the worst their bodies had faced in the last twenty-four hours was a dose of camomile tea and a lavender bodyscrub before breakfast. I began to wonder if I was right for Lamma. Beata had immediately blown my cover – I really was just a shifty, drink-soaked Scottish bloke. I didn't think it would take too long for her friends to twig on to me and shut me out. A couple of those who came in joined us at the table. They talked about finding a good yoga teacher, about tree planting, about some charity fun day they were planning and things that seemed way out of my league in the clean-living, making-a-difference stakes.

Outside the big glass window at the front of the restaurant, crowds of people continued to pass. I caught a glimpse of something that flitted between legs, scuttling past, something in a hurry. I almost bolted after him to escape the potpourri reek of the fit and healthy, escape back to some beer and debauchery, but I was continually drawn to Beata. She was luminous. The teak lustre of her hair glowed even in the partial light of the interior, sucking in the burn of the afternoon sun blazing outside.

So I hung on, wanting to have her company, hoping that I could build myself into a corner of her life, and, as the day wore on, other friends started to drift in, ones who had clearly had a longer night and were dragging themselves out for some recovery sustenance. The group at our table padded round with a blend of the shiny, happy people and the dirty and hoarse, struggling with daylight. Beata got on as well with the scruffnecks as she did with the hippy crowd. The conversation moved to a recent Lamma party all of them had been at and everyone bigged it up like some kind of mad beach rave – on all night, banging big tunes, and everyone screaming as the sun came up. Perhaps not everyone on Lamma was as pristine as I first thought. Perhaps there was a chance I could fit in. There might be a place for me in Beata's world.

We were opposite each other across the table, Beata and I, but had stayed connected by the space between us – an empty chair that meant we were still one side of the loop – until some tumbling mess of a dude called Steve spilled into the chair. I was annoyed with myself for not moving into that space, moving closer as the place filled up, and at him for jumping in there and breaking us up.

Steve caught the attention of the waitress. 'A Bloody Mary please, Joyce. And make it fiery, would you?' Then said generally to the table, 'Alright everyone?'

He shuffled around, pulling out a pack of tobacco and rolling a ciggie. Strands scattered on the table and poked out the end of his loosely packed rollie. A fringe of long unwashed hair hung over his face as he worked. Beata caught his attention at the end of the job and introduced me.

Steve studied my face. 'Here, weren't you at the Tinhead last night?'

'The Tinhead?' I looked to Beata.

She said, 'It's the pub just a little along this street, here. There's usually a big crowd outside on Saturday night. Were you there?'

Steve said, 'Yeah, weren't you with Janet? I saw you hanging out with her, I think. Weren't we talking? I'm not sure, I was pretty hammered, but it was you, weren't it?'

'Shit, eh, I'm not sure, but you're probably right. It was, eh... I was pretty battered myself, you know?'

'Fucking right mate, ha ha har. Tell me about it.' He slapped me on the shoulder and took a long pull through the straw of the drink that had been put in front of him. 'Ah, hooh, that's good.'

My hangover suddenly felt very dry, and my pockets very empty.

I eyed Steve and tried to summon a memory of him. From the way he went on, it must have been the same pub, but I couldn't remember meeting him. He spoke about Janet. 'Fuck me, she was in some state. Doesn't think that girl, does she, when she's in some state. No stopping her.'

Once everyone's attention had moved on to another talker, Steve said confidentially to me, 'Here, mate. You were in some state too, weren't you? You remember what you and Janet was doing?'

I had no idea.

Steve sucked the last of his Bloody Mary, leaving the red-coated ice cubes in the bottom of the glass. 'Oof. Not bad that. You should get one of those. It'll sort you out.'

The door swung open, but over the heads, I could not see anyone come in. It fell back again. None of the others turned to look or greet an incomer. It struck me as odd that nobody had noticed until a small, wizened head with a few straggly wisps of grey hair appeared around Beata's shoulder.

'William, whur the fuck huv ye been? It's taken fuckin ages tae get oottae that bastardin ghetto.' He gripped the iron spars at the back of Beata's chair. 'Iss is some shitey place this Lamma-hole, intit? Mon, lets get aff this fuckin dump.' My sunglasses were on his face. He took them off to peer round the group. 'Who ur aw these cun... Hauw, wait a minute.' His survey had brought him to the woman in the chair. 'Aw fuck, naw. No the fuckin frigid Scandy bitch. Whit the fuck...'

I said to Steve, 'Tell you what, would you mind shouting me one of those? I'm a bit skint and I could fair do with one.'

'Good for you mate. Here, Joyce!' He held up his glass and pointed at it, then held up two fingers. 'Two more.'

Davy acknowledged Steve, 'Orright mate,' and then squeezed past to get to me. 'Whit's goin oan here? I let ye get away fur a couple ae oors and ye've hooked up wey the fuckin ice-maiden. C'moan lets get the fuck affae this island.'

'I'm getting a drink.'

Steve said, 'You are, mate. It's what you wanted, yeah? Nice one.'

Davy shook his head, 'Naw, c'moan. Time tae boost.'

'I'm happy where I am.'

Steve said. 'Don't blame you, mate. Often end up in the Deli after a night out myself. It can get a bit comfortable if the booze keeps coming.'

'I'll drink to that.' Davy's hand was tugging at my t-shirt. I pulled it away. 'If I get a chance.'

Steve laughed. 'It's coming mate. It's coming.'

Davy squeezed up on the bench and poked me in the ribs. 'Fuck son, dinnae start fawin fur that cow agin. Widnae even gie ye yer hole.'

*   *   *   *

CHAPTER 13

I put my feet up on the railing in front of us, looked at the sparse fairy lights of Lamma as the ferry pulled away. The sun had set, and dark was falling quickly. I'd been hours in the Deli Lamma with Beata. We didn't bond. We didn't put our heads together and say, What have you been doing all this time? In fact, we were rarely alone. Her friends came and went, joined us and chatted. We hung out, and got on well. We had small moments of wonder at the chance of finding each other. She didn't deny me, didn't block me out. And when she walked me to the ferry, she gave me her phone number and said, 'Can you call me? Call me this week. I would like to see you and we can talk more.'

I told the wee man, 'This is it. Now's the time.'

'Whit ye oan aboot?'

'It's like, second chance, isn't it?'

'Second chance tae fuck her ower?'

Davy stretched his legs out and tried to get them up on the railing next to mine. His bottom slipped out of the plastic bowl of the chair, but he couldn't reach. I looked down on his liver-spotted bald head; the few wisps around the sides straggled overlong.

'I'm gonna stop,' I said. 'That's it, definitely. Stop getting caned, stop shagging about.'

Davy spluttered, spitting beer. I slapped his back to help him get his breath back.

I said, 'Davy, Davy. You're in this for me, right? And you know Beata's the one.'

Spittle hung from his lip. 'The wan whit?' His voiced rasped. 'Fuckin, sealed-up virgin?'

'I told you, this is it. I won't mess it up this time.'

'Aye, right pal. Right ye are. Whitever's best fur you.'

*   *   *   *

I invited Beata to meet me the following Friday at Club Sixty-four – a tatty pub in Lan Kwai Fong that I often fell into after work. It felt safe enough introducing her to some of the teachers I worked with at the tidy end of the evening. We were sitting out front of Sixty-four in rat alley, a pedestrianised lane with Thai, Malaysian and Chinese restaurants spilling out into it and a heady air of spices, beer and drains.

Davy had made himself scarce at the end of work. I'd hoped he was keeping away, but as I watched the alley, Tim and Al came ambling up the incline with Davy tagging behind. They swayed alley-wide, weaving between the crowds and past the restaurant hawkers trying to push menus into their hands.

Al didn't see us until he'd collided. 'Oh, hey. Orright, son. Wicked. Who's for a pint?'

'Sound,' said Tim, 'I'll just roll a number.'

Davy squeezed in close behind me. 'Huvin fun wey the Scandybitch, wur ye? I thought ye'd like a bit mair company.' As Davy wheezed in my ear, something dropped into my pocket. All I found there was my phone.

I said, 'Eh, boys, this is Beata. She's ... a friend of mine. We met in Australia. Beata, this is Al and this is Tim. I think I told you about them...'

She looked at me, surprised. 'Your friends from Scotland, right?' But quickly turned and said, 'Hi, nice to meet you. How is it you are here in Hong Kong?'

Al said, 'We couldnae leave the bold William havin all the fun,' then pushed into the ram-packed bar.

Tim lurched round to a seat squeezed in behind us. 'Wasn't long till we were following you out here, was it son? Old mates together, eh? We always go where the craic is.'

'Aye,' Davy had come round to my side. He rested a palm on my back. 'Wullie needs his boys aboot him, keep him on the straight and narra.'

I shrugged for Beata, held up my hands. 'They were on their way back from Australia, you see, and...'

Sammy came in like a tornado. She flung her bag behind us where it battered against the pub's front window. 'Took me bloody ages to get here. Thought I'd take a taxi through the tunnel, and then all the bloody traffic is jammed at Admiralty. Course, it's Friday night, and I should've known. It's always packed. Bloody taxi driver didn't have a brain. He got stuck and then he wouldn't let me out and...'

It took a while before I could introduce Beata.

'You? I've heard loads about you,' and bent to give her a kiss. 'So, are you coming out with us tonight? I'm sure we could squeeze one more in at William's.'

Sammy came round behind me and whispered in my ear, 'I got your text.'

'What text?'

She pushed something plastic into my palm, a small zip-lock bag.

'It's Charlie. One of my friends in Tsimsy sorted it for me. It's great.' She sniffed. 'When you asked, I didn't think I'd be able to, but you were right, it was easy.'

'But, I didn't…'

'Weeleeam!' The high-pitched keen sent a tremble down my spine.

'Oh, Christ.'

Jocelyn burst through the crowd waving. Her heels clipped on the uneven paving and she stumbled, oblivious to the shoulders she bumped and the beer arms she jostled. A couple of woman scowled as her long hair flicked over them. She was short and very blonde. Her lips were glossed deep red.

'Weeleeam, how you dooo-ing?'

'Eh, hi Jocelyn. Fancy seeing you here.'

'Isn't it? I was just leaving, but I met a friend of yours and he say you are in here'

'Who?'

'Oh, I don't know. A little guy. Over there.'

Davy was behind her, giving me the double thumbs-up.

I had met Jocelyn in Strawberries, a nightclub, the kind of place Davy loved, prime sleazy and a total cattle market. At least half the women were prostitutes and I was never quite sure about Jocelyn.

She asked, 'And what are you doing?'

'I was just having a drink with some friends.'

'Greaaat. I'll join you.'

'I… ah… yeah, I mean, sure.'

I made an attempt to stand but Jocelyn pressed down on my shoulder. 'No, no. You sit. It's OK.'

Davy said, 'Aw, this should be good.'

She held her hand out for anyone at the table to take. 'Hi, I'm Jocelyn. Oh, hi Teem.'

Tim looked up fearfully from his joint doings.

I said, 'Jocelyn, this is, erm, this is a friend of mine, Beata.'

'Hiiii. Did William tell you about me? I'm his friend too.'

'Hello Jocelyn,' Beata said, 'No, I'm sorry he didn't, but it's good to meet you.'

A voice called. 'Joss. Joss, come on!'

A muscle-boy approached – wide, tattooed and skinhead.

'Sweetie. What is it sweetie?'

'Fuck's sake Joss, what you doin?'

He pulled her to one side and bent to mutter in her ear. Jocelyn spoke clearly, 'These are my friends. We want to stay for a drink.'

He glared at me, pulling Jocelyn so that she was no longer pressed into my shoulder.

I looked at Beata and shrugged.

'No, sweetie. We don't have to.' Jocelyn was high-pitched and loud.

The skinhead said, 'Yeah, c'mon,' and dragged her away by the hand.

'Sorry William, goodbye. I see you soon. Goodbye Betty. Goodbye Teem.'

Davy was standing in the gap left by Jocelyn. 'Och, bollocks. I was looking forward tae that.'

'Who's that?' Beata asked. 'She looks like fun.'

Davy said, 'Aye, a lot mair than you.'

It was all coming at me, the state of my company, the depths I had sunk to. I crumpled inside, expecting Beata's horror.

Davy noticed the crackle in my palm, 'Oh aye?'

And I realised I was still holding the cocaine.

'Go on son, gwon gwon gwon.'

My hand sweated around the baggie.

'Gwon son, there's nothin like a wee toot ae the bingo if ye wannae keep up the patter, y'knaw, keep on chattin, impress yer bird.'

Beata was leaning across the crate to talk to Al. As she stretched her neck, trying to catch his words, her hair fell away showing a small tattoo just at the knuckle at its base. A ying-yang.

I pushed the packet into my pocket and headed inside.

Davy was at my heels. 'Right, we'll get doon a line each the noo, an see if we kin get some mair afore the ithers chank it all.'

Sixty-four was heaving. I said, 'Och, this is gonna take ages.' Getting through the crowed of drinkers was an effort. 'I don't know if it's a good idea.'

'C'mon son. She'll no notice ye've gone.'

'It might get me too wired, though. You know, like, too talkative?'

'It'll dae ye good.'

'She'll know I'm off my face or she'll think I'm some sort of pushy idiot.'

'Right then, here's whit we'll dae. Ditch the Scandybitch, get fucked up and heid tae the clubs.'

I went back.

I slipped the coke packet to Al, relieved to be getting it out of temptation.

Davy caught up, running right into me. 'Och, fer fuck's sakes. Wid you sort yer act oot?'

When I sat down, Beata passed me a spliff. She held it out at knee height, trying not to be too obvious. She said, 'Wow, Sammy's been telling about Jocelyn. She is something else.'

Sammy arched an eyebrow.

A wry smile curled onto Beata's lips before she took a swig from her drink.

Davy leaned in tight to my side. 'Lookit that face. She's goat ye sussed right oot. Ye've nae chance there.'

Beata said, 'It's good that you have your friends with you. It's... I'm surprised but it's nice, I know because you said before that you and these two were fallen out.'

'Aye, yes, yer right. It's great the lads are...'

'You know William, it's good to see you here. You have some nice people around you. I'm happy for that.' It sounded honest. 'But, there's one other thing you did not explain to me yet. What about your mother? You say to me in Australia that you...'

Sammy stumbled through the group. She'd been exhibiting the effects of the coke, bustling from group to group, chatting to everybody, but not staying too long, but now she pulled a stool over to the far side of Beata and settled in.

'So, Beata, William's told me loads about you.'

'Oh, yes, I was just saying to William how nice it is to see him here and see that he has some nice people to be friends with. Everyone's good fun.'

'Oh, well, I hope you count me in that group.'

I sat on the sidelines, left out of the female whirl of conversation. I needed another drink, something to blur out the anxious edges, so I went to the bar but I was twitching to get back and make sure that no other unexpecteds were heading Beata's way. She was in deep confab with Sammy when I returned. The pair of them clearly hit it off. Beata was a good listener.

Davy told me, 'Y'knaw Sammy's bin tellin aboot turning tricks. That's fuckin braw, eh? Ye go tae the bar fur ten seconds and Scandybitch's getting the lowdoon on how ye sell yer arse ower on Kowloon side. '

They had their heads close, speaking too low for me to hear. I put drinks in front of them.

Davy muttered, 'Sammy might get yer bitch oantae a bitae action. Mibbe that's it. Offer the bitch cash, that'll loosen her up. Thur aw hoors.'

I said, 'Hey, girls what's up.' Sammy was in flow and not for stopping. She was a torrent hard to hold back.

Beata said, 'William, let us girls talk. You go and smoke with the boys.'

When it got to midnight, and Beata started making moves for the last ferry, it was Sammy who said, 'Why not stay? I bet there's a ferry at six or something, right? Why don't you come out clubbing and we can put you on that one?'

Beata's resolve almost crumbled, but as she was considering, a Lamma friend came down the alley on the way to catch a taxi to the pier. Beata grabbed her bag and said, 'OK, you guys have a fun night.' She kissed my cheek. 'Hey William, thanks. That was fun and you have nice friends.'

I stood to watch her disappear.

Davy was standing next to me. He looked up from the height of my thigh and said, 'Mon then, we gonnae get a line ae that Charlie,' rubbing his hands together. 'Stick wey me, I'll see ye right. You knaw ye cannae dae weyoot yer wee Pal, Wullie.'

The next morning, I woke up next to Sammy.

'Ye cannae dae weyoot me. Ye knaw ye cannae.'

*   *   *   *

CHAPTER 14

Davy and I were standing in front of Mr Bang's desk as he filled us in on his plan, a smouldering cigarette between his waving fingers. Davy kept warning me to watch out for him, that he was playing us, but for once Mr Bang appeared to be keeping to his word. Friday was set as the day for our immigration trip and visa run. We had to cross from Pusan to Fukuoka in Japan, spend the day there, and come back on our new visas.

Paula perched on the edge of Miss Im's desk. Miss Im was twirling a pen around her thumb in a thoughtless, deft movement. Twirl, catch. Twirl, catch. Orla stayed at the back of the room.

I leaned towards Mr Bang, laying a hand on his desk. 'Am I right, you want us to... no... Do you want us to come here first?'

'Eight thirty o'clock, Miss Im money changie. Won, Miss Im changie dollar. You come take dollar. Immigration go.' He was more dishevelled than ever, no tie, shirt unbuttoned three from the top, a white vest showing. He looked like he had been up all night battering out the details with his gangster pals. Perhaps that was what he wanted us to think.

Miss Im continued to twirl her pen. She was obviously clued up already. I guessed Paula was too. Orla showed no reaction either, though I was sure that she knew none of this.

Davy said, 'Ho ho. Gettin the cash out tae pay aff the man, eh?' I looked down and saw him rub his hands together. When he caught my glance, he stopped and scowled. 'Ye up tae this?'

I asked Mr Bang, 'So, you want us to bribe them?'

He pointed to the chairs lined against the wall. 'Sit, sit. I talk.'

We pulled the chairs into a row in the middle of the room, Paula nearest Miss Im and me closest to Mr Bang. Orla crossed her legs, crossed her hands in her lap, and stared at the academy's advertising poster on the wall – a large picture of herself, all blonde hair and teeth.

Davy stood in front of Mr Bang's desk, crossed his arms over his chest and surveyed us. 'Yous look like naughty weans pullt up tae the headmaster.'

'I feel like one.'

Mr Bang said. 'Willim? Sorry?'

'Go ahead Mr Bang.'

'OK. We together taxi, immigration go. Interview immigration man. What you call immigration man?'

'Immigration man.'

'Hmf.' He shrugged. 'Immigration man, wah wah wah. One room Willim, one room Orla, one room Paula.' He pointed at us in turn then grandly gestured toward himself. 'One room Mr Bang, wah wah wah.' He used his hand as a gabbing mouth.

I interrupted. 'Why is Miss Im giving us dollars?'

He flicked hanging ash into an ashtray. 'You go immigration. Immigration man say how stay long time Pusan? You no money, how stay? You money packet... packet no.' He pulled a fat wallet out of his back pocket and flipped it open. 'What this?'

Paula said, 'Wallet.'

'Yes, you wallet show many US dollar, no problem stay Pusan. Visa no problem.'

'We don't pay the immigration man?'

'No no.'

Davy tutted. 'Whit you so pleased aboot? Fraid ae gettin yer fingers dirty, eh?'

Mr Bang continued. 'Finish immigration man, eleven o'clock, twelve o'clock. Airport go. Japan go. Fukouka you go to. Understand?'

'And tickets?' I asked.

'Airport buying.'

'With the money?'

'Yes.'

'All of the money?'

'No. More money, you keeping. Ticket, after, too many money, you keeping.'

'Is that our salary?'

'Yes. Now Mr Bang he pay.'

'All of it?'

He turned away as he worked his wallet back into his pocket. I looked at Orla, but she was still staring at the wall. She appeared to have no interest.

Davy came and stood between us. He looked at Orla as well. She was completely unmoving. Davy whispered, 'Yer Irish bint hus lost it, pal. She's fuckin flipped right oot noo.'

Paula asked, 'What happens when we go to Japan?'

'Japan, embassy go to. Visa change. Saturday come Pusan. Visa no problem. Hyundai Academy boss, no problem.' Mr Bang was pleased with the neatness of his plan.

'And Harry?'

'Sonofabitchie man?'

'Yeah, what's happened to Harry?'

'Sonofabitchie man no problem.'

I asked again, 'OK, but what do you mean? What's going to happen to him?'

'Me society brother sonofabitchie man finding. Wah wah wah. Harry very I'm sorry, I'm sorry.' Mr Bang was clearly pleased at his gangster prowess.

'What's happened to him?'

'Sonofabitchie man go. Fft, fft.' He waved Harry away like a swatted fly.

Davy chuckled, 'Ho ho, Harry's hud it. Cement wellies. Buried under a flyover.'

Paula shared a glance with Miss Im before she asked. 'Do we have to come back on Saturday?'

'Yes, Saturday come back.'

'But do we have to? Can't we come back on Sunday, or maybe even Monday?'

Miss Im said. 'Do you mean, Paula, that you want to take a short holiday?'

'Yeah. We're going all the way to Japan. We could have a little holiday.'

Miss Im spoke a few words in Korean to Mr Bang. He jutted his chin as he thought and nodded magnanimously. 'OK. Yes. Good. You stay. Monday come back. Mr Bang no worry. You have holiday. Toosday start teaching happy. Mr Bang happy.'

'Tuesday?' Paula checked.

'Yes, Toosday. OK?'

'OK. Great.'

Davy said, 'Hey William, ye hear that? A wee holiday,eh? Ye gonnae bring yer pet zombie?'

Orla remained catatonic. I had to take her arm and gently guide her out of her seat.

Miss Im stood to walk us to the door. She put her hand on Paula's shoulder. Paula reached back and touched her gently on the thigh before Miss Im returned to her desk.

Davy said. 'Here, whits goin oan between them two?' And jogged out the door after them.

Mr Bang waved us away and then reached for his cigarette packet.

I led Orla through to the staffroom. The rooms on the teaching side of the Academy felt emptier than they had been since we first started.

Paula clicked on the kettle. 'Cuppa?'

'Aye. Coffee thanks. How about you, Orla? You alright?'

She snapped out of her daze, briefly wide-eyed, and said, 'I'm fine.' As she sat, her blank inertia returned.

Paula looked chuffed; she lifted the jars of milk and coffee lightly, spooned with a flick. Her stirring gave a merry tinkle.

Davy tugged on my shirt sleeve, 'Here, ur her an Miss Im at it?'

'So,' I said, 'a holiday in Japan?'

Orla looked up at me. In that moment, I was the man who had shot her cat, trampled her flowers, farted at her father's funeral. Her voice was flat. 'Now's our chance to go.'

I took my coffee. 'But, he's getting us the visas.'

Davy sat on the chair next to Orla and gently rested his hand on her knee, looking at her with concern.

Orla said, 'We're not going to stay.'

Davy said, 'She's totally crumblin.'

Paula spooned sugar into her mug. 'Go? Where you going to go?'

Orla answered, 'We're leaving.'

Davy tapped his head. 'Get her tae a nuthoose.'

Paula asked, 'What d'you mean?'

She stared at me. 'You heard what he said, what he's done to Harry.'

I shook my head. 'Nah, all that gangster stuff, it's just rubbish. He's only showing off. I bet not even half of it's true. He's like a wee boy really.'

'A wee boy? How can ye be so blasé? He just said he had Harry killed.'

'He said nothin of the sort.'

Orla reached out and touched Paula's arm, letting her hand rest there. 'I'm sorry, but I just can't take it here anymore. We've got to use our flights to Hong Kong, and then try to get back to the UK from there.'

Orla's gaze dropped to her thigh where Davy's hand was sliding up it.

'The only hing you're gonnae get, hen, is locked away. We'll shut ye in the barmybarn an chuck away the key.' He threw an imaginary key over his shoulder.

I said, 'How about you Paula? We thought we should ask you if you wanted to come with us, but...''

'I'm staying.'

'That's kinda what we thought.'

She cupped her mug in both hands, lifted it up to her face. 'Miss Im is coming to Japan. We've been planning it. A short holiday together.' She took a swig then put the mug on the counter. 'Then back here and work.'

Paula was protected by Miss Im, the one person that Mr Bang couldn't do without. She would make sure that Paula came to no harm.

When Paula turned to put her mug down, Orla's hand fell from where it had been touching. Paula looked down on the back of Orla's sagging head. She sucked in her lips and furrowed her brow in silent inquiry.

I blew out, 'Aye, I think it's best if we get out of Korea.'

'Whit? Away fae the fuckin madness, eh? Away fae smelly food, smelly streets, noisy wee brats an starin grannies.' Davy laid his head on Orla's lap. 'How ye gonnae get away fae this useless sack ae mash, but?'

Orla began to lift from her stupor in the travel agents as we booked Friday evening flights. The agent scalped us for a booking fee, but that was little loss against the thought of getting away. The flights departed from Seoul, so we bought internals that left Pusan at three.

*   *   *   *

We arrived at the Academy early to pick up the cash. We had dressed down to go into immigration – jeans and sweatshirts – so that we looked more like scruffy backpackers than jobbing teachers. Davy had gone for the tourist look with Hawaiian shirt, big shorts and a floppy hat. I had no idea where he could have found those clothes, in his size, in winter Pusan but had stopped asking. His black thermals under the whole get up set it off a treat. Our packed bags were sitting in the yogwan, waiting to be collected for a quick taxi run to the airport.

Then, Mr Bang threw a large spanner into the works.

Some important new clients, staff from a local company, were keen to join our Academy but had requested a demo lesson before they would sign up. Mr Bang had decided that to secure their contract the demo had to be taught before we went away for the weekend.

'But the last flight to Fukuoka is at three pm.' I had no idea when the last flight was.

'No problem. Twelve-thirty o'clock teaching. One-thirty o'clock take taxi go airport. Mr Bang pay.'

Again the three of us stood in the office, but this time we were hard up against Mr Bang's desk.

Orla tutted. 'No.' In the last couple of days, she had made herself strong with thoughts of escape. 'If we finish at one-thirty, we won't have time to get our bags from the yogwan.'

Mr Bang was standing too, he backed towards the cabinet behind. 'No problem. William take bag. Orla go airport meet Willim.'

'How can I take the bags if I'm teaching?'

'Willim no teach. Orla teach. Company all man student.'

Like her old self, this news did not defeat Orla; it made her angry. 'You must be mad if ye think I'm stayin on me own to teach a bunch of men we don't know from Adam.' She spoke too quickly for him to understand, so she spelled it out. 'Orla, one woman. In school. Many men. Not safe.'

'But.' Mr Bang looked confused. 'Mr Bang in school.'

'Oh feckin great.' She shook her head. 'No, Mr Bang. I have to get to the airport.'

'Orla take taxi. Mr Bang pay.'

I could see her rage boiling. More importantly, this didn't seem workable against our schedule. I said. 'OK, Mr Bang, how about this? William comes back from Japan on Sunday. I can teach the demo Monday morning.'

His turn to shake his head. 'No. Orla teach. Today.'

I held up my hands. 'OK, we'll both come back tomorrow morning and Orla can teach the demo in the afternoon.'

Miss Im said, 'Oh, but William, that will spoil your weekend holiday,' in theatrically sympathetic tones. She looked to Mr Bang with pleading eyes.

'No. Today teach.'

Paula said, 'I'll teach it. I've got my bag here.' She held up a small holdall.

'No. Orla teach.'

$$* \qquad * \qquad * \qquad *$$

There was a partition, but it didn't reach head height. I could see Orla and Paula at desks in different corners of the open-plan office. Uniformed immigration officers at other desks chatted over stacks of files and sheaves of paper, or they watched us. I tried to ignore them, shut out thoughts of how my friends were coping, and concentrate on the fat, balding guy interviewing me. The hair he had stood up like black stalks in an encroaching desert. A greasy sheen on his forehead and cheeks reflected the striplights above. His expression showed mild interest, no antagonism or contempt.

'Hello Mr...' He bent back the pages of my passport to read my name. '... William. You are enjoying in Korea?'

'Very much, thank you.'

'And where have you been in Korea?'

I shifted in my seat, crossing and uncrossing my legs, unsure how to place my hands. 'Pusan mostly.'

He arched his eyebrows. 'Pusan? Then you are working?' He jabbed the question at me as if he thought to catch me out.

Davy was sitting on his desk, on top of the immigration officer's stacked in-tray. Davy had kicked off one of his flip-flops and with his big toe was slowly pushing paper clips out of their holder on to the desk. He muttered to himself, 'Aye. Workin fae the day he got here. No that you pricks ur any the wiser.'

'Oh no. I'm just a tourist.' I felt conscious of the neatness of my hair, the shine on my black shoes. I uncrossed my legs and lay my feet flat in front of me under the desk.

He flicked the pages and stopped to study my visa. 'But you have been in here a very long time.'

'Yes. Pusan is …' I licked my lips, scanning my memory for a reason for our stay.

Davy said, 'A shitehole. A fuckin misery. The arse end ae naewhere.'

I finished. '…very nice.'

'Hm. Yes. Thank you. I hope you have had a happy stay.'

'Yes, thank you.'

He put the passport down then opened a file in front of him. I could see my photo clipped on top of the page and my handwriting among the printed Korean text. Miss Im had translated the columns and boxes so we knew what to write. 'You have no friends in Pusan?'

Davy reached out his toe and flicked through the pages of the file.

'No. Oh, except the friends I'm travelling with. They're…' I lifted in my seat to point them out.

He waved me down. 'Yes, yes.' He ran a finger down to the box with my address. 'To stay in a hotel this much time must be very expensive. How did you afford?'

I pulled an envelope out of my pocket and opened it to show the officer the pressed ream of green notes. 'I brought enough money with me. I've been changing dollars when I need won.'

He leaned towards my wad and held out a hand. 'Then you have exchange slips?'

I drew the money back towards me. 'No. I never keep them.'

'He couldnae, could he.' Davy said. 'He husnae hud a bean since he got here.' He slipped his sandal back on then stood up. He began to do a soft-shoe shuffle over the files. I had to lean to one side to see round him.

The immigration guy ran his hand through the lonely stumps of his hair. 'Hm. This is not good. You know you should keep the slips for when you go out of the country, you can claim back tax on items you purchase if you show you change money in Korea.'

'Really? Thanks.'

Just as Davy stepped off it, he turned over the form and studied the next sheet. 'This… Mr Bang is your friend?'

'Right dodgy fucker he is, pal. Ye should meet him. Gangster. Mind you, mibbe you're a gangster n aw. You an Bang friends, eh? Pals ur ye?' Davy's dancing feet slipped a paper off the desk. It dropped to the floor.

'Oh no,' I said, 'I only met him last week.'

The officer leaned to pick up the paper, studied it, then asked, 'Then you are happy to stay in Pusan, to work for this man's school.'

'Pff.' Davy shook the ends of his baggy shorts like he was twirling a grass skirt. 'The school's shite, the weans are bastards, e'en the adults are a shower ae miserable cunts.'

'Oh well, I would really like to.' I fixed the guy with my most cheery and enthusiastic face. 'Pusan is such a great city. I would love to be able to stay for a long time. Who knows how long?'

'Awf, William. Where ever did ye learn tae lie like that? Whit wid yer mammy say?'

'Your working permit will be for one year only.'

'Fat lot ae use that is.' Davy lifted his thumb to his nose, wiggled his fingers and stuck out his tongue.

'Thank you.'

'You are welcome.' He pulled a sticky label off one of the sheets in front of him, and stuck it into a blank page in my passport. 'You know you must need to go out of Korea to validate this visa?'

'Ah, yes, I do.'

'You go Japan maybe.'

'Yes, I will.'

He put the papers back into the file and flipped it shut. 'Have a happy stay in Pusan.'

The waiting area was a small room with a high narrow strip of window and lots of fading posters and leaflets; claustrophobic after the open space of the office.

Davy knocked over a stack of leaflets on the low table next to the bench. 'Ye no think that wis jist a bit too easy?'

'No.'

He stood on the bench and pulled the corner of a poster away from the wall. 'I mean, wis yer pal in there no a bit ae a pushover?'

I took his shoulder and pushed him down to sit. 'I must have a trustworthy face.'

'Aye, a fuckin ugly wan. He must ae felt sorry fur ye.' Davy pushed another stack of leaflets to the corner of the table.

Paula came out next. She didn't say much, just 'That was pretty easy.' As she sat down she pushed the teetering leaflets back to the centre.

Orla was another ten minutes. She looked over her shoulder as she came through the swing doors, and briskly pulled her coat on. 'Christ. That was some grillin. You?'

Paula started to reply, but I spoke over her. 'Oh aye, yeah. Really tricky. They seemed to believe me though.'

'Fuck, I hope they did. Let's go.'

Mr Bang had a taxi waiting to take us back to the school.

I said to him, 'You were quick.'

He said, 'No problem. No problem,' but seemed discomfited. He sat up front in the cab and sucked on a cigarette, blowing smoke out the window.

Mr Bang began to talk loudly in Korean with the driver. Plumes of smoke blew into Orla's face. The three of us were squeezed into the back seat, Davy down by my feet.

A cold wind from the open window circled in the back of the cab. Orla pulled her coat tight about her and her teeth began to chatter.

Paula was between us, so I leaned over to say, 'Orla, are you OK?'

She stared straight ahead and shivered visibly.

Paula turned to her. 'Orla?'

Davy laughed, 'Oh-oh, here we go again. Aff the deep end. Whee-heeeeee, splash.'

Orla spoke slowly. 'I don't like this. I don't like being the one left behind.'

I reached across and put my hand on her leg. 'You're not. We'll be at the airport, and I won't go anywhere until you show up.'

'But what if I don't show up, William? What if I don't?'

'You're not planning on staying are you?'

Paula said, 'You'll be OK. Miss Im will make sure you get away.'

'What about him?' She nodded forward.

Mr Bang had stopped talking. He flicked his cigarette out of the window.

I said, 'Don't worry about him. Don't worry.'

Davy snorted in a dry, menacing laugh. 'Yer fucked, hen. Face it. Yer tea's oot.'

At the school, Orla focussed on getting her teaching kit ready. She hadn't yet prepared what she was going to teach, so she pulled out a couple of books and began to make some notes.

As I prepared to go, I said, 'So, you'll be OK, yeah?'

'Sure, no problem. It's just an hour class. Easy.' She tapped a textbook with her pen. When she looked up at me, her eyes were wide and sharp blue, beautiful eyes with lashes that peeled away, but sunk below a creased forehead. 'You won't feck about will ye? Just get the bags and get straight out there.'

When I left the Academy, there was still an hour to go before her class started.

*   *   *   *

Paula helped me lug Orla's and my luggage down to the lobby. The guy behind the desk watched as we piled up the bags, and then came out from behind his counter. He began to talk quickly in Korean, pointing at our bags. I could guess what he was saying, but our room was paid on account; if there were unpaid bills then it was something he would have to take up with Mr Bang. I strode out of the yogwan, down to the main road and flagged a cab, signalling for it to pull up the lane. By the time I got back to the lobby the reception guy had pulled his phone across the counter and was dialling. I put my finger on the hook to cut him off. He pulled the phone away from me and shouted.

Paula's Korean was better than mine, but neither of us had to understand to know what he was about.

'Look. Look. Call this number.' I scribbled down Mr Bang's number on one of the yogwan's business cards. 'Ask my boss for the money.' He looked at the numbers.

I tried again. 'Hogwan. Hogwan bossie. Hogwan bossie pay.' I mimed handing over money. 'You call hogwan bossie.' I mimicked a phone call. 'He pay yogwan money.' I did the cash thing again and it looked like he was getting it. 'But not call till Monday. Monday call.' His mouth hung open. 'Shit, how do you say Monday? Paula, do you know how to say Monday?'

'Wol yo il.'

'Wol yo il. Wo yo il, you call. Hogwan bossie. He pay.'

Paula and I grabbed the bags and dragged them out to the taxi. The guy stood on the steps holding the card and watching us load the boot. He didn't look convinced or pleased, but he wasn't dialling the phone.

The cab was heated, and I was already hot from the exertion. Sweat built on my face.

Paula said, 'Do you think he'll call Mr Bang?'

'He'll definitely call. I just hope he doesn't call now.'

'Do you want me to speak to Miss Im? She can maybe fend him off.'

'Aye, please do.'

As she called on her mobile, Davy, sitting snug between us, pointed his thumb towards Paula and said, 'I cannae believe she's shagging Miss Im. Fuck, it'd be worth hingin aboot tae see that. Fwoof.'

The taxi pulled into the busy main street and made its way towards the tollway that ran out to the airport, elevated above street level. Miss Im told Paula that Orla's class was starting a little late, but not to worry.

We worried. All the way out to the airport we talked about the timing, how close we could cut it and still make the flight.

We got stuck on a jammed sliproad. Car horns were blaring. I looked out the window at the cars pulled tight around us, no one going anywhere. 'I hope Orla doesn't get stuck like this, we'll be stuffed.'

Slowly the traffic pulled away ahead of us.

Davy was shifting in the seat, tugging at the crotch of his trousers. I nudged him with my elbow and glared at him. He said, 'I wis jist hinking. Whit if Orla's gettin stuffed at the school.'

I mouthed, 'What?'

'Jist that, ye knaw. She's in there on her ain. Fuckin Bang's awways been efter her. He's probly there wi his pals, shaggin her ower the desks. Bang bang. Eh, ye no hink? Bang bangs. Bang bangs the girl fae Bangor.'

I asked, 'Do ye think she's safe? It's really suss that he insisted on her teaching the demo.'

Paula said, 'He's just a sexist wanker. I'm not blonde enough for him. Don't worry, Miss Im will see she gets away alright.'

Davy had one thing in mind through. 'Paula's girlfriend's probly there an aw, wey the fuckin strap-on. Whahey.'

I dug him sharply in the chest.

Paula said, 'Are you alright? You're really twitchy.'

Davy sunk his teeth into my elbow.

'Ach!' Paula jumped at my shout. 'Aw, I'm just a bit worried about Orla.'

Paula looked worried about me. 'She'll be fine.'

At the airport, Paula bought a ticket for Fukuoka. She was flying half an hour before us. I went to our check-in desk and the lady there told me that the last check-in would be half an hour before the flight. To kill time we went in search of a coffee shop, but the service in the airport consisted mostly of rotten bowls of noodles and rice soup with chunks of long dead meat floating inside. Eventually we found one cafeteria where they poured coffee out of large cast iron urns. The coffee was over strong and gritty with undissolved milk powder. Drinking it set my nerves even more on edge.

Davy wouldn't sit at peace. He slipped down out of his seat and paced around the table. 'Right, yer jist gonnae huv tae go weyoot her. Gie her ticket tae Paula an she kin follae in a few days. Fuck it. Tear up her ticket an lea her here. Better idea.'

Paula kept checking her watch, and didn't touch her coffee. Eventually, she stood up and said. 'Good luck, Will. I won't see you when I get back.'

'Hopefully.'

She bent and kissed me on the cheek.

'Cheers Paula. At least this way it'll be easier for you to lie about not knowing what happened to us.'

'You just didn't turn up in Fukuoka, right?'

'Right.'

I went back to check-in, asked if I could check us through without Orla being there. No was the answer. We both had to be there thirty minutes before the flight. It was getting close to that.

'C'mon, lets jist fuck off. She's no comin. Mon, lets go.'

'I've got her bags.'

'Dump em.'

'Davy, shut up.'

I wheeled the baggage trolley away from the desk and started to run through contingencies: we could buy a later flight, hope to still meet the Hong Kong departure; we could reschedule Hong Kong – there must be somewhere in the airport I could rearrange the tickets; we could hole up in a hotel till the next flight; we could go to Seoul for a few days, I'd been told it was an alright city, a better city. I so wanted to be away from Korea though. This was the time.

My mobile phone was ringing. I dug around in my pack for it. It showed the Academy number calling. My heart sank at the thought that Orla had been delayed more; she wasn't going to make it on time.

'Hello?'

'Hello William?' It was Miss Im's voice.

'Hi. How are you?'

'I'm fine, but listen, William, there is a problem.' Our plan screwed. 'Orla, she…' She paused, unable to finish her sentence.

'What's happened? Is she alright?' Davy's sordid picture of Orla being raped ran through my head, then an image of Orla falling under a taxi.

'The students weren't from a company. They were sent by the Hyundai Academy. It was a trick so that Mr Bang would be caught with a teacher without visa.'

'Oh god.'

'Immigration went into the class before Mr Bang or me knew that they had arrived.'

'But, is it Mr Bang they were after?'

'Yes, but, they have arrested Orla also.'

And now the image came clearly to me of Orla been led away by uniformed men, her hands held behind her, her composure completely lost. She was a mess, hysterical, utterly broken and weeping.

Miss Im's voice kept coming out of the tiny speaker, but I held the phone away.

Davy grabbed at me. 'Whit? Whit's happened? He jumped up to try to snatch the phone.

I held it above his head, out of reach. 'Orla's been arrested.'

'Eh?' For a moment, even Davy looked stunned. 'Whit?' Then he cracked up laughing. His face creased up as his mouth spread wide and he barked laughter. He laughed so hard that he fell to the floor and rolled over with his legs in the air, revealing the lack of underwear under his baggy shorts.

The sight of Davy, and the thoughts in my head, made my stomach lurch. I held down the sickness, then felt pain, like I had been punched in the gut.

'That's fuckin… Och, och. I cannae stop.' He held his sides and slowly suppressed his laughter. 'That's fuckin hilarious.'

I could hear the voice in the receiver saying loudly, 'William? William are you there?'

I put it back to my ear. 'Yes. Yes I'm here.'

'You will need to come back. Orla will need help.'

Davy sat up and wiped a tear away from his eye.

I said, 'Yes, of course.'

'I'm sorry William. Did Paula go already?'

Davy began to lose it again, laughing loudly and letting himself fall back onto the floor. He was getting covered in dirt and dust.

I looked away from him, at the people who flitted past, all seemed to be keeping their distance from me. 'Yeah, she's gone.'

'Oh dear.' She paused, searching through her thoughts, practical Miss Im seeking a solution. 'Maybe I can't go to Japan. I will need to work this out.'

'Let Mr Bang sort it. He needs to fix this.' I shouted, suddenly angry. This was a mess. It was a mess for us, now it would be a mess for Paula too.

'Mr Bang has been arrested.' Her tone was terse.

'Of course.'

'You'll come back to the Academy?'

'Of course.'

'Then I'll see you soon.' She sounded as if she were annoyed, like somehow, something of this had been my fault.

When I hung up the phone, Davy was lying flat on his back, emitting chuckles. I stood over him, wanting to kick him.

'Whit? Whit ye lookin at me like that fur?'

'None of this is funny, Davy. It's definitely not funny.'

'Aw man, yer kiddin.' He picked himself up. 'Kin ye imagine the look on the silly bitch's face? This'll pit her right ower the edge.'

I started towards the exit.

Davy shouted, 'Hauw, whur ye goin?'

I kept moving. 'We've got to get back.'

I heard his feet coming quick and then his hand on the back of my coat. He stopped me dead in my tracks.

'The fuck we ur. We've got a plane tae catch.'

'Davy, didn't you hear me? The immigration department have got Orla. They've arrested Mr Bang as well.'

'I knaw. It's perfect.'

'What?'

'That's aw yer worries tied up in wan go.'

'How… Don't talk daft! Everything's a fucking mess now.'

'How is it? Now ye kin fuck aff an ye wilnae huv tae worry about Mr Bang or Orla.'

'You nasty little bastard! I can't just leave Orla.'

'How no?'

'How no? She's in jail. If I fuck off, who's going to look out for her?'

'Whit the fuck kin ye dae? Ye cannae go an bust her oot, kin ye? An if ye hing aboot, yer jist gonnae get stuck in the jail an aw. Whit the fuck good's that tae anywan?'

'I'm gonna meet Miss Im at the Academy. We'll sort it out together.'

'At the Academy? Ur ye stupit. How'd ye knaw thit thur no tryin tae trap ye? Mibbe Bang's foun oot aboot it aw an he's haudin Orla an waitin fur you?'

'Even more reason, I'll have to go back and save Orla.'

'Aw fuckin Superman, ur ye? It's a bit fuckin late, pal.'

'What d'ye mean?'

'You fuckin put me in bed wey her. Whit d'ye think that wis, ticklin? How come ye suddenly feel ye need tae protect the silly cow?'

'No, that's not… I don't know what you've been doing to her.'

Guilt filled the emptiness in my gut.

People were moving all around us, watching me as they passed. I had to look mad, shouting at an empty space. Was I? Was I talking to a tiny, vile man that no-one else could see?

I reached down and grabbed Davy by the neck. 'You don't fucking exist. You've done nothing to her.'

He brushed my hand away. 'Then who the fuck ur ye shoutin at?'

I had to get away.

'Stop ya prick.' His grip immobilised me. 'Thurs fuck aw ye kin dae, apart fae get arrested yersel.'

'I can't leave Orla.'

'Miss Im'll sort it. She's the only wan thit kin dae anyhin. She'll get her oot. The best you kin dae is get the fuck oot ae this country afore it gets aw the worse fur you.'

How could it get worse? The worst was already the fact that what he said seemed true. He always knew how.

I turned to him now, wanting to find out if there was a way that this could be done properly, safely, for all of us.

'It can't be that simple Davy.'

'It is. And Bang's the boy, int he? His pals'll huv thum both oot in nae time at aw.'

'But what's Mr Bang gonna do to Orla once I'm gone?'

'He wilnae dae nuhin. Ye knaw yersel that he's no a bad bastard. He's jist a dodgy cunt. A part-time gangster.'

'Aye, yeah, but… If it can be sorted, shouldn't I stay for Orla when she gets out?'

'Look, jist lea her a note, explain that ye huv tae go so you dinnae get arrested an aw. She kin spin Bang some story aboot you shitein yersel when everyhin went nasty.'

'But…' There was a kind of sense to it. Even if I wanted to, there was so little I could do. 'I suppose I could write her a note, explain why I've had to leave, tell her to come and join me in Hong Kong.'

The simple logic of it started to come. I turned the trolley around and headed back into the airport.

'Thurs no time fur that noo, ye've a plane tae catch.'

It felt like I could do it without really deserting her, without being the worst possible person. There was a lot to do in a short time. 'Right, this is what we're going to have to do: we'll get a locker and leave Orla's bags for her to collect.'

'Ye huvnae got time. Jist toss her bags an run through.'

'I cannae. I can't do that to her.'

'How no?'

'I'll put her ticket in the bag. I'll need tae get an envelope an post the key to Miss Im's house.'

'Whur ye gonnae get an envelope.'

'There's loads ae shops.'

Time was tight, but I found staff who could speak enough English to help, got an envelope and found the lockers. I had taken Miss Im's address as a contact for Paula. I had Paula's email as well, but I didn't even have an email address for Orla – we hadn't reached that point; we hadn't said goodbye. Her bag fitted easily in the locker.

I typed a text to Miss Im's number. 'Had to leave on plane. Orlas bag in locker. Will send key. U help orla pls. Send email later. '

Davy was twitching. 'C'mon son, shift it. We're aff oan oor big adventure again. That's the game, eh? Me and you, doin it thegether.' He started to sing. 'Just the two ae us. Dum dum dum dumpy dum. Jist the two ae us.'

I sent the text, switched the phone off, tossed it into the locker and shut the door.

Davy said, 'Hauw, don't be a twat, that'll be dead handy in Honky Konky.'

'No, Orla'll need it.'

'She wilnae need it in prison.'

'What? Davy, we said already… We know she's not goin to prison. She'll be…'

He dug a finger painfully into my thigh. 'Get the fuckin phone.'

'No, c'mon, let's go.'

His hand wrapped around part of my thigh. The bony fingertips dug in. 'William, dinnae be saft. Yer helpin naebdy here.'

'Ow. Get off Davy. Get off and we can go.'

'Dinna be daft.' His teeth-gritted anger frightened me. The pain in my leg was intense; I was starting to buckle as he said, 'C'mon ye fuckin stupit little arse-lickin wanker. Ye jist want Orla tae think thurs somehin decent aboot ye, but thur isnae. Yer a cunt, so jist enjoy being a cunt. Abandon her and take the phone.'

'I'm not abandoning Orla.'

'Whit d'ye hink yer daein? Yer daein a runner. A fuckin beautiful, sneaky, unnerhon runner.'

I pulled the door open. 'Go on then, get it.'

The pain left as soon as he let go. The strength came back into my leg.

Davy put a foot on the bottom edge of the locker and pulled himself up. 'I cannae see it. Whur'd ye put it, cunty-baws.'

'I chucked it in the back.'

'Whit the fuck d'ye dae that fur?'

Davy leaned right in, rummaging around. I hesitated, briefly, then pushed his back. Davy fell forward on top of the bag, tipping his legs up into the air.

'Hauw!'

The door caught his feet, jarring against them, but it pushed on to the latch. The key clicked the lock shut.

'Hauw. Whit the fuck!'

He banged hard against the door. The metal rattled solidly against its frame. There was a small area of mesh and what looked like the flesh of his lips pressed through in tiny pimples.

'William. William!'

I started to push the trolley away.

'William! Son!'

I had to move quickly; there were minutes until the gate closed.

'Ye cunt! Ye fuckin nasty little cunt!'

At the check-in, I addressed and stamped the envelope, dropped the key inside and asked the lady at the counter if she could put it in the post.

Davy was right. This was perfect.

*　　　*　　　*　　　*

CHAPTER 15

Hi Paula

How was Japan. I hope you are checking email and get this. I haven't been able to write til now. I don't have any way to contact Orla. Can you tell me what has happened to her? Can you give her this email address and tell her to get in touch. I'm staying at the Chungking Deluxe guesthouse in Chungking Mansions. I'm not sure how long I'll be here. I guess you are back in Pusan now and you should have got a key through the post at Miss Im's house. It's for a locker at the airport that I put Orla's bag in. Number 7136.

Take care

William

XOXO

I had written a few sentences to explain why I left and didn't go back to help Orla, but it sounded spineless, and I deleted them.

I was using a computer in a Chungking office that also did overseas calls. I gave the guy two hundred Hong Kong dollars and asked him to cut me off when it ran out. He took the number, dialled, listened until it was answered, started a stopwatch then handed me the phone.

I could hear her voice before I got the receiver to my ear. 'Hello? Hello? Is anyone there?'

'Hi mum.'

The delay was longer than simply time lag on the phone. 'Willie! Oh son. How are ye? Is everything alright?'

'Eh, yeah, it's OK.'

'Willie!' She sounded almost angry. 'My God son.' The Lord's name; she was angry. 'Where've ye bin? I've bin that worried since I got yer letter.'

'Don't worry mum.' I promised myself not to write her any more letters.

'Why didn't…' she began then went into a fit of coughing. She must have held the receiver away from her mouth, because the sound became distant.

'Are you alright mum?'

Her voice rasped, 'I just cannae understand what yer doing there. It doesnae sound safe.'

'Mum….'

'Yer sister says as much. But I suppose…'

'Mum?'

'… it must have worked out for you, if yer still there. Are you sure you're OK? And what about Orla?'

'I'm not in Korea now mum.'

'Eh? No?'

'No. I've left.'

'Are ye on yer way home? Where are ye?'

'I'm in Hong Kong.'

'Hong… What ye doing there? Is Orla with ye?'

'Eh… no. She stayed.'

'What?'

'She… She'll be following me after.'

'And what ye doin in Hong Kong?'

'Well, I'm trying to get back home, but… It's just… I don't have enough for a ticket at the moment … I'm probably going to have to get some work. For a while.'

'Can ye do that?'

'I'm hoping to. I've tried to get a teaching job, but that doesn't seem to be hapnin. And I'm trying to get some bar work. And then there must be something else I can try, though I'm not very sure what. In fact, I'm not…. Well. I'm sure I'll find something it's just that…' Every avenue brought a dead end. What could I tell my mum? But she was the first person I had been able to speak to. 'And I just… Well, I thought it would be easier here.'

'Oh.'

'Ye know, it used to be a British colony and all and I guess I thought there would be no problem for a British person to find work, but… Well, it's not. In fact sometimes it's hard to know it was a colony at all. I mean, the standard of English can be pretty awful and you'd think that would mean loads of work for English teachers, but there's not, as far as I've seen and…Well, without a work visa…'

'How ye gonnae get home?'

'I don't know.'

'Dae ye want me to send you out some money?'

'Do you have any?'

'No, but … Are you safe, Willie?'

'Aye, mum, of course. I mean, what's the worst that could happen?'

'I don't know son, that's what worries me. I mean, what're ye gonnae dae if ye cannae make money at aw?'

'I…'

'Would the embassy no fly ye back?'

'The embassy?'

'Aye, the British embassy, the Consulate or whatever. Would they no fly ye back if ye went tae them and said ye didnae have nothin left.'

'I don't know, I don't think so.'

'They would, I'm sure. I mind yer uncle Charlie wis out in Trinidad and the same happened tae him.'

'Was Charlie not extradited?'

'Naw. He…'

Mum started to cough again. This time the harsh barking and wheezing made me hold the phone away.

The man in the office waved at me and said, 'One minute.'

When mum came back on she said, 'Sorry son. Sorry.'

'I'm sorry mum, I didn't even ask you how you're doin.'

'Och. It doesnae matter.'

'That cough sounds pretty bad. Are ye down with something?'

'Och, ye know I don't like to complain, son. But tae tell the truth, I've no been that well.'

'What's the matter, Mum?'

'It's… well, the doctor says it's Emphysema.'

'Oh, Christ.'

'That's what the doctor says anyway… Ye cannae really trust what they tell ye. I mean, I thought it was just… all those bad colds, ye know?'

'But is that treatable?'

'They think so. It's just mostly, ye know, there's medicine I have tae take, and I need rest… they say.' I noticed how laboured her breath was, how slow and difficult each sentence was.

'What about Helen? Has Helen been there to help?'

'She does what she can, but she's no even in Glasgow that much. She's eyways down in London. But she does what she can. She came and stayed last week. For a night.'

The guy got my attention. 'Finish now.'

'Mum. My money's up. Mum…'

He pressed a finger onto the hook of the phone before I got the chance to say goodbye.

I left Chungking, bought a half bottle of vodka and started walking. It was evening, but the heat was oppressive and the crowds still blustered around me, dragging me in directions I didn't fight against.

*   *   *   *

I hadn't been to the waterside before, hadn't realised that the street I was staying on, ran down to a concrete path along a harbour wall next to a churning stretch of water.

The pace diminished down there. Tourists, young romantic couples and Chinese families drifted or gathered by the water's edge, snapping snaps, pointing out features of the skyline, wondering at the brilliance of being there – that picture postcard line of glistening, glowing, flashing skyscrapers in the background, a short distance away. The only thing frantic was the constant motion of the water, in which the lights of the city chopped and shattered. The waves had no flow or direction; there was just ceaseless agitation.

I climbed some steps to a raised viewing area. Only a few canoodlers or other loners were up there. I sat on a ledge and cracked the vodka. Its ammoniac fumes hit my sinuses before the acidic burn hit my throat. After a momentary retch, the alcohol settled in my gut and radiated out to my limbs.

The lamps above the promenade were yellow-tinged, giving a secluding dusky half-light. I felt unobserved, separate from anyone, distant. No-one would care to pay me attention. If anything they would rather look away.

Something came back to me that I hadn't thought of for a long time and I took another swig of the vodka.

In my last year at school, one day, with my head in a comic, I had ignored my registration teacher, Miss Quinn. In a fit of pique she told me that she knew what my prospects were. She described an old tramp who slept rough around Queen Street station in Glasgow, whom she often saw hugging a bottle and begging money. She said she knew that this old boy was an ex-professor, intelligent and well-connected. His successful career had been lost when he lost the plot. He had pushed away his family and his colleagues because he was too involved in himself, too deep in his thoughts to engage in the real world, or so she would have it. She saw me ending up just like him; too smart for my own good, and the maker of my own ruin.

Across the water, the line of the land stretched with buildings and streets, lit up with more life. Above the buildings there were hillsides, tall and dramatic, high and steep enough to be undeveloped and wild. I had seen so little of this city. My area of vision had been restricted to a few blocks. Buses left continuously from outside Chungking, but I had been too afraid to explore.

A huge tanker crossed my line of vision. A ferry service was leaving from near where I sat, making a repeated journey over to the opposite shore. Ferries passed each other in both directions full of yet more people. There must have been lots of reasons to journey across. There was a lot over there that could hold potential, the potential for me to find a way out, perhaps. But

I knew the journey would only bring a new set of challenges that I couldn't meet.

I was left with only the image, the retina stimulus of the skyline, as I fixated on the central cluster of buildings, fifty, sixty storeys high, their edges trimmed with sparkles, their peaks capped with halogens and lasers shooting into the sky. A land of fantasy, it ought to speak of adventure and intrigue among the rich and famous; to me the scene was inhibiting. The power of all that light filled the atmosphere, clogged it and prevented any star breaking through the night sky, as if there were nothing beyond the confines of the city. While the laser beams tried to reach out to an expansive and far distant universe, the ambient glow brought everything closer in around me. Hong Kong held me tightly within its bounds and kept me wrapped in tension and fear. While the skyline appeared to grow wide with possibility, the pressure of the city crushed me into a tiny enclosed space. I couldn't bear to watch any longer. The only place I knew to be was in my room. Not exploring. Not connecting. Just lying fearful.

*   *   *   *

A young Chinese woman got out of the lift on the twelfth floor behind me. She was petite and pretty, with her hair cut short in a boyish way, short back and sides. She smiled. No-one else was around, so she was smiling at me.

She said, 'Hi.'

I said, 'Hi,' and walked away with thoughts only of collapsing into bed.

She said, 'Do you stay here too?'

'Yes. Yes, I'm staying in there.' I indicated the dorm room.

'Are there other guys in there?'

'Well, there are some, I dunno if they're in just now. I was just going to bed.'

'Oh, I'm sorry.' She walked towards me. 'It's only, do you have a plug? I'm staying in here.' She pointed to the single room. 'And I don't have one and I would like to listen to some music.' She was a head shorter than me. She had thin arms that ran smoothly to her wrists. One hand held out an eviscerated electric plug, hung by one screw with its pins hanging loose and no fuse. 'Just for a short time and then I could give it back to you tomorrow.' Her eyes were marked round with heavy eyeliner.

'Em, no I don't, but I think one of the guys in the room has. Let me see.'

The room was dark and I shuffled far enough up the centre aisle to see that none of the beds were occupied. I flicked the light on and looked among the dope dealers' gear. They had a stereo that they used to play dub reggae. I hesitated only briefly before pulling the lead out of the player and disconnecting the plug from the wall.

She wasn't in the lobby, but I could see light in the far corridor. I crossed, prepared to knock, but the bedroom door was wide open. She was bent over the bed flicking through a pile of CDs. Her high heels lifted her calves and pulled up the back of her short skirt.

'Eh… Is this the kind of lead you need?'

'Oh, hey. That's great. Thank you. Are you sure you won't need it?'

'Well, it's not mine and, well… no, it doesn't matter.'

'Thanks.' She crouched to push the lead into her player. 'I don't know how I broke the other one really. It just fell apart.' She laughed as she pressed play.

I heard the opening chords to Blur's Parklife.

I said, 'Great,' and turned to go.

'Do you like Britpop?' She asked.

'What, you mean indie music?'

'Yeah, like that.' She pointed at her stereo. 'I really like that.'

'Yeah, I guess I do.'

'Are you British?' She asked.

'Yeah.'

'Cool.'

'Are you?'

'British?'

'Yeah, I mean, your English is very good.'

'No, that was just school. They taught us using English, you know, they thought that was important. They don't any more. They don't think it's that important anymore.'

'What d'you mean, anymore? What changed?'

'Oh, like the British going and stuff.'

'What, since the handover?'

'Yeah. Chinese rule and stuff. They want us all to be like super-Chinese now.' She raised her hands as if to say, big deal. Her diction and mannerisms were very natural.

'So, have you never lived in Britain?'

'God, I'd love to live in England, but it's so expensive, and I've only got a BNO passport.'

'A…?'

'So, they won't let me just go and live there easily. Hey, would you like a drink?' She unscrewed the cap on a bottle of red wine, swigged from it, passed it to me, then kept talking. 'But it's not like I hate Hong Kong or anything, its just that I've been here all my life and I kinda know that there's lots of cool stuff out there, so I'd really like to get the chance before I'm like too old.'

'But you can't be that old.'

'Well, I'm maybe older than you think, but anyway I'm old enough to know. Do you want a ciggie?'

'No, thanks.'

She blinked as she lit the cigarette and smoke wafted in her face. Her lips pulled away from the filter with a light kiss, leaving red lipstick marks.

'Hey, I'm going out for a drink. You want to come?'

'Oh, thanks but, I'm a bit tired. I was about to go to bed.'

'You're not that old either. Come on, you'll be fine once you get out.'

'Well, it's just that I don't really have much money.'

She looked at me, at my backpacker clothes, my unfed body. 'Well, how about this. I know where we can go and only rich guys pay. You can drink all night and no one will ask you to buy a beer.'

'Oh, look, thanks for the offer, but I don't think I can do that.' She cocked her head, looking at me as if I was daft. 'Well, I guess it's just the way my mother brought me up, not to take anything for free, you know? Work for your money and pay your own way.'

'That sounds like my Pop too.' She drew on her cigarette again, but hurried it, sucking hard to get the drag over and say, 'But that's a load of poo.'

'Ha!'

'It is. It's rubbish. You know these rich guys, especially rich guys in Hong Kong, they love to show off their money. They would hate it if you tried to buy your own drink.'

'That's OK for you. You're a woman.'

'Girls, guys, anyone. I tell you what. I'll take you to a place where I know some people. We won't have to hit on anyone or anything like that, we'll just go in and say hi, and then have a drink and a laugh, and maybe a dance. Do you like to dance?'

'Sure. I…'

'You'll need to dress a bit better than that though. Do you have any… tidy clothes?'

I couldn't imagine going somewhere that I had to dress up, didn't think I had the energy for it either.

'Are you sure? I mean, you're not…' Looking at what she was wearing meant looking at a lot of flesh. '…that smart or…'

'But I'm a girl. Go on. Go quick and we'll get moving.'

I went.

I dug in my pack and pulled out clothes that I would normally only wear for work. I wondered what the hell I was doing, but didn't stop. Somehow this girl had got me on a roll I wanted to keep on; fixing on what to wear, wondering where we could end up; it prevented anything else from occupying my mind. When I got back to the room, she had tidied all of her CDs into a neat pile on the floor, cleared the bed, and was stretching the bedclothes out straight.

She swept her hand across the flattened sheets then held it out to me. 'I'm Sammy.'

'William.'

'Hey. One more drink and then let's go.'

She took a long bubbling swig and I copied. Between us we had almost finished the bottle. The wine mixed with the vodka and I felt drunk, light enough to go with the flow. Sammy led me purposefully out of the building. The human contact – an arm on mine, a person talking – lifted me, carried me through streets I hadn't been down before. We crossed another main road, into an area of pedestrianised malls. Her neat, quick heels clipped on the pavement, giving rhythm to her continuous talk, chattering of music, about bars she frequented, people she'd met. She sometimes asked about me, but it was easier to answer short and allow her to continue.

We came to the gaudy entrance of a basement bar. The stairs were barely lit, just a strip along each step like the direction markers on the floor of a plane – in case of emergency. The doors swung into a dark, crowded nightclub. Heavy aircon blasted down over the entrance making a wall of cold air you had to walk through and sending a chill down my back. The darkness and engulfing noise were disorientating.

Sammy took my hand and led me across the middle of the dancefloor. Guys in shades watched us pass. Beautiful woman ignored us. Wrists and necks were draped with gold that stood out against the black of the shirts or slim dresses. I quickly realised that I was the only non-Chinese.

After the dancefloor, we came to the back of the club. Sammy reached out a hand and pressed the wall. It gave way. This new door led into a smaller room. It was less frenetic in here. As the door swung back into its snug frame, the bassbeat of the dancefloor was reduced to a muffled thump. The walls were padded in dark velvet on their bottom half, covered in small squares of mirror on top. Black leather couches ran around the walls with low tables and armchairs or stools. Most of the seats were occupied, but there was no crush; no-one was standing except the waitresses taking orders from the tables. There was no bar. I immediately felt uncomfortable.

Sammy, still holding my hand, scanned the room until she recognised someone and pulled me to a corner. I saw many tiny reflections of myself looking awkward and scared as we crossed.

The group we approached were listening enrapt to one of their members who was talking animatedly, gesticulating and sloshing the drink in his hand. The man talking was wearing white.

We stood at the back of the company, facing the talker. Sammy didn't interrupt, but she bobbed up and down in place until he noticed her and stopped.

'Sammy,' he said and then spoke in a long string of snapped Cantonese. He smiled broadly and Sammy grinned and chuckled as she talked with him. I stood behind, squirming under the gaze of everyone else in the group.

'Oh, hey, and this is William.' She stepped to one side and forced me in amongst them. 'He's like this old friend of mine that I haven't seen in so long.'

'Welcome William. My name is Terence Tang. Very nice to meet you.' Terence rose from his seat, putting his drink down and reaching out to shake my hand. I was wearing a white shirt as well, but the off-the-peg cut of it looked tatty next his. 'Please, sit.' He directed me to the end of the couch that he was sitting on. Sammy sat between us.

The couches were deep and I sank far back. Terence introduced me to the rest of the group, and I had to shift forward and lean across my knees to shake hands.

'This is Miss Wong Mei-ling, this is Michael Li, Mr Yuan.'

They greeted me with a great show of friendliness, smiling and speaking some politeness in English, but I felt like my rightful place in this company should be to take their order and move on to the next table.

Terence introduced the last member of the group, sitting directly opposite me.

'And this is Ah-Fai.'

Ah-Fai was wearing a loose silk shirt unbuttoned quite low. When he leant forward I saw his chest and stomach were flat and toned. He held my hand overlong, forcing me to hover uncomfortably, my knees aching. Eventually, he said, 'It is very nice to meet you,' and let go. His hair was thick, spiked and fully black, belying the lines of age on his face.

None of the men in the group could have been younger than forty though Mei-ling looked ages with me and Sammy. She didn't show any interest in Sammy or any sign of recognising her.

Terence asked, 'And what would you like to drink?'

I really wanted beer. I was thirsty after the vodka and wine, but there were only spirits on the table, so I asked for a vodka and coke. Sammy had the same.

Terence asked me, 'So William, are you visiting Hong Kong, or do you live here?'

'Well, I…'

Sammy interrupted. 'He's just passing through. His family know my Pop, you know, business partners and all that, but he's been coming through for like years. It's been, what? What's it been William? Well, it's been like years, hasn't it?'

As she spoke, Terence smiled and nodded. At first he directed his acknowledgements to me, as if I still had a part in the conversation, but slowly his attention was fully drawn to Sammy. She slipped back in to Cantonese, and I slipped further back into the couch, sipping from my glass.

The rest of the group drifted into their own conversations, forgetting about me and leaving Terence to his new focus, apart from Ah-Fai, who leant across the table again. 'You like Hong Kong?'

I had slouched too deeply to struggle forward again, so I shouted, 'Yes, very much.'

He smiled but clearly could think of nothing else to say. I didn't know if his English was limited or if he didn't have the imagination. I was glad that he had tried to include me, but I couldn't dig deep enough in myself to find any way of contributing. Eventually Ah-Fai sat back and looked to his companions for some conversation to join.

I really didn't know what I was doing there or why Sammy had brought me along. I stayed and was handed another drink when my first ran out. Other than getting drunk, I couldn't see a reason to stay. Getting drunk seemed good enough.

At one point Sammy asked, 'Hey, are you OK? We'll go and dance soon, yeah? And you can get another drink if you want.'

Mostly, she was occupied with Terence. Others got involved in their conversation. I thought that perhaps they were trying to prise Terence away from her, but eventually they drifted off again, and mostly it was Sammy who rattled away at him. While Terence listened, his hand sat on Sammy's knee, close to the hem of her skirt. She seemed unaware. She had her elbow up on the back of the couch, flicking the ends of his hair.

I slipped into a drunken daze. I was smashed enough, and in such an uncommon situation, that my thoughts did not want to travel far, did not go back into the current state of my life. Now that people were ignoring me, I could gaze vacuously around the room, unengaged. If I was going to be stuck, I might as well be stuck, drunk and oblivious.

As I neared the end of another drink, Ah-Fai stood up and leaned over the table to say something in confidence to Terence. They talked and laughed for a moment before he sat back down, and Terence went back to talking to Sammy.

Ah-Fai smiled at me. He raised his drink and spoke to me again. Though I didn't hear what he said, I raised my glass in distant cheers, nodded and tried to smile.

Sammy nudged me in the ribs and said, 'You know, Ah-Fai says he likes you a lot. There's maybe a chance you could make some money if you like him as well.'

'Eh...'

'You said that you don't have a lot of money.'

'Yeah, but...'

'Well, you are young and good-looking. You know there are some very easy ways to earn some extra cash.' She grinned as if she was telling me a cheeky little secret.

It was a few moments before it really dawned on me what she was saying. I felt so dumb. I hadn't even thought it, but it seemed so thick that I hadn't realised. Sammy was buying me these drinks. This bright young thing, these older men. When she had straightened her sheets, it wasn't some tick of fastidiousness; she was getting ready. But surely guys like these had plush pads of their own to go back to. Yeah, and wives and children. Sammy was renting for the night and would be gone in the morning, a little bit richer, and still with that same buoyant step, still vivacious and chattering, happy and hopeful.

And she was suggesting I could do the same.

She did it for fun, but me, I had a need. I really needed money. I needed a way out, and if this was the way that was being presented, then maybe I had to take it, just this once. Maybe it wouldn't be so bad, not if it was just once. Getting myself through.

And then I flashed on the image of my own naked flesh in Ah-fai's hands, or another nameless man, old and powerful, overpowering, pushing me down into bed sheets; amorphous blurs of skin enveloping, hurting; pulling myself up, gulping for air.

The headrush made me feel too drunk, sick with it.

Terence was saying something to Sammy and she nodded, smiling at me.

I was being put on display, to sell, to show myself how far I'd sunk. A wall was collapsing on me, pressuring me back into my cell. My route out of trouble was debasement. Abject degradation.

Ah-Fai leaned across, pointed at my empty glass and said, 'You want one?'

'Yeah I do. I just have to go to the toilet.' He scooped his fingers into a bowl of peanuts on the table as I lifted out of my chair. 'I'll get my drink when I come back.'

He nodded. 'Sure. Great.'

I know he turned to watch me as I walked away.

I pulled the shining handle on the velvet padded wall. The door was heavy and I managed to open it only enough to squeeze sideways through.

The dancefloor was packed. I looked for a space, but my head throbbed with the heaviness of the beat and swayed as the booze churned into my system. The crowd were heaving up and down. As I tried to pass, I got bumped to the side, pushed away. All the dancers were totally unsmiling. There was a lot of contact, bodies on bodies, and a lot of beautiful woman showing the full length of their suppleness, arms, legs and backs, and bellies, but it was all too serious, too vulgar. None of it was fun.

I stumbled towards the door, twisting and sidling, mumbling to excuse myself and came up behind a leggy woman who was dancing with more enthusiasm than any of the other forlorn girls. As I edged past her, trying not to make contact with her flying elbows, I saw that she was dancing with a man wearing a white suit and black shirt, shaking his body and thrusting his crotch at his scantily clad partner. A tiny man.

I came around the woman just as she bent down to hear something the little man had to say. He grabbed her neck and put his mouth close to her ear but even from where I was standing I could clearly hear him say, 'Wait tae I get ye hame, doll. I'll show ye whit a real man keeps in his troosers.'

*   *   *   *

CHAPTER 16

I was preoccupied and fumbling at dinner. Davy stayed wrapped tight around my shoulders, knocking things out of my hands and whispering in my ear. I ordered a bowl of muscles and Davy stole them from the shell as I lifted them to my mouth. He slurped them or let them slip onto the tablecloth so that I had to say to Beata, 'I'm sorry, I dunno what's up with me today.'

She laughed, 'You are … with no hands.'

'Handless. I am that.'

'Fuckin feckless, that's whit ye ur.'

I wrenched Davy from my shoulder and threw him to the floor.

'William!' Beata stood from her seat and reached out to me, as if she thought I was going to fall. She frowned and said, 'It must have been a very big weekend for you if you are still so... shaking on Tuesday.'

'Oh, it's not that. It's just…' Despite the proximity of the two, my weekly phone calls to mum had never come up during my regular Tuesday night dinners with Beata. 'My mum's not well.'

'No?'

'I told you everything was fine, but it's not. I just couldn't really talk about it, but she's really ill. Has been for quite a while now.'

'What is wrong with her?'

Davy picked himself off the floor. 'Aw, naw. Pass the fuckin hanky.'

'She's got emphysema.'

'I don't know what that is. Is it bad?'

'Aye. Or yeah, well it could be, it's to do with her breathing.'

'Don't you want to go back to Scotland?'

'I cannae fuckin listen tae this.' Davy lifted the edge of the tablecloth and stepped underneath.

I said, 'I don't really know why I haven't gone back already.' I wanted to be around Beata, wanted to be able to meet with her, every day if I could. 'It's shitty, I know, but I've got a place in Hong Kong. I don't think I'd have that in Scotland any more. I'm almost scared of going back, of getting stuck there.'

'But you could go back for a short time.'

'I know... It's just... I know.'

I stared at the empty plate in front of me, but I knew Beata's face would be placid, calm.

'Couldn't you send her money?'

'I should, but I'm so skint. It's like, life in Hong Kong sucks up all my money. Every day, it just disappears and I don't seem to be able to...'

'What are you doing now?'

'Whit?' His voice rose from under the table. 'She fuckin stupit or somehin.'

'You are here eating in a restaurant.' Her tone slipped low into a touch of anger. 'You are even saying that you will pay for the bill like you are a gentleman or something. And all the time you are partying and clubbing and spending so much on drinks.'

'Aw, here we go, the anti-bevvy rant.' His hand came over the edge of the table and lifted Beata's wineglass away.

'Yeah, I know, I...'

She took my hand across the table. 'William, I know you care very much about your mother, and you shouldn't be so bad to yourself, because you need to live your life as well. But sometimes you are a bit stupid.'

'Hawwwww, there ye go.' The glass came back empty.

A waitress came to collect our plates, forcing us to split hands. I waited for her to finish before I looked Beata straight in the eye. 'I don't really know what I'm doing with myself.'

'Fuck's sakes.' Davy's head thrust out from under the tablecloth, right between my legs. 'Wake up tae yersel!' He slid back under.

I said, 'I have fun here, but it's kinda pointless as well. I'm still just doing the same thing week in week out.'

'Dae we weep or puke?' His head popped out beside me. 'Ditch the bitch! Let's head tae the boozer.'

I brought my fist down hard on the table. My wineglass toppled and landed with a donk on Davy's head. White wine spilled over him.

'Ah, ya cunt, I'm soakin.' Davy stomped off in the direction of the toilet, wine trailing off him.

Beata shook her head, watching me fumble after the glass, and then calmly said, 'Why don't you move to Lamma?'

'What? Why?' A flood of notions overcame me, and hopes.

She said, 'How much do you spend on rent every month?'

'Five grand.'

'Well on Lamma you will get a room for two thousand, maybe two thousand and five hundred. And also, if you live on Lamma, maybe you would get on the last ferry a few times and not stay out all night spending so much money.'

'I… Yeah, maybe, I mean…'

Moving to Lamma? What she said made sense, but I was struck far harder by what she was not saying, what I understood to underlie that plan.

A waiter came over with a cloth to wipe around the table and floor, and I excused myself to the toilet.

Davy was standing at the hand-dryer, twisting his head under the hot air.

I shouted across the noise. 'You see?'

'Whit?'

'You see? I told you.'

He pointed at the dryer. 'I cannae hear ye.'

'She wants me, Davy.' I held his head between both my hands and pulled him away from the machine. 'She wants me close. That's what this is about. She wants me around her all the time, and away from everyone else, away from the parties and clubs. That's why she wants me on Lamma.'

'She wants whit?'

'I knew it. And I tell ye whit, I'm gonna do it. Definitely. This is it. I'll do anything she wants.'

I shoved him back under the dryer.

As I sat at the table, Beata said, 'Hey William, there is one thing I have mean to ask.'

I held my breath in anticipation.

She said, 'What is it with you and Sammy?'

Air released from me in a stream.

'You know Sammy, she really like you, and I don't know why the two of you, you are not together.'

Davy arrived back from the toilets, his hair blow-dried flat across his scalp, just in time to hear Beata say, 'I think you and Sammy, you could make a really good couple.'

He cackled, 'Aw, she's aw yours mate. Nae fuckin doot aboot it. Hoohoo.' Then floored himself laughing.

'No, Beata, no. It's not like that. It's only been, sometimes…'

'Ho. Hahaha. Fuckin brilliant.' Davy slapped the floor. 'Go on Willie, tell her. Tell her ye love her.'

'Beata, you don't understand. When you said about moving to Lamma, I thought…'

Davy climbed onto my lap. 'Ye thought she wis gonnae suck ye aff.'

'To Lamma?' Beata looked confused. 'This was advice, to save money.'

That was obvious, that was clear. Of course that was what she had said, but I had seen so much, in her face, in her body language, in the growing intimacy of our conversations. 'But no, Beata. I thought that now, after all this time, that you and me would…'

'Tell her ye want tae fuck her.'

'I've always wanted to be with you Beata.'

The moment of release, the moment I could never come back from; putting it out into the open, declaring myself to the world, to her, revealing what she must already know.

She didn't miss a beat. 'You haven't.' No shock or surprise. She just shook her head. 'You think you have, but you haven't.'

'Numpty! Kicked in the bawbag every time.'

She reached again for my hand. 'You have many ideas William, many thoughts that you perhaps shouldn't follow.'

'Noo ye kin tell her whit a bitch she is.'

'My thoughts tell me that I want to be with you.'

'Ma thoughts tell me she disnae gie a flyin fuck.'

She had to understand. We had gone so far in Australia, and now we were closer. We'd got past my mistakes. I felt it so clearly, so deeply. We were ready. She had to know it, which meant she had to be hiding it. She was fighting it.

'You're hiding it because of Sammy. I know you don't want to hurt her, but Sammy will understand.'

'No William. That's not what I want. Not now.' Beata remained impassive, showing no recognition of my wrench. 'You make this life for yourself, what you do in Hong Kong, and I'm happy I can be part of it, like we have. We don't need it to be more.'

'Willie, she's fuckin wey ye.'

I started, 'I don't really understand how you couldn't…' But she did know. She must. 'So much has happened. We've spent so much time together.'

'Because we're friends.'

Friends. Perhaps I should have been grateful for that much. It was far more than I had been left with in Australia, but it felt like scraps from the table, a regal handout to the undeserving. I was being fed a titbit to keep me hanging on, begging for more, more scraps of affection, more sniffs at the banquet, but never indulged. I'd never get close enough to the table.

Davy stood at my side. He patted my back. 'Tell her, son.'

I pulled my hand away from Beata's. 'You never let me get close.'

'She's fuckin frigid.'

'You don't do affection like other people.'

'William, stop.'

'Yer never gettin any ae whit she's got.'

'Why don't you ever fuckin give anythin away?'

Shock was beginning to take her face. 'What are you saying?'

'An there's poor you, pittin yer heart in her handbag.'

She knew, but was making me spell it out, rend myself. 'It's so fuckin obvious. How could you not see? I would do bloody anything for you.'

She shook her head, said, 'I know,' and turned away.

'She disnae care.'

I snapped, 'No, you don't.'

'I do.' She had to face me again, to force her face into compassion. 'I understand how you feel, but...'

She pitied me.

'God.' I couldn't help my finger pointing. 'You must be hard.'

'That's it son. That's ma boy. Tell her.'

'Or cold. If you can see me like this.' My teeth were clenched. 'If you know, and you still don't let me near, then what sort of...

'Cunt. She's a cunt.'

'What sort of a...

'Virgin. She's a nasty dried up virgin.'

'You're just a...'

'William?'

It came out of me and Davy in the same breath. 'Scandy bitch.'

*   *   *   *

CHAPTER 17

Dear William

It is easier to write this letter to you because you act something funny when I have try to call you. I would want to meet to talk to your face but I think now it is difficult because of what we say before.

You were very nasty to me. I know there are many reasons why this. But really it doesn't matter because I like you. I really like you, I always do. I am happy to be your friend because you are funny and good to be with. You are a good person with a good heart. I can feel that from you.

The problem is the other side. There are times when something dark is in you, when you are not yourself, and you let yourself be cruel and nasty. You push too far. Then you hate yourself for take it too far. Something take you over, a different William, and that person is someone you wouldn't like. If you sat down next to that person in a pub you would be right off the loud, aggressive, show off person that you become. I want you to understand that if you will be like that, I do not want to be with you.

Now you are cruel to Sammy too. She do not know why this happen and it is not her fault. Even if you do not want Sammy to be your girlfriend, she is your friend. You will lose her unless you speak with her.

You have so much to be happy with, your good job, your friends, the fun you have in your life, but so often I see that you are unhappy or angry. It is like you only let yourself go so far, so good, but then you have to stop yourself from being happy. You must be in control of that side of you. You are strong enough person, I think. I have seen that too. It is for you that you need to work, William. You may be better to help yourself if you can.

Do not avoid me anymore, William. Do not avoid Sammy and do not avoid yourself.

With love to my friend
Beata

*   *   *   *

We topped up our wineglasses and moved from the table to the comfy chairs. A cool breeze blew in through the open balcony doors. I was on the edge of the couch while Sammy spread herself across the rest, her head rested on a cushion on my leg. 'Aiya! Ho bao.' She patted her stomach. 'Thanks, Will.'

'Ho, Willie.' Davy stood right in front of me. 'Ho, Willie, son.'

Sammy lit a cigarette. 'So, guys, how are your travel plans?'

I said, 'Well, we've decided when to go, and it's not long, eh?' Peripherally, I could see Davy waving.

Beata placed an ashtray on the floor next to Sammy. 'No, really not. Only a few weeks.'

'I wish I was going with you.' A column of ash built on the end of her cigarette. 'Couldn't you wait a while so I could get the cash to come with you?'

Davy shouted, 'Hey Willie, look.'

I shook my head. 'What, a year? Three years.'

Sammy reached over her shoulder and gently slapped my arm. 'That's not fair.'

'Willie, son, look ower here.'

Beata said, 'I think there will be another time.'

Davy started to sing, 'Thur wis a wee cooper who came frae Fife.'

'I hope so. It's unfair, going to Europe without me.'

Davy continued, 'Nickety, nackety, noo, na, noo.'

I turned to Beata, 'So what do we have to do now?'

'And he hud gotten a bastardin wife.'

'Well, as far as I know, we need to go down to the agent with our passports.' She mimed the actions. 'Pay there and pick up the tickets.'

Davy bounced into view. 'Hey Willie Wallacky, hey John Dougal, alane, quo rushity roo, ra, roo.' He was doing a rubbish attempt at a highland fling, arms flailing.

I asked, 'Is it genuine?'

'I think so.'

'It just seems so cheap.'

'Yeah,' Sammy said, 'but how many stopovers have you got?' Her tone was, who-would-want-to, sarcastic. She sucked on her cigarette

Beata shrugged. 'Quite a few.'

Sammy blew out a grey fountain. 'Where first?' A mosquito flew through the smoke above her.

'Dakar?' I was pretty vague on the details.

'Where?'

Beata said, 'Bangladesh.'

'Uh?'

She explained, 'It's the flight, Biman Air. That one is a company from Bangladesh.'

'Oh shit, pack your parachute.'

Davy bounced into the space between us, shunting against the small coffee table. The glasses trembled. 'She widnae fuck an she widnae blaw,

'Nickety, nackety, noo, na, noo.

'So he smacked her heid aff a fuckin waw,

'Hey Willie Wallacky, cunt John Dougal,

'Away ya bastard, roo, ra, roo.'

Sammy asked, 'So Beat, have you decided? You definitely not going to Scotland?'

'No, I fly London to Stockholm. My mum is mad to see me.'

'It's a shame though. Wouldn't you like to see it?'

I said, 'I'm not even going to be there that long myself before I head over to Sweden.'

Davy jumped up onto the table, gritted his teeth, clenched his fists and stared hard at me. 'He kicked her in her dried-oot cunt,

'Nickety, nackety, noo, na, noo.'

His foot stamped on the table. Spit flew from his teeth. 'He bent her ower an gied her a shunt,

'Hey Willie wankery, yer a cunt John Dougal,

'Away an fuck yersel, roo, ra, roo.'

I smiled, 'Hey Sammy, do you not need to get down for the ferry?'

'What time is it?'

'Just gone nine.'

'It's really early.'

Beata said, 'But don't you go to your mum's tonight?'

'Yeah, yeah.'

'Come on then.' Beata jumped up. 'We can walk you down, and maybe we will still meet Steve in the Deli.'

'Oh, very nice for you.' Sammy stubbed her cigarette and sat up.

As I stood, I bumped into the coffee table, knocking the glasses flying and sending Davy tumbling backwards, shrieking. He cracked his head off the tiled floor.

The girls both shouted, 'William!'

As we cleaned up the mess of glass and wine, Davy sat glowering, rubbing his head.

The night breeze blew against us as we wound down the hill from Tai Peng Tsuen, the village that sat on the hilltop above Yung Shue Wan and the bay with the ferry pier. The way was dark between the arcs of street light and occasional lit verandas. The valley below us bellowed with an abundance of horny toads hidden in the marshes. We enjoyed our tumbling walk, legs falling along the slope so that our feet slapped on the concrete until we slowed as the path levelled out and we reached the village. We said hello to a few faces sitting outside the Fountainhead – beer-handers, lazily happy – and others passing through on their Saturday night, going-nowhere, drift.

At the pier, Sammy said, 'Right, I'll see you guys on Tuesday.'

'Great.' I pecked her on the cheek. 'Your place, yeah?'

Beata did the same. 'Does Andy know?'

'He'll be happy.' She clicked through the barrier and bounded off towards the ramp, turning and walking backwards for the last few steps. 'And don't have too much fucking fun without me.'

Beata and I took our time going back through the village, not stopping with anyone in particular, just smiling hellos, raising a few waves and passing through. The smoked glass doors of the Deli showed that it was pretty packed inside. Already the music was cranked up, Janet was dancing between the tables, Steve was standing on the cushions of one of the benches, waving his pint.

I asked, 'Do you feel like going in?'

'Not really, no.'

'You wanna walk?'

We followed the path through the village and out towards the beach. We backtracked along the route where I had first pursued Beata, and then beyond, where the density of the housing began to thin and the trees and bushes thickened. We walked close together, picking our way through the dark. A pair of African drums rattled and bomped, drifting out of some rooftop or porch, jungle-deep on the hill. And then the trees dropped away on one side and opened up a view of the powerstation. At night it sparkled. It was sprinkled with floodlights and beacons studded the three chimneys, a thin stream of pale blue smoke rose from one, catching stray light.

The view obscured as our path rose over a crossing path and then delved downhill. A tunnel of tree canopy created fifty yards where we could barely see ahead and, after a few paces, lost the circle of light behind. Beata grabbed my hand and picked up speed, pulling and tugging until we both started to run blind, feet again slapping, laughing until we burst out into space at the beach.

A spread of fine, clean sand rippled in front of us, each bump and dip given contrast by the streetlamps that looped round the back of the beach. Beata and I headed straight out, away from any electric glow. The moon was not far above the horizon, only a slim crescent between passing clouds. I kicked off my flip-flops to feel the cool sand. The thin powder crunched under my steps. Outcrops of rock framed either end of the short beach and we aimed ourselves dead centre, right at the breakline where new waves licked a little at the dry sand.

Then, as we crossed the sand, the powerstation came into view again. It's yellow and white lights blurred together, giving a massed glow. Though faint with distance, we could hear the constant grating of its gears and pulleys. We were separate from it, in surroundings of nature – sand, the sea, rocks, trees, a breeze on our skin and waves that rolled almost soundlessly – and yet it was almost impossible not to ogle the powerstation.

I said, 'It's kinda beautiful, isn't it?'

'What, you think the thing that burn up coal and smoke out to the atmosphere is beautiful?'

'Well, not that, exactly. But just look at it. From here I sometimes think it looks like a miniature city, a whatsit, you know? Like you get in museums.'

'I don't know. It's your language.'

'A diorama.'

'A what?'

'A diorama, it's like, you know a model, a miniature city all lit up.'

Beata said, 'Yes, you know, I did think this, one time when I was at a party on Powerstation beach. I sat looking at the lights and I thought then that it was quite nice. You know, weird but pretty.'

'Aye, but what were you on at the time?'

'Ha, no, it wasn't that.' She flicked sand that fell on my feet and legs. 'You see the glow it gives in the sky around it?'

'Yeah. Is that cause the sky's so hazy?'

'I don't know, but you have it too, do you know? You have a glow in the nighttime.'

'Shit, d'ye think I'm radioactive?' I patted my body, checked for a heartbeat. 'Maybe all this time living near a big generator does ye in.'

'Aff, I think you are alive. It's a glow everyone has. I think you see it best when the sun is come up or go down. When it is half-light?'

'At twilight?'

'Yes, twilight, that's it. Thank you.'

'Everything glows in twilight though. All the colours are brighter. I thought it was just the effect of the sun being low, near the horizon.'

'It could be, yes, I don't know. But I like to think it's the time when we best can see the glow of the energy in everything.'

'Like the powerstation over there?'

'I suppose it is.'

'You know, you're a bit of a raging hippy, aren't you?'

'And you're a moron.'

'True.'

'You are too much of a doubter, William. You can't think any of it to be true.'

Beata picked up a handful of sand and I flinched away. She cast it across an approaching wave. She was right, I did doubt. Usually, I thought it was a strength; I had been brought up to question, to have an open mind, and that made me free. But right there, I so wanted to believe. I so wanted to listen, hear, believe and be part of what Beata was.

As the wave drew away, Beata said, 'I remember one time before we talk about energy. We talk about how energy join us all together and we were sitting on a beach that time too. Do you remember?'

The evening flashed before me, the beach and the night spent on the floor of a half-built house, sleeping bags and zips.

'That time I think you listened to me then, but maybe it was only that you thought you could ... How is it you would say? You wanted to get into my pants?'

'Ah ... eh ... no.'

But she was smiling. She knew how to tweak my buttons, how to gently wind me up.

I said, 'No, I'm listening. I'm always listening.'

'So,' She pointed at the powerstation, 'You see all the air around the lights, they have an orange glow, like a halo and each piece of metal, it's like it has energy that it is ...' She waved a hand in front of her, searching for the word. 'It's giving ... It's feeding it into the air.'

'But that's ... just ... lights.'

'Perhaps, but that's what it makes me think of. We have energy all around us, energy that spread out and touch other thing, touch everything. That's what I feel like when I sit next to you.'

'I like that. I don't know if you are right, but I like it.'

'Of course you don't know.'

'What, because I'm such a moron?'

'No. Well, maybe yes, but no. It's always important for you to know, isn't it? But sometimes it's important to just believe.'

'I don't think I'm very good at that.'

'Anyway, it is very hard to know anything, really. There is only one thing that we always know.'

'What, our own stupidity?'

'No, stupid.'

'Thanks.'

'We know that we are here. Look.' She let a handful of sand run through her fingers. 'Can you feel it?'

'Yeah, but, I don't even know it's real. That old existential thing, I think therefore I am. I only know I exist.'

'That was Descartes.' She pinched the skin on the back of my hand.

'Ow.'

'Can you feel that?'

'Course I can, but ...'

Her hand rested on top of mine. 'So you know that you are here with me.'

'Yes.'

'And you know that now, right now, you feel OK?'

'Yeah. Really, yeah.'

'People spend so many time sorry for what they done in the past, or they worry about what they do in future, and so they are unhappy. I think, if you check and see, I'm happy now, right now, what do you need more than that?'

'But what if you're not happy?'

'Most often, if you stop to look to yourself, right in this time, there's nothing to be sad about.'

'I've been sad.'

'Yes, but why? Sad for something you don't have or because your life should be better? Maybe you are sad because of something you done, but if you can check, you are alive, you are not in pain, and if you are in pain, you will be so much in the pain you will not think am I sad or happy or not.'

Beata's voice, Beata's touch, Beata's warmth and her beauty all spoke of a person capable of happiness.

She said, 'Look at yourself.'

'What, five-foot ten, straggly hair, freckly skin, big nose.'

'No.' She squeezed my fingers underneath hers. 'Feel inside yourself. Think how you feel in this moment, how your body feels, how your mind feels.'

'Right now?'

'Yes.'

The water rose and fell, slight white spangles of phosphorescence glittered in its tiny breakers. Beata's hand still rested on top of mine.

'I feel great.'

She drew herself closer. I put my arm around her back and felt the warmth of her body press into my side, though the sand had grown cold and damp under my backside. Where my hand came round her waist, there was a gap between her top and skirt and I could feel where the flesh rolled at her tummy and tucked towards her hip.

I noticed for the first time that Davy was still with us. He had been sitting nearby, immobile, staring away, but when I looked, he turned, grinned, gave me a wave, and then jumped to his feet. While Beata and I shared a silent moment, holding each other, breathing in unison, Davy stripped off and ran into the sea. He frolicked at the waters edge, jumping and splashing like some attention-seeking toddler.

Beata leaned further in and rested her head on my shoulder briefly. Then she said, 'Come on. I think we can go home now.'

CHAPTER 18

On the way back towards the village, she took my arm. We walked slowly and quietly taking the long route, following the Cable Road down past Powerstation Beach and stopping to look at the grinding metallic beast's reflection in the sea, its whites and yellows glinting off the water, and glowing hazily into the sky.

On the main path, not much into the village proper, we came to the foot of Snake Path, a dark lane that curves up to Tai Peng in a much gentler slope than the one that climbs out of the centre of Yung Shue Wan. Beata's flat was near the bottom of Snake Path, so we parted there.

'Are you sure you want to go that way? It's too dark.'

'Don't worry, I think the snakes are more frightened of me.'

'Good night then.'

We kissed goodbye. Our lips lingered and our faces held slightly apart a moment longer.

Beata smiled. 'Nice night.'

'Yeah, really nice night.'

'See you tomorrow.'

'For sure.'

Snake Path was lit for the first couple of hundred yards. After that, only a little moonlight found its way through the overhang. Still, I skipped along the way. Beata's kiss tingled on my lips. I licked them.

The foliage fell away on the left of the path allowing me to see the village and the ferry pier below. It was a clear night, and the view stretched out to the lights of the shipping in the channel and even the distant Tsing Ma Bridge that carried travellers to the airport.

I was startled by a rustling in the bushes behind. My heart skipped, thinking of some unseen creature, but I turned and saw Davy dragging his hand through the branches as he walked.

'Bloody hell, you nearly gave me a heart attack.'

The wee man looked forlorn. His head hung and the tips of his pointy shoes dragged along the ground. A little seawater still glistened on his scalp.

I let him catch up. 'What was that earlier with the dancing and the nickety nackety?'

'Jist a wee song.'

'C'mon Davy, you can do better than that.'

'I just like a wee song is aw.'

'And what the hell's with the breeks and the shirt and that? Are ye pinin for the hameland?' He was wearing baggie britches, a frill collared shirt and a tight tartan waistcoat.

'Go fuck yersel. I kin dress how I want.'

'What's the matter, Davy, feeling neglected?'

'We jist dinnae dae nuhin any mair.'

Davy had been withering for a while now, taking on the flaccid grey pallor he wore when I had first pulled him from the soapsuds in Tully. A lot of the time I was barely aware of him, unless his behaviour was so erratic or so desperate that I couldn't ignore him.

The flat was empty. Steve was still in the pub, and undoubtedly not back till well on. I poured the last of the wine into a glass, put on some music and set about tidying from the meal, clearing and cleaning the dishes.

Davy sat in front of the telly, the picture on but the sound turned right down. When I'd finished straightening the place, I sat at the other end of the couch. 'What's on?'

'Fuck all.'

'You wanna watch anything?'

'Fuck all.'

I turned the volume up a little and flicked between the two English-language channels. He was right, there was nothing on.

'William?' His voice was small, almost timorous.

'What?'

'How come yer nae fun no more?'

'Get off, I am.'

'No yer no. Ye jist fuckin walk tae the beach and go tae yer bed. Whit fuckin fun is that?'

'That's not true. I still enjoy a night out.' I held up the wine glass. 'I still enjoy a drink.'

'How come yer no in the pub?'

'Sometimes there's other things to do. If I get a good sleep tonight, I can meet Beata at the beach tomorrow. And there'll probably be volleyball if enough people make it down.'

'Whoo-fuckin-hoo.'

'This is a good life. A better balance.'

'It's shite.'

He sat next to me, twisted up tight, his arms crossed over his chest, his legs under him. His brow furrowed down and his lips pushed up, squashing his nose in wrinkles. Even his ears drooped.

I leaned back, stretched my legs in front of me and reached for the control to turn the telly up further.

The phone rang. It was on the floor, within reach.

'Hello.'

'Eh, hello, can I speak to William, please?' It was a Scottish voice, one I recognised.

'Hi, this is William.'

'William, it's Helen.' My sister.

'Wow. Helen. Great.' It was so unlikely; I hadn't spoken to her for almost two years. 'It's been ages.'

'I know.'

'Hey, what? Are you coming out to Hong Kong?' She was a businesswoman, an accountant. Accountants came out all the time. 'Do you have a business trip? It'd be great to see you.'

'No William. Listen, I'm sorry, but it's about mum.'

Of course it was. What else could it be?

Davy sat bolt upright. His cheeks lifted. His ears pointed.

I asked, 'What's happened?'

'I'm sorry.' There had been joy, hope and pleasure in life building inside me, filling me up. They all drained as Helen said, 'Mum's dead.'

The words bumped against my head.

'It was yesterday.'

Something forced its way to my throat. It flowed and flushed my face. It filled my ears till they buzzed. It pushed against my eyes until tears welled.

'I'm sorry that I didn't phone you sooner, but I didn't have your number and in all the fuss, I hadn't had a chance to look out her address book till today, and then it took me ages to find, you know how she keeps the place, everything has a special spot, but no-one else knows where it is.' I could picture exactly where Mum kept her address book – in the shelf under the unit she used as a tea-stand next to her armchair in the living room. I could see it, long and thin, marked throughout in an eccentric mix of felt-tip colours that bled through to the page behind making everything hard to read. I could even imagine where she would have written my number, where my previous numbers, all the ones I'd used since I'd left her house, would be crossed out, leaving only the most recent; mine written under Uncle Alek's, her brother who had died three years before. I knew his had never been crossed. I knew she would not have changed for a newer book.

The buzzing made Helen's words, the words in which she told me how Mum had died and how she had been found, hard to hear. It was like cicadas brought into my room and dotted around the walls, spread over the floor, and stuck on every inch of the sofa, surrounding me. I couldn't find any sound of my own. All that came out of me were tears. They wet the receiver that I pressed against my head.

I didn't want to watch Davy, but he had grown. He crawled across the couch, grinning, then stood. He loomed. His stature had swollen. His face was wide and horrible. It dominated the air before me. He surrounded me like a dark smoke.

I pulled my legs to my chest, wrapped my arms around them and lowered my head to my knees. I said, 'I'm sorry,' before I dropped the phone.

I heard Helen distantly. 'William. What did you say? William. I can't hear you.'

I closed my eyes, but could still see his face. The buzzing in my ears became the hissing of his breath, and I saw his teeth, his teeth clenched and grinning, stained, yellow, spittle strung between them spreading with his breath. His wheeze distorted. It stuttered and blew in his throaty voice. It burst with his rasping laughter.

*   *   *   *

PART IV: SCOTLAND

CHAPTER 19

Mum was buried in the morning, but the sun never got high. At this time of the year, the days are short, the clouds are low. The air was thick, cold and damp, continually on the verge of deluge.

Beata controlled me. She steered me from place to place, person to person. She was the one who greeted and condoled, bright but respectful, subdued enough to show that she knew it was a funeral, that a dead person was there. She knew that dead person was my mother.

There weren't that many. A small, grey, blank gathering of people who vaguely marked the path of a woman's life, showed the faint outline of the shape she had cast. I recognised Mrs Teal from next door and managed some words with her. The care nurse was there, and made herself known. There were a couple of old dears, probably ages with Mum or older, the kind that haunt every funeral. There was one old fella there that I had never seen before, and Helen, with a man. Beata did not steer me towards them. They did not approach.

Davy, though, would not leave me alone. At every step he was tugging on the panels of the ill-fitting suit I had dug out of mum's cupboard. I don't know why the hell I had worn it. It had to be Dad's.

The service was grimly Catholic. The priest talked about God, not my mother. Though she was devout, I don't think she had been well enough to attend the chapel regularly for a long time, and so the Father knew little of her, passed her on as another soul that had to be given up to the greater good, the greater God. Her spirit was pushed on. I could only hope it was on to what she believed. I didn't. I couldn't feel it. I felt no presence, except Beata by my side, and Davy muttering obscenities into my ear. It was something I couldn't bear.

At the end of the service, Helen approached. Her man, comforting her by the arm, was tall and broad and smiling, while Helen slouched. Her mouth was wrinkled tight.

She said, 'This is Mum's funeral, not some merry little jaunt for you to swan through.'

'What?'

'How come when I went into our mother's house I found that wee tart raking through her cupboards? Pick her up at the airport, did ye?

'What? ... Don't you dare.'

'You may want to bring any sort into your life, but don't bring it round here.'

'You knew we'd be in the house, but... Don't dare say that about Beata. And anyway, what do you know about my life?'

'What do I care? You left. I don't know why you've even bothered to come back.'

'But you ... You phoned. I'm your... I'm her son.'

Helen stared. Her face was hard and aged far more than it ought.

Her man took our moment of glowering silence as his opportunity. 'Ah, hello. I'm Damon.'

Helen said, 'Damon's my ...'

'Fiancé. So I guess we're going to be brothers-in-law, aren't we? Very good to meet you.' He continued to grin as he held out a hand like a pack of sausages. His accent was quite-posh English, his handshake very firm. 'But of course, very sorry about ... you know, about ...' The sausage-hand slackened. It was slightly damp.

I put my hand on Helen's arm. 'Helen, I didn't come back for a battle with you. I just want to ...'

'Fuck aff Willie.' Davy pushed violently between my legs, causing me to tip back, away from Helen. He said, 'Ye've nae chance wey her. She's yer ain sister.'

'... I just ... I was hoping to ...'

'Ye should let a real man huv a chance, eh? Fuckin only wan ae them aroon here.'

'Stop it!'

Helen turned on me. 'Stop what? You want to stop what? Your own guilt? I don't want you here. You were no good to her alive and you are no use to me now.'

'Hey, hey, that's you numbered, pal. Little Miss Sis means business.'

'What you talking about? I ...'

Davy said, 'Cannae blame yer sister, but.'

I said, 'And what about you? Where were you?'

Helen glared at me, her face hard. 'What d'you mean?'

'I mean, you were in the country right the way through. It doesn't sound like you were around much.'

'Don't you come it. I work. I work bloody hard. Me and Damon both. I'm not some bloody perpetual student like you.'

'What?' I couldn't take it in.

'You think life's such a laugh, don't you? It's just a joke to you. Well, some bloody joke it is now.'

'Aye, well, she's goat a point. It is but, intit? Good fuckin craic if ye knaw how tae.' Davy was at my feet, twisting between my legs. 'It cannae be that bad, eh? Nothin a bevvy wilnae sort. Ask yer sister if she wants tae head oot fur a pint.'

'Shut up!'

Helen's mouth opened, but her next comment hung on her lips.

It was clear Helen thought herself better, holier than me. I said, 'What's so special about you and whatsisface anyway?'

'Nothin. That's it, but. Nothin's special. It's just you that thinks life's some silly game, running round the world like yer the only one that matters.'

'Aye, son, she's spot oan again.' Davy pinched the thin skin on the muscle of my calf. I swayed as I flinched away. 'Yer nuhin special. Fuckin sure yer no.'

'And I'll tell you something,' Helen said, 'Damon's a successful man. That's what working hard in the real world gets you. A rich man, the kind of man that you couldn't even hope to be.'

'He's goat money, eh? She's probably right there, then. Ye've nae hope. Feckless shite that ye ur.' He turned his fingers, twisting my skin between them. I arched away from the pain, and stumbled, catching my feet against each other. I fell to the floor of the chapel. Helen looked down on me, making no move to help or word of comfort. The light from the high windows shone harshly on her head giving her features unnatural shadows.

Davy laughed.

Beata helped me up, took me by the elbow and walked me out to our hire car.

I gripped the steering and took deep breathes, staring at my knuckles, while the mourners departed. Then I drove. Away from the Church and out of Glasgow. We talked very little. Or, Beata and I talked little. Davy continued his incessant prattle from the back seat.

'Why ye fuckin botherin? Urs nae point drivin naewhere. Nae point daein fuck aw. Ye knaw yer a useless, shiftless, feckless wee shite. Naedby cares aboot ye Willie.'

'Beata does.'

'Aye. But how much longer?'

I know Beata was looking at me, but she didn't speak. I decided to keep quiet and tried my best to ignore Davy. Despite the circumstances, Beata and

I had decided to tour a little while we were in Scotland. I concentrated on the tight winding highland roads as we travelled up the side of Loch Lomond through Crianlarich, across the Rannoch Moor and down between the dark hills of Glencoe.

He stood on the back seat, leant forward and spoke directly into my ear. 'Ye knaw, son, ye've jist aboot hud it, hun't ye? Cannae sink much lower. Whit fuckin use ur ye tae any cunt? Nae family, a bird that wilnae shag ye, nae fuckin life at aw. Ye might as well jist dae yersel in, dae us aw a favour. Mon, stoap aff at the Spar, we'll buy ye some bleach tae drink.'

We travelled through Fort William and on to skirt the banks of Loch Ness. We had eaten our supply of crisps and pre-packed sandwiches, but the hunger wasn't enough to make me stop the car in Inverness, even though the dark was settling over.

Davy moved and leant towards Beata's ear. I could hear snatches of his whispers directed to her. 'Course if he hud any baws at aw, he'd ... Dae ye no think we should dae that fur him? ... Or we kin awways ...'

She remained impassive, no longer staring at me. Her head lolled to the side; her gaze fell out the window, though there could have been nothing to see save her own reflection in the darkened glass. Davy moved again. He whispered between her ear and the window, away from me, further from my earshot so that he could fill her head with all the evil that I was. Davy knew it all. Davy held it, and now, finally, he had decided to share it. A way to kill off anything that may have spawned between Beata and me. He was going to talk to her, and her alone, until she was sick fed up, the sight of me unbearable, my presence enough to make her skin crawl.

The night was black as our headlights flashed across the sign for Elgin.

Beata said, 'I need to stop now. Can we find somewhere to stay here, please?'

Davy said, 'We're stoapin. Och aye, we're stoapin.'

*   *   *   *

I awoke in my single bed, still exhausted. The morning was chilled; the covers were bunched to one side. During the night I had found the tightly tucked blankets smothering and pushed them away. The damp morning mist was now seeping into the room. I pulled the blankets back around, pressing my eyes shut, willing myself back to sleep.

As we had cruised Elgin looking for rooms available, I had hoped we would be offered a double bed, through necessity or the presumption that we were a couple. The thought of Beata's closeness, of her warmth through the night had buoyed me; comfort and hope. At the B&B we found, there were none, though the pinched Presbyterian face of the landlady suggested she may be judging our unmarried state too dangerous to allow it.

I lay, eyes closed, with my back towards Beata's bed listening to a soft susurration. There were tiny, sibilant sounds in the air, arriving from no direction, a tiny voice whispering syllables gently under breath. It came to me that there was another, another voice reaching me. It may have been my strained mind trying to build something new, something that could speak to me and reassure, but it felt tender, playing against my ears.

I turned and through the meagre light saw Davy on Beata's bed, curled close to her face at her pillow. They were whispering; the two of them. They were chatting, thinking I wouldn't know. They thought I was asleep.

'What are you saying?' I sprang out of bed.

Beata started and flipped onto her back, knocking Davy off the pillow. He glided across the sheets, slipped to the floor and afforded me a sneer before he hid under the bed.

I shook her. 'Beata. What were you talking about?'

'I … What? William, I'm sleeping.'

'No you're not. I heard you. I saw you talking. What were you saying?'

'Nothing. I was asleep. Maybe I was waking only… Was it in Swedish?'

I got dressed. I couldn't discuss it, to delve into her duplicity, to open myself to the crushing failure of my attempts to win her over. Now she was lost to me, enrapt by a stronger force. A malevolence. Davy would allow me no quarter, no freedom, nothing that would support or strengthen me.

She followed me down to the breakfast room. I filled my plate with black pudding, bacon and sausage, far more than I wanted: a greasy meat barrier between me and my vegetarian companion.

Beata ate cornflakes and flicked through leaflets and brochures for local tourist attractions. 'I would like to visit something today.'

'I want to drive.'

'Yes, that's fine, but let's see something first, OK?'

She reached across and put a leaflet in front of me. Spynie Palace. Photos showed a castle that looked like any other Scots castle – crusty and dilapidated. Her hand took mine. Bacon dangled from my fork. Beata held my face with her eyes, imploring me.

I said, 'Sure. Fine, we'll go.' I knocked her hand away. 'Soon as we check out.' The meat dragged painfully down my throat, barely chewed.

The morning became bright and fresh, the cold air crisp, less oppressive, perhaps because we have come so far from the city. As we stepped out of the guesthouse, I had to pull my jacket tighter around me but also to reach for my sunglasses.

Leaving Elgin, we were quickly into countryside. Here the land is far more open and flat than in the steep, rugged banks of the west-coast lochs. Trees and hedges line blank winter fields. Dark, unflowered furze and heather lie thick on any short hillside or bank. Occasional houses – square blocks with little sign of ornament or garden – billowed chimney smoke but showed little other sign of life. The road ran straight and I drove in a mindless way while Beata watched the passing blandness attentively. Davy talked. 'Wee fuckin day-trip? Whit's the use? S'no as if ye'll be aroon tae hink back an mimember, whit a lovely day oot I hud wey the Scandybitch an ma wee pal the day efter I pit ma maw in the groon. Away and find a ...' We passed a hedgerow into view of a distant, ominous brown stone tower. 'Whit's that?'

'That is it.' Beata pointed. 'It must be. Here says only three miles from Elgin. You think we drive three miles already?'

'Aye, I spose.'

The palace passed from sight again but a sign came up quickly directing us off the main road. We turned into a gritty single track that trundled us through woods to a rough parking spot. There were no other cars.

Davy fell out on my side before I managed to swing the door shut on him. 'This place'll be shite. Nae point bein here. Bit like you, eh pal?'

'Give it a rest, will ye?'

Beata stepped out on her side. 'You had enough rest already, come on.'

I followed her. Davy followed us. 'Aye, ye could dae wey a rest, right enough. Get fuckin well arrested. Lock ye up, stoap ye takin a harm tae yersel.'

'Shut it!'

'Sorry?' She pointed at her ears. 'I think, the wind blowing, I can't...'

Beata strode off, leaning forward. The trees bent towards us.

Davy said, 'Fuck's sakes, bawbag, how we pissin aboot here? Gonnae find a bridge tae jump aff or somehin, get it ower wey. Mon, me an the bird'll lea ye tae it.'

Davy paced forward and took Beata's hand, leading her faster ahead, pulling her along a path worn across the grass.

I called after, 'You don't even know it's this way.'

They moved from sight around a copse of trees. I stepped after and the castle came into view.

A tall, flat, faceless wall, presented to us.

Davy and Beata were already approaching a high archway further along the façade. I rushed to keep them in sight. Passing through, I discovered that the grim solidity of the outer wall gave way to decay.

The palace was in ruins, with low remains and fallen stones scattered around the plan of an ancient courtyard. Some taller walls stood at the corners, but on the inside, where they faced us, they showed the hollow remains of doorways and holes where floor timbers would have been struck through. Grass has been allowed to intrude throughout and has been closely cut – to increase the comfort of visitors. To me, it intensifies the sense of voyeurism. Casting round here is like treading on a life ended and eviscerated, gaping at the cold embers of life that must have thrived between these stones.

It was all the more striking then that one sizeable building, what must have been the largest part of the castle, appeared intact. This was what we had seen from the road, a dappled, square-sided block, built tightly in neatly mortared stone. There were five stories of narrow glassed windows running up its sides and a low window at its foot. The rooftop was lined with ramparts. I had been to this kind of highland castle before, seen the dark panelled wood, suits of armour and the ancient livery mouldering in rarely visited halls. The family undoubtedly were dissipated now to warmer, more forgiving parts of the world.

Davy and Beata had stopped at an information board sticking out of the grass.

David's Tower

This impressive stone tower was built by Bishop David Stewart with work completed in the late 15th century. It is likely that the Bishop, who had excommunicated the Gordon Earls of Huntley, built David's Tower to protect himself from retaliation. The Bishop's palace was a highly fortified and easily defended castle.

'Hows aboot that? Davy's Tower. Fuckin braw, that is.'

The entrance was in the same narrow style as the windows, with a traditional wooden door hung on black iron hinges. It swung open easily. We stepped through and found inside an empty shell. The walls were exposed stone apart from occasional patches of plaster. Beneath our feet, a flat concrete floor had been put in, but there were no floors above. A wooden stairway had been fitted against one wall leading up two stories to a platform, and then further still, as if it went right to the ramparts. Where I had expected a complete roof, wooden and tiled, there was an ugly construction of perspex covering the opening. Despite this, the interior was gloomy and chill.

Beata shivered, sucking a breath through her teeth.

I wanted to climb and get onto this roof, to push my legs, tackle the effort, drive myself into the exertion and see what reward I could get from reaching the height of this gutted old tower. I wanted to see how far the view could extend

'Head on up, son,' Davy said. 'Have a swatch at how lang's the faw fae the tap.'

'It's too nice today.' Beata took my arm and steered me away from the steps. 'Let's walk outside.'

I felt my arm and shoulder tense, but I let her lead me out. I thought I was trembling.

I had never seen her look at me in the way she did then, wary, as if she were checking me over, sizing me up – my sanity, my safety, my threat.

Davy was holding her other hand. He stuck two fingers up at me.

The ruined parts of the palace were scattered before and to the side of David's Tower. We wandered, and again Beata looked at me again, gauging me. That look on her face. I pulled my arm away and let her hand slip off. I clambered over a low wall, putting it between us, and walked away.

She called, 'William.'

Davy was with her still. 'Hoi, dickheid.'

I didn't turn.

'William, can we talk?'

'Dickheid, the bird wants tae tell ye yer finished.'

I followed the crumbled remains of an outside wall until it came to what may have been some great hall or church. Within its plan, there was a small space, a priest-hole or anterior room that allowed me a nook to conceal myself. I had no idea if they had watched me, but I went inside. I lowered myself almost to the ground to get below the height of the top stones. Once there, I peered back through a gap. The pair of them were strolling amiably; they weren't searching or caring what had happened to me. Her left hand reached down and held Davy's right. Beata continued to look ahead as she walked, but Davy turned his head to her, enrapt. He was wearing an oversized pullover and loose hanging trousers that made him look, from a distance, like some moribund child walking with his mother, except his feet were bare on the cold, damp grass. He was talking, rattling away. I could see his face working and hear the undertone of his voice. They were too far for me to hear his words.

They separated. I watched Beata sit on some low stones and take her pack from her back. Meanwhile, Davy scuttled along the course of the wall and came into the space of the church. I let him draw nearer, waiting until he rounded the corner of my nook. 'You!'

'Willie! Ya prick. I near shat masel.'

'What you been sayin to her?'

He backed away. 'Whit the fuck you aboot?'

I got him into the corner. 'I thought you hated her.'

'Whit ye talkin aboot? I wis naewhere near her.'

'I know what you're doin, and ye can quite it. Leave her alone. Let her be.'

'Fuck ye.' Davy had regained composure. 'I'll dae whit I like.' He pointed a finger and stepped at me. 'An don't hink ye kin trap me in yer wee corner.'

He touched a huge stone to the side of him and it tipped in place then tumbled from the wall. Crumbling debris fell behind it. Beata looked over, startled, then crossly at me.

Davy had gone.

I was an idiot, crouching behind rocks, playing hide, with nobody seeking.

Beata lifted a hand and beckoned me. I conceded. Rather her company than Davy's, or my own. I was making myself more foolish and despicable. I sat on the other side of the wall from her.

When I refused her water, she put the bottle to one side and laid her hand on the pile of rubble. 'I love this history. Everything so old. It talks to you,

you know, about all that happen in the past. Don't you want to know about what happened here?'

'Buy a fuckin brochure, hen.'

I leaned over and saw Davy hidden on her side. But I had said that, not him. With no thought, I had let it slip out.

Beata's eyes widened; her face was stony. 'William, I can see that you are not right.'

I almost laughed. 'What d'ye expect?'

She looked me over again. 'William, I want to ask you something. Is it ok?' She paused, but when I didn't respond, continued, 'Are you angry with me?'

I was. I resented her. I resented them. I said, 'I've seen you.'

'Seen me what?'

'You and him.'

'Who.'

'I've seen you and him chatting away. Becoming real pals, int ye?'

'Chatting with who?'

'To him.' I pointed. 'Davy.'

She looked at the wee man, but said nothing.

'You're ganging up. Between you, yer working out how to fuck me over or …'

'William, what are you talking about?' She reached over and put her hand on my back. 'There's no one.'

Davy climbed up on the wall between us. He wrapped an arm around Beata and pressed his head into her side.

I said, 'Oh aye. You want me to think that, don't you? You want me to think that you don't see him, so that I must be mad. It's been a while now, hasn't it? It's only now you're letting it slip. You two have been at it for ages, but you don't want me to know because if it's only me, then I must be mad.'

Davy's voice was low and level. 'Ye ur mad son. Lookit her. Lookit her face. She disnae knaw whit yer talkin aboot. Yer a fuckin mental case, an noo she knaws it.'

'I'm sorry, William. Your time now is very difficult, and you are upset about many thing, but it sound like you think I am with another guy … Is that … Do you think I have a boyfriend or … You and I are not together … still … but I have not another man and I just … I hope you are not upset with me.'

Davy said 'Noo's yer chance son, tell her how much ye fuckin hate her. She hates you, she telt you already.'

'No she …' I swung for him.

Beata's look was fearful. She was frightened for me or worse, frightened of me. I was falling apart in front of her and my sight or my presence was horrifying.

I said to her, 'I'm not.'

'Aye ye are. She's a bitch.'

'I'm not upset with you. Really, I can't.'

'Then why do you talk like that? Why do you look at me like you think hate.'

'Cause she's a fuckin two-faced bitch, tell her.'

'No.' I let her hand rise up to touch my cheek. 'I'm sorry.'

'Don't be sorry. There is no need for you be sorry at this time.'

'Tell her to shut it.'

'No, Beata. I'm sorry for dragging you all the way here. I'm sorry that you've had to go through all this misery. And all the time I'm just going fucking mad. I'm losing it and dragging you along for the ride. I'm sorry I drove you all the way to this place. I don't even know why the fuck we're here.'

'It don't matter. I want to be here for you. I want to help you.'

'Tell her jist tae fuckin shut it. Shut her face.' Davy shouted. 'G'won son, shut her face fur her. Slap her wan.'

I told her, 'It's me. I'm angry with me. I'm angry because … because I know I've messed up. Again. That's what I always do. I'm not much good … to you.'

'Ye kin say that again, yer fuck all use tae nae cunt.'

'William, it's …'

She leaned towards me, pulling me into her embrace, but pushing down on top of Davy. He tried to push her away. 'Shift it, bitch!'

'It's a difficult time for you. I know this, and it should be. It is right that now is difficult because you have suffer so much.'

'Suffrin your fuckin Scandy wittrin, ya silly cow.'

I had to ignore him, shut out his nasty proddings and fix only on what Beata had to say.

'Please, don't be too bad on yourself, and know that I will help you. I am here now and I will stay here with you.'

'But … But I don't think you will, Beata. You left before, and that was right. I'm not a good person. I know that so well. Everything around me turns to shit, and that's right, that's what should happen to me. I don't want you to have to go through all that as well.'

'I'll help you any way you want.'

'But why?'

'I love you William. I do. It's not just because you are upset or unhappy and it's not only about I want to help you. I really do love you and I want you to know that.'

*   *   *   *

CHAPTER 20

Beata pushed her backpack aside, scrambled over the rocks and reached her arms around me. I let my face fall into her shoulder and her warmth curled over me, binding her words to me. 'I really do love you and I want you to know that.' It was like being wrapped in a towel just off the radiator. I drew on her sweet untainted smell and felt fortified. She pulled back just a little, encouraging me to lift my face to hers and Beata looked at me. She searched my eyes. The tension in her face showed her worry for me, but under the concern, there was that spark of brightness; between the furrow in her brow and the straight set of her lips there was the shine in her eyes. She touched my face. Gently. A soft whisper of her skin caressed mine, warmth fleeting over in this cold place.

I had known that I was never going to feel joy again. I had lost the capacity for it. My life had seemed so drained, so desperately worthless, that there was no point prolonging it with happiness. But it returned. An intense ripple of joy flowed through and filled me. It is still here now, that bubble, that inflation, buoying me in the belief that I can get through because perhaps I have been doing something right. It isn't all wrong, it hasn't been, something of me has created good – good moments, good intentions. I do have good intentions, I'm sure. I was well meaning in all of this. Perhaps only for most of this. But in that, I know I can take strength. There are ways in which I have failed. I failed Orla, for sure. I can't help feeling I failed Mum, even though she wouldn't blame me. But I have left a positive imprint in places. There are people who don't detest me, who probably feel it's been good to know me. And Beata loves me.

Beata's declaration of love struck me so intensely, I was dumbfounded. A silence grew between us in which the joy in my love for her was so apparent that it hurt. It filled my chest and pressed against my ribs. It filled my head.

The shrill shriek of horror and disgust that had overpowered me when I learned that mum was dead now dissipated and faded away. It was replaced with the presence of this woman. She had been there since I had first watched her coming down the guesthouse fire-escape in Tully. I had been in awe of her then, and I had thought her unapproachable. Now she was not just part of, but all of my life. The greatness of it was that she didn't want to control me, steer me or use me; she wanted me to be with her as myself. Beata has given me the strength to decide my own path.

I knew in those silent minutes that I didn't need Davy any more.

I excused myself, telling her that I wanted a moment on my own, some time to clear my head. My crisis point had come. Now was the time to finally set myself free. I left Beata and headed towards the place I knew he would follow, the place where I feel that we can now bring this to an end. I went to climb the tower.

It has six stories inside, which is high for the north of Scotland, though paltry for Hong Kong. Were I there, I would have been in a lift. Here, my legs can take me up, and they hurt. I thought I was fit. Lamma life involves a lot of walking, but the climb up those stairs bit sharply into my thighs and calves. My knees ached.

When I set out, I wanted to see if I could get on to the roof, if the stairs really did lead out on to the ramparts, and they do. I have access to one edge. The wide flat lands of Moray are spectacular from here: its green slight hillsides, its sparse fields and far off waters. It's spectacular. Beata would enjoy it, but I won't call out to her or let her know. It's better if she doesn't.

'Enough. It's enough.'

Davy is here, beside me, panting. It seems his strength is not what it has been. 'Davy's Tower, it's a grand place, intit? Brilliant. A wee treat, so it is. It's ma place.'

'This is the end of it Davy. We're not doing this any more.'

'Ach, the stairs are no that bad.'

'Shut it. You know what I mean. This is the end of it all, Davy. This is the end. I don't need you. I have her.'

'Shut up yersel, ya dick. Ye hink ye kin fuck me aff jist cause some Scandy bitch says a few nice hings?'

'I've had enough. I don't need you. You don't help me. You are not part of my life any more.'

Davy was back in his idiotic traditional garb. The cartoon goblin. Rumplestiltskin. Just to mock me. He held his fists up, turning them in front of him. 'Fuckin, come ahead, pal. Gie it yer best shot.'

'You know, back in Tully, I felt sorry for you. I couldn't believe someone could do that. Shutting a tiny wee man in a washing machine. Poor, defenceless little goblin thing. What is it you said, a Brownie, is that what you are?'

'Fuck aff.'

'I don't know what the fuck ye are.'

'Ah telt ye, I'm jist ...'

'Ma wee pal. I know. But it's shite, Davy. You're not my pal. You're the thing that turns everything nasty.'

'You couldnae wipe yer erse weyoot me, pal. Yer fuckin feckless. Ye need a wee bit ae guidance. Words ae wisdom, eh? So ye need me. I made ye. I kin make ye again.'

'If I let you, you'd destroy me.'

'I'll sort ye oot.'

'I know what you are Davy. I know how vile you are, how nasty and manipulative. You want to destroy me. Or you would, but for how I can serve you – no, what I can serve you. Alone and vulnerable, weak and pliable, that's how you want me.'

'Ye dinnae have to be feart ae me, laddie. We're oan the same team. Jist, ye knaw, ye huftae toe the line, screw the bobbin, keep the heid, ma son.'

'I don't need you, Davy. I'm beyond you.'

'You awways need me. Yer addicted.'

'I have Beata.'

'Aye, like fuck. The Scandy's nae use tae ye. She's in ma poaket noo.'

'It's all lies. You want me to believe you've got power over her, but you don't. C'mon, come here with me and look. You watch, little man, and you'll see a beautiful, powerful woman passing among those rocks and trees. She won't be fretting, she won't be fearful, because she has faith. I don't know how she has it, I'm not sure I understand it, but Beata has faith in life, and faith in me.'

'Fuck her. She's a fuckin frigid, tight-cunted, stinking fuckin Scandy bitch.'

'No. No she's not. Ye've always been wrong about her. And ye know what? Now I know I'm right. I've always been right. Today. Today, I got myself back.'

'Whit fuckin bollocks ye talking, pal?'

'I know what you are, Davy. Rapist. Abuser. Incubus. Now I won't have to live it again. I don't believe in you.'

'Aye.' He grabs a lump of flesh on the back of my hand and squeezes it tightly between thumb and bony finger.

'Aah!'

'Fuckin, believe in me noo, dae ye?'

I slap at his hand. 'Get away from me.'

His fingers wrap entirely round mine. His grip is tight, squeezing the bones of my fingers together, turning them on each other.

'I'm as fuckin real as you need. Fuckin no believe in me? That's you, that is. Nae fuckin baws tae see whit's in front ae ye. That bird there, fuckin Scandybitch, ye couldae fuckin fucked her a lang time ago. That fuckin mither ae yours, ye couldae sorted her oot fuckin easy, but ye cannae see whits in front ae yer neb, ya twat.'

I'm pulling at my hand, trying to wrench it away from him, but it won't break free. 'Stop. Now. It ends now.'

My fingers have slipped from his and I'm stumbling. The wall digs into my thighs.

Davy's mouth gapes. 'You wanted this.' It's obscene, too large. 'Aw ae this. Aw I dae is gie ye whit you want.'

'No! It's only ever what you want.'

'Ye made yer ain choices. Ye cannae blame me, pal. An it's too late tae change noo. It's this or nuthin.'

His other hand has grabbed my wrist. His fingers cut in like ropes.

I'm wrenching, and tugging but I can't get free. 'It's nothing, then. Ye hear me, Davy. I want nothing.' I'm backed into an archer's cut in the parapet, the point where the wall drops low. The wall is on my thighs. His pressure is tipping me backwards. The edge is too near.

'Yer a wee toad, so ye ur. And a fuckin shitebag. If ye could admit who ye ur, we'd jist get oan wey enjoying wursels. I'm the bastard? I'm the abuser? Rapist? Look tae yersel, son.'

'You are not real. You are not here!'

Using his own grip, I can lift Davy. If I twist, I can push him in to the dip.

'Aw no.' He's scabblin, his legs are kicking at me. His bare feet have nails like talons. 'Yer no pittin me ower.'

'You are gone.' If I push, if I push hard enough. 'This is the end.'

'No on ma ain.' Davy's digging his heels in. He wants me up there with him. 'You fuckin watched son. You pit me in there wey aw they birds. Ma plays or no, you played thum.'

I can make the decision. I can do this for myself.

'You cannae dae fuck all!' Davy is growing. He's swelling. His whole figure is building. He wants to loom and threaten, his stature is growing. But with a lunge, I can grab him, both hands on both his arms, and suddenly he is tiny again, just a midget of a man, struggling and wrestling to get free from my grip. But I will only let him go once he is over the edge and beyond saving.

You're right Davy, god fuckin help me. The wretch. The narcissist. The bastard abuser with the twisted unquenchable lust. That's me. And this is where it ends.

Because she loves me.

'No Willie. Dinnae dae it. Ye cannae!'

I step into the cut and, with a final twist, and a hurl, he's gone.

'I'm yer pal!'

He's gone. But I'm toppling. The effort to hurl Davy has unbalanced me.

As Davy falls towards the hard ground, his limbs curl, his howl is fading, but I'm teetering.

Davy has ended. I know.

And I'm free. Finally. Suddenly, I am me. I am strong, maybe for the first time, but my new will is taken from me as I struggle to regain balance and feel the tug of gravity pulling me after. My decision is made.

And from here, I see Beata strolling at the edge of the woods. She is so beautiful, uninhibited and serene. And, as the emptiness grabs, she sees me.

- THE END –

WEE DAVY EXTRAS

You can find a bunch of extra Wee Davy stuff online. Visit:

http://weedavy.co.uk

There you will find videos of the author, Andrew Doig, reading excerpts from the book, and audio files of Andrew reading the first three chapters. You will also find some extra unpublished materials, sections that, while not essential for your enjoyment of reading the events of Wee Davy, will give you interesting insights into aspects of the story such as:

- What was the full story of the night in Cairns?
- What happened in Korea?
- What happened when William first arrived in Hong Kong?

There is also a selection of illustrations by gifted artists, bringing to life episodes from the novel.